A Matter of Trust

Nick Udall

ISBN: 978-1-916696-45-7

PublishNation
www.publishnation.co.uk

For Dodo. As ever, my inspiration.

Chapter 1

It was the milkman. He always woke her. The clink of the bottles, a cough or sometimes, regardless of the early hour, a whistle. Then the sound of the milk float as it stuttered on its way down the cobbled street. Kate turned over and looked at little Rosie sleeping in the bed beside her. Yawning, she slowly sat up and stretched out her arms above her head. She glanced at the alarm clock on the bedside cabinet and saw that it was almost six o'clock. The sun was already rising, peeping through a chink in the curtains. The light played across Kate's face as she edged towards the side of the bed, careful not to disturb Rosie. Her daughter had been upset during the night. She'd had a bad dream and got into her mam's bed. Swinging her legs out from under the covers, Kate tentatively reached down with her feet to find her slippers, her toes shrinking away from the lino on the floor, that even in the summer was cold to the touch. How she would love to have carpets for the upstairs, but such luxuries were beyond her means. Putting on her dressing gown, Kate quietly turned the handle to the bedroom door. Opening it, she stepped out on to the landing. Moving the board placed across the stairs to stop Rosie from falling, she stepped through the gap and replaced it behind her.

Descending the steep stairs, Kate reached the bottom and pushed open the door to the kitchen of her two-up two-down terrace house in Bright Avenue, Ardwick. The light was streaming in through the net curtains, illuminating the kitchen and creating a welcoming atmosphere. Kate walked over to the draining board and picked up the kettle. She filled it from the cold tap at the sink and then placed it on top of the cooker before lighting the jet of gas beneath it. The flame spluttered into life, slowly boiling the water with which to make the first brew of the day, the cup of tea she enjoyed the most. It was a time when Kate could be certain that she would have a moment to herself. It was an opportunity for quiet reflection, before she would turn on the radio, wake Rosie and get them both ready for the day ahead; Kate to go to work and Rosie to her nan's.

Lately, Kate's thoughts had turned towards her husband Joe. It was now two years since he'd been gone; June 4th 1959, just a few months after his hero, Buddy Holly. He'd been found dying on the pavement outside a Manchester nightclub, the victim of a vicious assault. The police had never found the assailant. Devastated by her loss, Kate had been inconsolable. Yet somehow, she had found the strength to recover from the tragedy. She realised that she had to carry on for the sake of their daughter, vowing at Joe's graveside that she would do her utmost to make sure that Rosie would never go short of love and attention. It wasn't long however, before Kate began to suspect that Joe had been hiding a secret. The suggestion came when she began to notice the averted eyes and apologetic looks of her friends and neighbours. At first, she had assumed that it was the result of their embarrassment. A sense of unease at not knowing what to say to her following Joe's death. Yet these were people she'd known for years and their reactions didn't seem to make any sense. Then, on the day when she finally felt able to sort through Joe's clothes, she found the note in his suit pocket. It contained only a single name and number, but for Kate it was another cruel blow. *Jane Blackfriars 673.*

It had taken her a week to summon the courage to make the call. Afraid of what she may discover, she felt that it was perhaps better if she didn't know. Yet it could never be that simple. If she failed to act, the doubts about her husband would always remain. Kate knew that she had no choice. She would have to find out. When she had rung, a man had answered the phone. No, he told her, Jane no longer worked there and they weren't sure where she'd gone to. She had just left without warning several weeks ago. It seemed a dead end, but then there were those looks and Kate began to wonder if her friends knew more than they were saying. Was that why so many of them seemed unable to look her in the eyes? She decided that she would ask her best friend Sarah. If anyone knew, she would and Kate felt sure that if she was gentle but insistent, she would get the answers she sought.

Sarah, Like Kate, was twenty-two and also lived in Ardwick. Kate had known her since their days at Ross Place Infant School. A spirited and pretty young woman, Sarah had beautiful, long black hair. Both she and Kate had no shortage of admirers, yet Sarah had a steady boyfriend, Len, to whom she was getting engaged. Sarah worked for the same bookmakers as Kate. Based at their Head Office in Piccadilly, she had tipped off her friend about the vacancy in Levenshulme, where Kate now worked.

When Sarah had next visited and Rosie had gone to bed, Kate had the opportunity to question her. Waiting for her moment, Kate hesitated. As such the two women sat on the settee chatting casually for some time, until Kate's voice suddenly sounded a more serious note.

"Sarah," said Kate.

"Yes Kitty."

"Will you promise to be honest with me if I ask you a question?"

"Well," said Sarah, wondering why Kate had made such a strange request. "I hope I can always be honest with you. After all, you're my friend."

Sarah waited. She felt Kate's piercing green eyes searching her features for any signs of discomfiture. Finally, Kate responded.

"Thanks. I really need to find out the truth. A few weeks after Joe died, I went through his wardrobe and in his suit jacket I found a piece of paper with a woman's name and phone number. I've rung the number but she's no longer there."

Kate paused, uncertain as to whether she should continue but, taking a deep breath, she did.

"You see Sarah, it's the way that most of the women around here look at me. It's as if they know something that I don't."

Once more, Kate hesitated. Sarah could see that she was struggling to find the words that she wanted to use.

"Go on," said Sarah, quietly.

Kate sighed, she was finding it difficult and was beginning to doubt her resolve. Perhaps, after all, she couldn't face up to finding out about Joe's secret. Yet something in her mind drove her forward. She just couldn't leave things as they were.

"Tell me Sarah," said Kate. "Have you heard anything?"

Once Kate had mentioned the piece of paper, Sarah thought that she would have no difficulty discussing the matter. After all, it was now out in the open. But it wasn't that straightforward. Her best friend was asking her to confirm that the husband she loved, had been cheating on her. Sarah felt a sickly feeling inside. Her heart seemed to jump and her chest tightened. Right now, she wished that she were anywhere but here. But she realised that there was no way out; that she was committed to telling Kate what she knew. Reluctantly, she gave her answer.

"Yes."

Kate could see that her friend was distressed. She knew that Sarah believed the news would upset her and feared that she would be angry at not having been told about Joe before. In fact, she was wrong. Kate felt a sense of relief. She had wondered about Joe's fidelity for so long, not wanting to believe her worst fears about him, but increasingly resigned to the probability that he had betrayed her. She had married a handsome young man in Joe. Before they had gone out together, Kate was aware that he'd had many girlfriends, some of whom had a reputation for being 'easy'. Joe had been desperate to go out with her, but she had always turned him down. Finally, he had convinced her that he was finished with his casual relationships; that he would be faithful to her if only she would give him the chance. Kate had finally relented, won over by his cheeky smile, his constant attention and his sense of humour. Joe had made her laugh. She was happy in his company and most importantly, he had been true to his word. It seemed to Kate that Joe really had changed. The two of them were inseparable. Joe was kind, considerate and loving.

The two had married over four years ago, when they were both eighteen. They'd needed their parents' consent, which for Kate proved difficult. She hadn't seen either her mam or dad since their separation when she was sixteen. She had finally tracked down her dad, who turned up to give her away at All Saints Register Office. Initially, their marriage had gone well. Joe went out a couple of nights a week with his friends but until Rosie was born, always returned after 'last orders'. Every week he and Kate went together to the 'Pictures' or the 'Richmond', a pub just around the corner. Yet with Rosie's arrival, Kate slowly began to notice changes. Joe started going out to the clubs in town. He would turn up at home in the early hours, often drunk and disturbing Rosie. He seemed less caring; almost resentful of their daughter's arrival. Although Kate tried to reassure him, giving him lots of love and attention, she sensed a growing distance between them. Soon, their weekly nights out together became a thing of the past. Unable to work for the first year of Rosie's life, Kate found it hard to manage the household expenses, relying as they now did, on Joe's wages alone. Yet Joe gave her very little, spending his money on fashionable clothes and nights out, giving little thought to the needs of rent, food and bills. It crossed Kate's mind that Joe was simply too immature to handle fatherhood, but she did wonder why he was so keen to dress in the latest fashions. Was he trying to impress the women in town? Yet, choosing to dismiss her concerns, Kate assumed that eventually, Joe would face up to his responsibilities. After all, she had seen the good side of his nature and was optimistic that it would, in time, return. With his death and her subsequent grief, Kate had lost her concerns about Joe's behaviour, only for them to be resurrected with the discovery of that fatal piece of paper. Now, with her simple answer, Sarah had confirmed her worst fears.

"How long did you know?" asked Kate.

"Since shortly after Joe died," replied Sarah. "Please understand Kitty. I couldn't tell you. You were utterly devastated. I didn't think that you could cope and with Joe gone, did you need to suffer any more?"

"I know," said Kate. "I know you thought you were protecting me. But I'm glad that you've finally confirmed it. It's for the best."

Kate moved along the settee and hugged her friend. She felt a sense of relief.

"I can put it behind me now Sarah. And at least I know that I wasn't imagining the way that people were looking at me. I did have moments when I thought that I was."

"It's only because people care about you Kitty. They don't like to think that Joe treated you badly."

"Yes, I suppose so," said Kate. "Come on, let's talk about something else."

With that, it had been over for Kate. She had gained some kind of closure. She would never again revisit the circumstances of Joe's death, but as she sat drinking her tea, she recognised that it had changed her. She was sure that she would never trust a man again. She would, in that way, ensure that nothing could threaten her or Rosie's happiness.

Chapter 2

"Mammy! Mammy!"

Kate could hear Rosie's voice coming from the top of the stairs. She had just woken up and with her mam missing, there was a hint of concern in her voice. Putting down her cup, Kate rose from her seat and strode quickly towards the foot of the stairs.

"Okay darling. I'm coming," said Kate.

Quickly, she climbed up to meet Rosie, who was stood behind the board on the landing, with her arms outstretched.

"Hang on, I'll soon be there."

Reaching the top, Kate moved the board and picked up her daughter. Holding her tightly, she carefully descended the stairs. Rosie was now three and a half. She could, with care, negotiate them herself, but Kate decided it was easier to take her down. It wouldn't be long though, before Rosie would be too big for her to do it anymore. At the bottom, Kate kissed Rosie on the cheek and put her down on the floor.

"Come on Rosie, let's get you some breakfast."

"Yes, please Mammy," said Rosie, excitedly.

A huge smile lit up her face. It was a smile of youthful innocence and warmed Kate's heart. Rosie trotted over to the table and climbed on to her chair, raised up by a big cushion that Kate had attached to it. She was just big enough for her arms to clear the table, so she had no trouble eating her breakfast. Kate put a bowl on the table, filled it with cornflakes and added the milk.

"Do you want to put your own sugar on Rosie?"

Rosie nodded her head, clearly pleased at being given such an important responsibility.

"Well, I'll hold the bowl. Remember, just one big spoon."

Kate watched as with almost comical concentration, Rosie very carefully placed a large dessertspoon in the sugar bowl, slowly withdrew it, so as not to drop any sugar off the edges and carefully moved it towards the bowl, before shaking the sugar over its contents. All the while, her little tongue had been protruding from the side of her mouth, only to be withdrawn, with some sense of satisfaction, when the job was complete.

"There you are," said Kate. "Aren't you a clever girl?"

Rosie looked up at her mam and smiled. A smile that beamed across at Kate. Although others may consider her opinion biased, Kate was convinced that her daughter was just like a little angel. With her sparkling blue eyes and blonde curly hair, her cheerful disposition could brighten up any day.

"Are you looking forward to going to Nanny May's?" asked Kate.

Rosie looked up at her Mam, swallowed the mouthful of cornflakes she'd been eating and nodded.

"Well, you need to get your breakfast finished and then you can get washed and changed ready to go."

Having attended to Rosie, Kate left her playing with her dolls on the settee, whilst she got washed and changed herself. Kate had always been, like all young women, very particular about her appearance. Working at a bookmaker's, she was expected to be well presented and she never failed to satisfy either the punters or her bosses. Her beautiful, long chestnut hair framed her pretty face, with its green eyes, cute nose and soft lips. She dressed simply but effectively. A crisp blouse and knee length skirt with heels. It was no surprise to Kevin, her manager, that Kate's window was the one at which most of the punters lined up to place their bets, the other female clerks having far less work to do.

Ready, Kate put Rosie's coat on and holding hands they set off for May's house on nearby Parker Street. May was already waiting for them at the front door and seeing her, Rosie couldn't help but get excited and started to pull on Kate's arm in order to get to her nanny.

"Mam! Mam! Look. Nanny May."

"I know," said Kate. "Slow down. We'll soon be there!"

Just before they reached her, Kate released Rosie's hand and she charged into her nan. May put her arms around her, then picked up Rosie and gave her a big kiss.

"Anyone would think that you've not seen me for ages," said May. "You were only with Nanny yesterday!"

Rosie buried her head into May's neck, clearly content to be reunited with her once more. It was obvious to Kate just how much Rosie loved her nan.

"Have you got time for a brew before you set off for work Kitty?" asked May.

"Yes, I should be all right for about twenty minutes. I cashed up for Kevin last night and he's told me to come in a bit later this morning."

May turned and carried Rosie through into the front room and on into the kitchen. Like the houses on Bright Avenue, those in Parker Street were two-up two-downs. Yet unlike Bright Avenue, not all of the houses had a front garden and May's was one of those. Put down in the kitchen, Rosie went straight to the settee and picked up the colouring books and crayons that her nan always left there for her. A budding little artist, Rosie was soon occupied. It gave Kate and May a chance to talk and the latter was always prepared to offer some help and advice.

May was Joe's grandmother. Her daughter, June, had been deserted by her husband when Joe was a baby and the shock had led to her disappearance, leaving May to care for him alone. Already widowed, the stress and effort had prematurely aged her. Now in her mid-sixties, May's hair was grey and her features haggard, yet humanity and kindness shone through her wrinkled face. Always subsisting on the breadline, any extra money she earned, had been spent on her grandson. Now, although Kate begged her not to, her meagre pension was carefully eked out so that she could buy toys and clothes for Rosie. May desired little for herself. She was happy to wear the handful of skirts, tops and blouses that she had possessed for many years. May had just one pretty, floral dress in her wardrobe, bought for Joe and Kate's wedding and kept for special occasions such as Rosie's christening.

May had been delighted when Joe married Kate. Kitty was kind and considerate and the two women quickly became friends. After Rosie was born May felt that Joe had let his wife down. Like his father, he had no sense of responsibility. May had helped but she could only do so much. After Joe's funeral, Kate was determined that she would provide for Rosie herself; she wouldn't rely on claiming benefits. May seized the opportunity to support her, looking after Rosie so that her mam could go out to work. Kate had quickly got a succession of jobs: in shops; as a machinist and finally, working in a betting office.

It was a job in which Kate was thriving. It was July 1962 and betting shops were a new phenomenon, only legal on the high streets for just over a year. Working for a growing firm of Manchester bookmakers, Kate had quickly impressed Kevin, her manager and the bosses down at Head Office in Piccadilly. She was already taking on more responsibility than her job as a counter clerk entailed and she would frequently open up and close the shop. She had learned quickly and was soon charged with the task of reporting the daily profits and losses. Head Office, having identified her aptitude for the business, had already asked her to move to Piccadilly. Kate though had declined. She was far happier having contact with the punters. There were so many weird and wonderful characters and parted as she was from little Rosie, they made the day pass so much quicker. Kate loved people and the job gave her every opportunity to enjoy their varied company.

Now sat at the kitchen table, May and Kate shared a brew. As Kate had come to expect, it wasn't long before she faced the almost inevitable question.

"Have you met a nice young man yet Kitty?"

"No."

"There's still no one at work?"

"No May. Anyway, as I've told you, most of them are already married."

"Oh," replied May, with a hint of disappointment. "Aren't there any nice customers?"

"Not anyone I would ever go out with. Besides, I'd be too concerned that they'd spend all their money gambling. I wouldn't go out with anyone unless I felt they were responsible."

"A pretty thing like you Kate, surely you must have some nice men interested in you."

"Well, I've been asked out a lot, but I just tend to laugh it off when it happens. It's for the best and most of the punters take it in good part. It's not like I'm being too serious and it means that I can still get along with them."

"Well, Kitty. I know our Joe wasn't as considerate and sensible as he should have been, but don't let that put you off, there's bound to be some decent blokes out there."

"Yes, I'm sure that there are, but then there's Rosie. How many men will want to take on someone else's child? Rosie will always come first, so I'm quite happy to stay as I am. She's not being pushed to one side, like I was as a kid. Rosie's far more important than any man."

Kate looked across at Rosie and back at May. Her eyes shone fiercely; a protective young mother not concerned about anything other than the welfare of her daughter.

"Look at the time," said Kate, glancing at the clock on the mantelpiece. "It's nearly ten thirty. I'd best be getting off."

Kate took a last sip of tea from her mug. Putting it down on the table, she pushed her chair back and stood up. May rose with her.

"Rosie, give your mam a kiss," said May.

Engrossed in her colouring, Rosie looked up, got off the settee and held out her arms to her mam. Kate picked her up and kissed her on the cheek before putting her back down.

"Be good for your nanny, Rosie."

"Yes Mammy," said Rosie, settling back on the settee.

"Remember Kitty, if you do meet someone and want to go out, I'll have Rosie at any time."

"I know you will," said Kate smiling, but as she walked out through the front door and made her way down to the end of Parker Street, turning left down Syndall Street towards the bus stop on Stockport Road, she thought that there would be little chance of taking May up on her offer.

Chapter 3

It was eight o'clock on Monday morning and Ed was leaving his flat on Errwood Road in Burnage. He was on his way to catch the bus into Piccadilly. It was the beginning of July and his degree course had finished. He knew that the summer would have to be spent working. He needed to earn money to supplement the grant he would receive for his postgraduate teacher training. His friend Chris had seen the advert. It was up in the Students Union, a place that Ed rarely frequented. A firm of local bookmakers were looking for temporary staff to cover their employees who were away on holiday. The job was guaranteed throughout July, August and into September. The wages were reasonable and Chris had already telephoned to arrange an interview. Ed had followed his lead and had been asked to turn up at the firm's Head Office in Piccadilly, at nine o'clock on Monday morning. Ed's grandparents had been keen gamblers and as a young boy they had often taken him to greyhound meetings at Owlerton, in his home city of Sheffield. Sometimes they had allowed him to pick a dog, placing a small bet on it. They had given him the winnings if it was successful. As such, Ed had no aversion to gambling and was intrigued by thoughts of what the job would be like.

Catching the bus on the Kingsway, Ed made his way into Piccadilly and soon found the company's offices. It was a dingy entrance. A narrow doorway, through which there was a steep flight of stairs with a large room at the top. Inside, the walls of the room were covered with large boards on which newspapers were displayed. Extracts from the 'Sporting Life' and 'Sporting Chronicle', which on closer inspection, showed the runners and riders for the day's race meetings.

"Can I help you?"

Ed looked round. The voice came from a pleasant faced and balding man stood behind the counter on the far side of the room.

"Yes," replied Ed, walking towards him. "I've been asked to arrive at nine for an interview. My name is Edward Deane."

"Oh, you've come about the summer jobs. You're a student from the University then?

"Yes," said Ed.

"Okay. Hang on."

The man came out from behind the counter and walked over to Ed.

"Follow me."

Ed followed the man through a door in the corner of the room, into a passage with smaller rooms leading off to the sides and then through a door at the end into a spacious reception area, where a bespectacled, middle-aged woman was sat at a desk.

"Hi Bill," said the woman, smiling.

"I've got a young man here to see Arnold. He's come about the vacation jobs."

"Oh, right," replied the woman.

"I'll leave him with you then," said Bill.

With that, Bill turned on his heels and departed.

"What's your name love?" asked the woman, looking up at Ed over the top of her glasses.

"Edward Deane. I'm supposed to be here for nine o'clock."

The woman looked back down at a large diary open on her desk and moved her finger slowly down the page, carefully checking the details. The finger suddenly came to a stop.

"That's right," she said, looking up. "Edward Deane, nine o'clock. Take a seat and I'll tell Mr Sheldon that you're here."

The woman got up out of her chair and disappeared through a door to the rear of her desk.

Ed moved to the side of the reception area and sat down on one of the comfortable chairs that were situated behind some low tables. On them were placed copies of the day's racing papers. Sitting down, Ed looked around the room. Hung on the walls were a series of pictures showing scenes of happy employees gathered at various company functions. The company's owners clearly wanted to create the impression that this was a friendly, family business.

After a short time, the woman re-emerged through the door. Holding it ajar she beckoned over to Ed.

"Would you like to come through? Mr Sheldon will see you now."

Ed rose from his chair and moved quickly towards the door. The woman smiled at him as he slipped past her and then shut the door behind him as he entered the room, leaving the two men together.

"Hello. Mr Deane?"

Ed nodded affirmatively.

The words came from an elderly, grey haired man behind the desk. He had sharp features; piercing eyes and a long, pointed nose. His cheeks were drawn and as he rose from his seat, Ed could see that he was small and thin. His clothes however, looked expensive. He wore a silk tie, shirt and waistcoat; his jacket placed over the back of the chair. He held out his hand to Ed across the top of the desk.

"Arnold Sheldon. It's nice to meet you."

Ed took his hand and shook it firmly. All the while, Sheldon's eyes moved across his features, weighing the young man up and down. Apparently satisfied, Sheldon disengaged his hand and motioned to Ed to sit down.

Well, what are you studying at university Edward?"

"I've just finished an American Studies degree. I'm waiting to start a postgraduate teacher training course in late September," replied Ed.

"Rather you than me," replied Sheldon, with a wry smile. "I wouldn't fancy dealing with some of the little hooligans in Manchester. Never mind, I suppose you can't go wrong with all those long school holidays, can you?"

Unsure of how to reply, Ed merely nodded.

"I assume that you saw the advert in the Students Union then?" continued Sheldon.

"Yes, one of my friends did. He told me about it."

"Oh, so you don't mind working in a bookies then?"

"No, not at all."

"Do you gamble yourself?" asked Sheldon.

"No," replied Ed.

For a moment he was about to mention his grandparents, but thought better of it.

"It's better that you don't," continued Sheldon, "because we don't like our staff gambling, especially at work. We want everyone focused on the job and looking after the punters."

"Right," said Ed.

"Have you done any other part-time work?" asked Sheldon.

"I've had temporary work in a couple of factories in previous vacations."

"Okay," said Sheldon, seemingly satisfied. "You'd be employed on what we call 'Relief'. You'll be filling in for staff all around our Manchester offices when they're on holiday or ill. It means you could be working in two or three locations every week. Don't worry though, we'll pay for your bus fares. All you have to do is keep hold of your tickets and just hand them to the shop managers and they'll give you the money back. We don't expect you to be out of pocket. You live on Errwood Road, don't you?"

"Yes," replied Ed.

"Well, you won't need your bus fare for the first couple of weeks, because I'm sending you to our office in Levenshulme. It's on Stockport Road, near the junction with Moseley Road. It's not far from you. Just off the top of Errwood Road. You start at ten-thirty and finish after the last race, once the manager's cashed up and the money's correct."

"Okay," said Ed.

"I'm assuming that you still want the job," said Sheldon. "Starting today."

"Yes, very much so. Thank you," confirmed Ed.

"Right then, if you just fill these forms in, I'll ring Kevin, the manager at Levenshulme and let him know that you're on your way."

Having filled in the details of his name, address and national insurance number, Ed said goodbye to Sheldon, shook his hand and walked out of the office to catch the bus to Levenshulme. He felt relatively pleased with himself. He had secured the job without difficulty and the extra money was really going to come in useful. He could stay in Manchester and save up a fund to help him through the coming months. The sun was shining, which added to his sense of contentment. What he had no way of knowing however, was that Sheldon's decision to send him to Levenshulme, based on his desire to save the company some money on the cost of bus fares, would lead to a meeting that would change Ed's life forever.

Chapter 4

Getting off the bus at the junction to Moseley Road, Ed walked back up Stockport Road until he reached the betting office which was nestled among a cluster of shops. It had a long, glass frontage, behind which was a screen containing a picture of a galloping horse and jockey. The door, to the side, was heavy and had to be pushed firmly before it would open. Containing painted glass, it was impossible to see into the shop from the outside, as the law of course required. Entering, Ed saw that the layout was very similar to that he'd seen earlier in Piccadilly. Boards pinned with newspapers covered the walls and underneath them were shelves where the punters, after studying the form, could write out their bets. Along one side of the room was a raised walkway, above which were a series of vertical white boards. On them were attached large sheets with the names of horses that were running in various races. On the opposite side of the room, Ed could see the shop counter, with its glass windows that rose towards the ceiling. Walking over, Ed looked through and saw a man sat at a desk in the corner.

"Excuse me," said Ed, calling through the gap at the bottom of the window. "I'm Edward Deane. I've been sent on relief by Mr Sheldon."

The man looked round. He appeared to be in his mid-thirties. He had black hair and a ruddy complexion. He smiled and got up from his chair.

"Yes, Arnold's been on the phone. You've got here pretty quick, haven't you?"

"Yes," replied Ed. "The bus didn't pick up many passengers. It's still quiet after the rush hour."

"Come to the end of the counter and I'll let you in. My name's Kevin by the way. I'm the manager."

Kevin smiled again. He seemed pleasant, which reassured Ed, given that he knew that they would be working in close proximity for the next fortnight. Reaching the end of the counter, Ed turned the corner and went through the door that Kevin had opened up for him. Kevin locked the door behind them.

"It's for security," said Kevin. "Obviously we take in a lot of money, so bookies are targets for gangs. We've been okay though since I've been here and if there's any sign of trouble, I can get straight on the phone to Longsight police station."

"Oh, okay," said Ed, uncertainly.

"Don't worry," said Kevin, laughing. "I'm sure we won't be getting robbed today! Anyway, would you like a drink of tea or coffee?"

"No thanks," said Ed. "I'm fine."

"Well, the kettle, mugs and everything you need is over there," said Kevin, pointing behind him. "You can make one anytime you like."

Ed nodded appreciatively.

"Well, I might as well get on with showing you what you have to do," continued Kevin. "You'll soon get the hang of it."

Kevin showed Ed how the till operated. How it stamped on the betting slip the amount of the stake and the time that the bet was placed. Kevin stressed how important it was to put each bet through the camera between the tills and stamp an 'off slip' when each race had started, before bringing the bets to him to settle. This guarded against paying out on 'winning' bets placed after the result had been declared. The time and number on the off slip didn't lie. No matter how much a punter may argue, it was obvious if they were trying 'to pull a fast one'. Kevin showed him how the bets, winners and losers, were filed. He warned him to be careful just before 'the off', as punters would rush to the window, throw their money on the counter and often attempt to short change the staff in the process.

"Remember, it's their fault if they leave it till the last moment and can't get their bet on in time," said Kevin. "But as I said, I'm sure you'll learn quickly and no doubt Kate will keep an eye on you at first, to make sure that the punters don't try it on because you're new."

"How many other people work here Kevin?" asked Ed.

"Through the week, just me, Kate and Sue. On Saturdays, our busiest day, I have another settler who comes in to help me with the bets and a member of the relief staff to work on the counter. Kate should be in soon, I told her to come in a bit later as she closed up for me last night. She's full-time, then there's Sue, who you're covering for, who's part-time. She doesn't come in until one, just before the first race."

As the two of them had been talking, an elderly punter had entered the shop. He had walked straight to the boards at the far end of the room and had been quietly studying the form, before writing out his selections on a couple of betting slips. Having finished, he walked slowly over to the counter.

"Here you are," said Kevin, as the old man approached, "let's see how much you've remembered. I'll wait while you take his bet."

Arriving at the window, the old man exchanged pleasantries with Kevin. He was a regular. He always bet small amounts; sixpence win, each way or doubles. For him gambling was a pleasure that gave him an interest in his retirement. He would look through his morning newspapers, study the form and then set off for the bookies so that he could put his bet on. He had no desire to win big, but always got great enjoyment out of seeing his horses occasionally come home to beat the bookie.

"Who's this then?" the man asked, looking through the window at Kevin.

The man was small with glasses and a cloth cap. He had a jacket, shirt and tie and was immaculately turned out.

"He's the relief for Sue," said Kevin.

"Oh," replied the man, clearly unimpressed.

"Edward, this is Sam," continued Kevin, turning towards Ed.

"Hello," said Ed.

"He's a student, isn't he?" asked Sam.

"Yes," replied Kevin.

"Can always tell," continued Sam, still directing his comments towards Kevin rather than Ed, who sensed that the old man had little time for students.

"Never mind lad," said Sam, finally addressing Ed himself. "At least you're prepared to do a bit of work. Unlike most of the lazy so-and-sos."

As he took Sam's bet, Ed fortunately remembered everything that Kevin had told him and he was able to hand a stamped copy of the bet back to Sam and take the money without any errors.

"Seems to know what he's doing, doesn't he?" said Sam, with a feigned look of surprise. "That's not usual, is it? Not with students," he continued, smiling.

Ed wanted to tell him that he wasn't really a student now, but decided not to bother. Any explanation would clearly be wasted on Sam who, he believed, would have no interest in it.

Folding his betting slip up and putting it in his wallet, Sam said his farewells and turned to leave, Ed and Kevin watching him as he made his way to the door and disappeared outside.

"Sam's okay," said Kevin. "Once you get to know him."

With that Kevin went to sit back down at his desk. A serious gambler, once he'd opened up the shop and completed the paperwork from the previous day, Kevin would quietly scrutinise the 'Sporting Life' to determine his selections for the day. Although Head Office didn't encourage their managers to gamble, as long as they placed their bets at their competitors' shops, they ignored it. Ed thus found himself sat on his stool in front of the till waiting to take the next punter's bet. As it would be fairly slow until just before the first race, Ed was able to stave off the relative boredom, by reading the shop's copy of the 'Daily Mirror' that Kevin kept behind the counter.

After a while, Ed glanced up at the clock on the opposite wall. It was eleven thirty. Just then, the outside door opened and a figure breezed into the shop, gliding rapidly across the floor and over to the end of the counter. Turning towards him, the figure stopped and smiled. She was beautiful. Ed couldn't help but be struck by the petite young woman, her long, wavy hair framing a smiling, attractive face. She looked very pretty in her short coat, blouse and skirt, her heels accentuating her shapely legs and figure. Ed, stunned and unable to respond, felt himself going red with embarrassment. Kevin, noticing Ed's discomfiture, smiled. He could see that Kate had gained yet another admirer.

"Hi Kate", said Kevin. "I'll just let you in."

"Thanks," replied Kate, walking around the end of the counter.

Kevin opened the door and stepped aside as Kate entered.

Ed didn't know where to look. Fortunately, as Kate stopped to remove her coat, she and Kevin struck up a conversation about the previous night's takings. This allowed him to glance down at the newspaper he had laid on the counter in front of him. Gradually, Ed began to regain his composure, his face returning to normal as it lost its flush of embarrassment. He knew that he must now look up if he didn't wish to appear rude and he was eager to make a good impression. Raising his head, he saw Kate glance towards him.

"Hello", said Kate. "Are you the relief for Sue?"

Ed nodded.

"This is Edward," said Kevin. "Edward. This is Kate."

"Hello," said Ed, getting off his stool and standing respectfully before Kate. "Most people call me Ed", he added, uncertainly.

"Not Eddie then?" asked Kate, smiling.

"Er, no," replied Ed, uncertain how to respond.

"Well if you're sure Ed," added Kate, playfully.

Ed found himself smiling too. He couldn't help it. Kate was so radiant, so lovely. He realised that she was teasing him and he loved it. Her smile electrified him; made him feel a tingling sensation. He couldn't understand it. He had never felt a reaction like this before. He hardly knew her and yes, she was beautiful, but he'd seen other beautiful women. Yet none of them had made such an immediate and unique impact upon him.

"Kate. I need to take the winnings over to the bank and run a couple of errands. Can you look after things for a while?" asked Kevin.

"Yes, sure," replied Kate.

"Okay, thanks. I shouldn't be more than an hour."

Kevin put on his coat, took the bank bag with the takings and put it into a holdall to hide it from any prying eyes. As he exited the counter, Kate locked the door behind him and turned towards Ed.

"Well, are you going to make us both a brew then, or am I going to die of thirst?"

"Me? You want me to make a brew?" asked Ed, hesitantly.

"Yes. You can make a drink of tea, can't you?"

"Yes, of course," replied Ed, secretly pleased that she had asked him. Although he didn't want a drink himself, he thought he'd best make one for both of them. After all, he had no desire to appear unfriendly.

"The tea and sugar are in the cupboard above the sink. The cups are on the draining board. The electric kettle's there too."

Kate pointed over to the corner where they were and sat down on the stool in front of the other till.

"Don't rush Ed. We don't start getting busy for over an hour."

Ed, feeling more at ease now, duly made the drinks and brought them over to Kate. Placing the mugs on the counter between them, he sat back down on his stool. It was quiet, with just a couple of punters in the shop studying the day's races. Kate took a sip of her tea. She smiled and took another.

"Well, Ed. I'm impressed. For a man you can make a good cup of tea."

"I've been making drinks of tea for years," said Ed, with a sense of satisfaction. "I can cook too," he added, with a hint of pride.

"You're quite the modern man aren't you, Ed? How come?" asked Kate, more than a little intrigued by the young man who had been sent as cover.

"I've helped around the house as long as I can remember," replied Ed. "My grandma taught me how to cook."

"Your grandma?" asked Kate.

"Yes, my parents died when I was young. It was my grandma who brought me up. She always expected me to do my share of the household chores. Keeping my room straight, washing the pots, running to the shops. I did lots of jobs around the house. My grandma said that men should be able to look after themselves; they shouldn't expect their wives to wait on them hand and foot. It certainly paid off for me, as I've had to look after myself these last three years in Manchester."

"Your grandma must be very proud of you."

"Yes, she was, but I lost her just over a year ago."

"Oh. I'm sorry," said Kate.

"It's okay. You weren't to know."

"And you have no other relatives?" asked Kate.

"Not really. I have a couple of cousins, but I never see them."

Changing the subject, Kate continued the conversation.

"Well, I am surprised that you cook for yourself Ed. I thought you students just lived on fish and chips."

"No. I can cook anything at all," said Ed, proudly.

"Oh," said Kate, sounding suitably impressed. "I'll have to put you to the test sometime."

"Yes. Any time," replied Ed.

Kate smiled at him, her beautiful green eyes alighting on his face. Ed felt that she was gently teasing him and blushing once more, he quickly turned his face away to look towards a punter who was busy writing his bet out on the far side of the shop. Kate was touched. She liked him. He had made a favourable impression on her and when he had overcome his shyness enough to look directly at her, she felt that he was quite handsome. She realised that he was a little embarrassed; that he wasn't sure of himself. She decided to help him out by once more changing the subject. Following his gaze towards the punter, she re-opened the conversation.

"No, there's not many punters around at the moment Ed. Don't worry though, you'll soon be rushed off your feet once the racing starts."

Ed turned back towards her. She was indeed a picture. He couldn't help but be aware of just how lovely she looked. Her pretty face with its cute little nose and soft, inviting lips. Her high cheekbones and beautiful, graceful neck, adorned by a simple necklace that dropped towards the slight opening at the top of her blouse. Crisply pressed and brilliantly white, her blouse was neatly tucked into a black pencil skirt that went down to just beneath her knees. She looked immaculate, yet there was nothing 'showy' about her. She wore very little make-up, just the smallest amount around her eyes. She dressed conservatively, yet this only served to accentuate her gorgeous figure, which he had immediately noticed when she had taken her coat off on her arrival. Ed was sure that she was one of the most beautiful women he had ever seen. It seemed unbelievable that he had met her today of all days, in a betting shop in Levenshulme.

"How long have you been at the University then?" asked Kate.

She was keen to continue the conversation, wanting to put the young man at ease. She wasn't naïve, she knew full well that his previous embarrassment had been because she had made a significant impression on him. Waiting for his response, she gave him an encouraging smile.

"I've finished Kate," said Ed, after a short pause. "I've done three years for my degree and I'm now getting ready for teacher training."

"Oh," replied Kate. "I hope you're going to be a decent teacher. Too many of them weren't when I was at school. We need good ones. I don't want my daughter putting up with what I had to when she goes to school."

Ed was stunned. He'd assumed that Kate was single. He felt a sense of disappointment, but for the moment, he didn't fully understand why. He now noticed her left hand. There, on the third finger, was a wedding ring. He hadn't registered its presence before. There was no reason why he would. Hearing Kate tell him that she had a child, was a surprise. Had he heard her correctly?

"A daughter?"

"Yes, Rosie. She's three and a half and I love her to bits," replied Kate. "She's at her nan's whilst I'm at work. I do miss her, although I feel better that I'm earning the money to provide for us both."

Ed was intrigued. He wanted to know more but his natural reserve and his unwillingness to appear nosy, meant that he had no intention of questioning her further. But he couldn't help thinking. Did 'both of us' mean that Kate's husband was no longer with her?

Kate could see the quizzical look on his face. She was warming to Ed and had no hesitation in opening up to him.

"You see Ed, my husband passed away two years ago. Once Rosie was old enough to be left with her nan, I was determined to come out to work to support us. I don't agree with relying on 'social.' I'll look after my daughter first and foremost, before anything else."

Ed looked at her as she spoke. The more time he spent with her, the more at ease he felt. Everything she said increased his fascination and respect for her. He listened as she told him about her life with Rosie, not realising that subconsciously Kate's recognition that she had made an impression on him, had led her to talk about her role as a mother. Kate had known many men who were attracted to her, but hesitant once they knew about Rosie. As Ed may react the same way, she was letting him know about her situation from the start. Yet Kate also sensed that there was something different about Ed; something she couldn't quite put her finger on. He was quiet, shy and not too confident, well certainly he didn't seem to be around her. He wasn't like Joe or his friends; so sure of themselves and often arrogant when dealing with women. He was placid, calm and his words and actions were considered. He hadn't once made any inappropriate comments and although he wasn't strikingly handsome, she found his gentle nature endearing. It seemed ironic that she had told May, that very morning, that there was no chance of her finding romance. As yet, Kate didn't know whether she would. Nevertheless, she was certainly looking forward to working with Ed over the coming days.

Chapter 5

Kevin returned at one thirty, fifteen minutes before the first race. The shop had become busier, the punters gathering for the day's entertainment. Many hoped that today would be their time to celebrate; that they would deliver a blow to the bookies and strike it rich. Ed was amazed to experience the tension and sense the punters' expectations rise as the loud speaker crackled into life and the runners and riders were announced for the one forty-five at Haydock Park. Andy the Boardman was in place. A rugged, respectable Scot, he had retired from his job as a mechanic at the bus depot on Hyde Road, but had found a new lease of life in the excitement of this gambler's den. He rapidly got to work scribbling down the odds, as the loudspeaker updated the betting markets at a relentless rate. Ed was swept along by the heady atmosphere. The smoke that filled the room from hundreds of cigarettes, that men sucked on as they craved relief from the tension of waiting for the exact moment to place their bets, at what they hoped would be the best odds possible. It seemed illogical. A roomful of men and a board with horses' names and prices. Nothing to look at, only the opportunity to listen to a race commentary, blaring through in a shrill metallic drone from the solitary loudspeaker. The human mind, thought Ed, how brilliant it was. How imaginative. It was amazing how out of such limited stimuli, it could create such enthusiasm, as men cheered, shouted and groaned, pleading with their horse to make that last ultimate effort over the final furlong, as the commentator excitedly relayed the action.

But Ed had to be on the ball. Kate had warned him before the first race was off.

"Ed. Once Andy starts to write down the prices, you have to be careful. The punters know you're new. They'll try it on and ask for a higher price. If it's just before the off, Kevin won't have a chance to notice and it will cause a big row when he refuses to pay them out."

Nevertheless, at first it seemed to be going well for Ed. The majority of the punters went to Kate's window and it meant that there weren't any problems for the first race. Ed, seeing Kate working far harder than himself, felt a little guilty.

"Why are they all coming to you Kate?" he asked.

"They're superstitious," replied Kate. "They think I'm lucky, when actually I'm not. You're new. They think you'll be bad luck."

With a few more races having passed, Ed had got into the routine of taking the bets to Kevin and then filing the winners. Having paid out a couple of successful punters, Ed was beginning to feel confident. He was soon to be tested however, when a middle-aged man in a smart suit and hat thrust a betting slip towards him, demanding a price of ten to one. As he had been taught, Ed looked at the horse's name, noted the race and then looked up towards the boards across the room.

"Come on, hurry up. The race is going to be off. Just give me ten to one."

The man was being quite aggressive and his attitude threw Ed out of his stride. Finding it hard to concentrate on the board, he was unable to locate the horse.

"Crikey! Where have they got you from. Just give us ten to one," continued the man. "What a complete idiot!"

Floundering, Ed was about to write the price on the betting slip when he felt a hand on his shoulder. It was Kate, who was now stood beside him. She took the bet off him and turned towards the man.

"You know better than that Bill. There's no way that Kevin is going to pay you out if it wins. It's five to four. Do you want the price or not?"

Ed looked at her. She couldn't be much more than five feet tall in her heels, yet she was stood erect, a determined look on her face and she was putting Bill firmly in his place.

Unable to sustain eye contact, Bill looked down towards the floor. Slowly raising his head, he looked sheepishly at her, unable to speak.

Ed, looking around, realised that Kate had left a queue of customers at her own window to come to his rescue. They were all desperate to get their bets on for the next race and they weren't happy.

"Get over here Kate. We're going to miss the off," shouted one.

Kate turned to them.

"I'll be there as soon as Bill here stops playing the clown."

With that the queue quietened as all eyes turned towards Bill. Ill at ease, Bill seemed to shrink into himself and meekly responded.

" Yes, I'll take five to four Kate. I'm sorry. I don't know what got into me."

"Okay Bill. Let's just forget it."

With that Kate took his money, stamped his bet on Ed's till, put the money into the tray and handed the ticket to Bill. Without any comment she went back to her own till and rapidly took the bets off the waiting punters, all of whom were dealt with before the field were under orders.

Wow! thought Ed. What a confident young woman she was. Totally in control. She had defused a situation that for him, was liable to become quite nasty and she had done it simply, directly and without anything other than a quiet, calm assertiveness. She had helped him out without any fuss whatsoever. With a brief respite offered by the running of the race, the punters all engrossed in listening to the commentary, Ed turned to thank her.

"Kate, thanks for helping me. I made a bit of a mess of that didn't I?"

Kate looked at him. She liked his vulnerability. She wasn't impressed with arrogant and aggressive men and she appreciated how Ed had shown no signs of anger towards Bill.

"It's okay Ed. Don't worry about it. He tried it on because you were new. Don't take it personally. You're doing fine. Most people new to this job take a lot longer than you have to settle in. We don't normally let anyone go on the pay out until they've been here at least a week. We all make mistakes and whilst you're getting used to the job, you're bound to have some problems. It's normal."

Kate smiled at him reassuringly. Ed smiled back.

"Ed. I'm a bit low on sixpences. Have you got many?"

Ed looked in his till.

"Yes Kate. I've got loads."

"Here's five bob. Can you give me ten sixpences please?"

Kate handed two half-crowns to Ed who took them and placed them in his till. He then collected the sixpences and holding them out in his hand, offered them to Kate. Ed felt Kate's fingers lingering over his palm as she took them from him. The touch was electrifying. Her fingers were so soft, that it felt to him almost like a caress. He felt himself blushing once more and he knew that Kate, smiling at him once again, her eyes sparkling and her lips parting slightly, had noticed.

"Thanks Ed," she said, softly.

There was no time to dwell however. The two of them had work to do and there were still many races to get through. As the afternoon wore on, Ed didn't really have the time to think about what had happened, but somehow, he felt different; a warmer, satisfied feeling coursing through his body. And then it came. The next, almost inevitable mistake and it was a huge one. Taking a bet for a shilling win, Ed rang up £10 on the till, a monumental amount that only the biggest and wealthiest gamblers would ever put on. Noticing what he'd done, Ed panicked. He realised that his till would now be £9 19 shillings down. What could he do? Holding on to the ticket, he froze, the punter looking expectantly at him not knowing what he had done. It was Sam, the old man he had met earlier that day. He often popped in during the racing to put on a couple of extra bets. Finally, Ed spoke.

"I'm sorry Sam. Could you just hang on?"

Sam looked at him but fortunately for Ed, nodded and then spoke.

"Okay lad. What have you done?"

Not registering Sam's question, Ed felt that there was only one thing he could do. Turning to Kate, he waited for her to finish taking a bet and then spoke.

"Kate. Help!"

Kate turned to him and saw the pleading look on his face.

"What's the matter," she asked, reassuringly.

"I've over staked Sam's bet. I've stamped it £10 rather than a shilling."

"You daft thing," said Kate, her face opening up into a smile. "Don't worry," she added, noting Ed's look of horror and desperation. "I'll sort it out. You come on my till whilst I deal with it."

Kate changed places with Ed and moved quickly to reassure Sam.

"Hi Sam. Ed's made an error on your bet. I'm going to have to cancel it and then issue you with a new ticket."

"That's all right Kate," said Sam, smiling.

Like most of the older punters, he was fond of Kate. She always had time for him. She laughed and joked with him, would listen to his troubles and always remembered what he had told her. She never failed to ask after his wife and family.

"These students hey," said Sam, shaking his head. "He seems a nice enough lad, but like all of 'em, he might be intelligent, but he's got absolutely no common sense."

Quickly, Kate addressed the problem. Sam got his new ticket and Kate put a note in the till attached to the old ticket to cover the over-ring. The race off, Ed and Kate swapped back to their own tills.

It's strange how something seemingly so trivial in the great scheme of things, can mark such a departure in someone's life. In so many ways, the incident crystallised the feelings that Ed had experienced over the short time that he had spent with Kate. She had dropped everything to help him. She had told him to go on her till, something she wasn't supposed to do. She had shown compassion for him and once again, had resolved his problems with understanding and without any hint of ridicule or blame. She was an angel. No one had ever been this kind to him before. And she didn't even know him; she had no reason to be so nice. It would have been easy for her to dismiss him as foolish. To take the attitude of so many he had worked with in the past. Those who resented his academic background. Eager to condemn him for any mistake he made and insistent that he would never succeed in the real world; 'the university of life.' Kate was so different and she was also so beautiful. When he had thanked her, she told him to think nothing of it. She had smiled, patted his arm and praised him for doing so well on a difficult first day.

At the end of the racing, the shop emptied quite quickly, just a few punters remaining to write out some bets for the night's dog meeting at White City. Having cashed up, the tills, pay out and takings all tallying, it was time to go home. Ed said his farewells, smiling at Kate as the two of them left the betting shop; Kate to catch the bus back to Ardwick, Ed to walk back to his flat on Errwood Road.

"I'll see you again in the morning Ed."

"Yes Kate. Thanks again for everything. You saved me more than once today."

"Don't be silly Ed. You've done really well. Actually, most of the students we get take a lot longer to learn the job and most of them don't seem to do more than sit at the till. You had a go at dealing with everything, so I'm more than happy to work with you."

"Thanks Kate. Bye."

"Bye Ed."

Kate smiled and set off to the bus stop.

As Ed walked down Errwood Road, he felt a sense of contentment. He hadn't expected this. The job was simply going to be a means to an end; an opportunity to make money to stay in Manchester and hold on to his flat in Burnage. Now he realised that he couldn't wait until tomorrow. He wanted to be back at work. And the reason for that was simple. He couldn't wait to spend more time with Kate.

Chapter 6

Ed was already waiting outside the bookies when, at ten thirty the following morning, it was time to open. As the door was unlocked however, he was in for a surprise. It wasn't Kevin standing there to welcome him, but Kate.

"Hello Ed," said Kate, smiling. "Are you all right?"

Taken aback, Ed hesitated, unable to get his words out. Although he could only have been silent for a few seconds, to Ed it seemed like a lifetime before he finally blurted out a response.

"Yes. Yes, Kate. Fine, I'm fine."

Ed felt a fool and thought that he saw a gleam in Kate's eyes. He feared that she may see him in a humorous light. In reality, nothing could have been further from the truth. Kate was pleased. His hesitancy was a clear sign that he liked her and she felt flattered that she'd made such an obvious impact on him, after such a short period of time.

"Come on in then," said Kate. "Or do you intend to stand there all day?"

Ed realised that he'd remained stationary at the door, leaving Kate to hold it open.

"Oh, yes. Right," he replied, following her into the shop.

"Are you going to make us a brew then Ed?" asked Kate, after the two of them had made their way behind the counter.

"Yes, of course," replied Ed, pleased that Kate was giving him something to focus on.

Whilst Ed made the tea, Kate was busy filing the losing bets from yesterday. Turning to look at her, Ed was careful to ensure that his eyes didn't linger for too long. She seemed even more beautiful than yesterday. Her long hair was immaculate, her face radiant and so, so pretty. She had perfect poise, a stunning figure and a calm elegance about her as she gracefully placed the slips in to the separate compartments on the wall.

Kate understood that men found her attractive and she was used to their attention. Aware that Ed was watching her, the young graduate's interest was pleasing. Kate found it refreshing that he admired her with such reserve. He was a quiet and considered young man; someone who was showing her the utmost respect. If anything were to develop between them, she would be the one in control. It was clear that although she was only slightly older than Ed, there was a gulf between them in terms of their experience. Kate had had it tough. Brought up in Ardwick, life had been a struggle, but she'd adapted and survived. She learned her way around, was confident and assertive. She had overcome her parents' divorce and the crushing loss of her husband in tragic and suspicious circumstances. She was determined to build a new life for herself and Rosie. Ed however, came from a more stable background. He'd lost his parents at a very young age and as a result, he couldn't remember much about them. Although recently he'd had to face the passing of his grandmother, he had chosen to shelter himself from the travails and tragedies of everyday life, by withdrawing into a world inhabited by books and education.

Nevertheless, Kate could see that Ed had a maturity that Joe never had. He was serious and focused on his future. Ed could look after himself and was financially responsible. One glance at his clothes told her that he wasn't like Joe. He wasn't obsessed with the latest fashions. He wouldn't be wasting money on a desire to look trendy, in an effort to impress young women. He wore a simple plain shirt and tie. A cheap coat along with trousers that had been poorly pressed. She smiled to herself when she saw them, but also noted the fact that he had tried to iron them himself. He wasn't like most of the men in Ardwick, who expected their wives or mothers to cater for their every need. Yet at the same time she had to admit that his air of vulnerability, did make her want to put a reassuring and protective arm around him.

Having made the tea, Ed took the mugs over to the counter where Kate was sat on her stool. It was only now that Ed finally registered the fact that the two of them were alone. Kevin wasn't there.

"Where's Kevin?" asked Ed.

"He's had to go to Head Office," replied Kate. "He goes once a week to take copies of the accounts."

"Oh."

"So, there's only you and me here," continued Kate. "I don't expect Kevin back until just before the first race, so you're going to have to put up with me this morning."

Kate smiled. It was a warm and inviting smile.

"That's okay," he replied.

Almost immediately, Ed felt concerned that his words may be misinterpreted. Once again, he felt foolish. Quickly, he attempted to rectify his error.

"I mean, it's nice to be here with you Kate."

Ed went red. Kate laughed softly.

"It's okay Ed, I know what you mean."

"I just meant that I like spending time with you. I...."

His words ran out. Kate could see that he was flustered, desperate not to upset her, but also not to make her feel that he was being too forward. She had never come across a real 'gentleman' before. Could it be that Ed was one? Observing the concerned look on his face, she knew that she had to rescue him from his awkwardness. She had no wish to make Ed feel uncomfortable and so quickly changed the subject.

"What are you interested in Ed? Outside of your studies I mean?"

"Well. Football, cricket and music" replied Ed, pleased that Kate had once again put him at ease.

"I used to go to watch United when I was younger," said Kate. "Since I've had Rosie, I've not really been as interested. Who do you follow Ed?"

"Sheffield United."

"Why?"

"Because I'm from Sheffield."

"Oh," said Kate, sounding surprised, "you don't really sound like it. I went to Sheffield to watch the Reds play Wednesday when I was sixteen. It was strange on the buses, hearing the accent. So different to Mancunians. How come you've not got much of an accent Ed?"

"I don't know really. My Grandma certainly had an accent. I've never given it much thought. Perhaps I should sound more like a Sheffielder."

"No. You're fine as you are Ed. I think you speak nicely. You don't need to change, just be yourself."

Kate's words made Ed feel good. He wondered if she knew just how much what she had said had pleased him. She was such a nice, friendly person. It seemed so natural for her to find a positive in almost anything.

As the morning passed, the two of them, only infrequently interrupted by the few punters who came to place their bets, talked continuously. Their conversation ranged over a variety of subjects. They were getting to know one another, sharing an intimacy that would have seemed unthinkable when they had first met yesterday. It seemed to Ed that no time at all had passed before Kevin returned and the first race was about to begin. The afternoon sped by, Ed revelling in every moment he spent in Kate's company. However, when it was time to say goodbye at the end of the day, Ed was to be in for a disappointment.

"I'll see you tomorrow morning Kate," said Ed, holding the door open for her as they left the shop.

"No, I won't be in again until Thursday. It's my day off tomorrow. Every Wednesday. I get it off in place of Saturday."

"Oh," said Ed, hesitantly.

Unable to hide his disappointment, Ed hoped that Kate hadn't noticed, but of course she had and realised now just how much of an effect she was having upon him.

"I'll be able to spend some time with Rosie. I can take her to the park and into town. I want to buy her a couple of summer dresses," added Kate, again making Ed fully aware that she was a young mother whose primary responsibility was to her daughter.

"Have a nice time," replied Ed. "I'll see you again on Thursday then Kate."

"Yes. Bye Ed."

"Bye Kate."

Ed smiled and turned to walk home. After a few steps he looked back to see Kate crossing the road to the bus stop. She looked lovely. He was certain that it wouldn't be as enjoyable at work tomorrow without her.

Sat on the bus home, Kate thought about the events of the last two days. She was well aware that she'd made an impression on Ed. The signs were plain to see. The way he blushed and averted his eyes from her in shy embarrassment and his eagerness to please. What had surprised her though, was her own reaction. He wasn't physically tough in the way that many men in Ardwick were. He was gentle, considerate and unselfish, yet determined too. They were qualities that she found attractive. So, what should she do? She knew that she would have to make the running if she decided to go out with him and that, she'd never done with any man before. After Joe had been unfaithful to her, Kate knew that any attempt to find love would become a matter of trust. She would only be prepared to take a chance on someone, if she really believed that their relationship could become serious. When she had talked to Ed, she had made it clear just how important Rosie was to her. Perhaps she had done this to try and push him away. She therefore decided that she would wait to see how Ed reacted over the following days. She would give him a chance to get over her. After all, she may only prove to be a passing infatuation for him. Nevertheless, she couldn't help thinking that her time with Ed had proved surprisingly enjoyable.

Chapter 7

For Ed, Wednesday was just one of those days. It had to be got through in order to reach Thursday, when once again he could spend time with Kate. Yet as he walked up Errwood Road on Thursday morning, he wasn't sure what his sense of anticipation really meant. Kate's own assessment of him was correct. He was inexperienced where women were concerned. Whereas his friends boasted about their 'conquests', real or imagined, Ed wouldn't go out with someone for the sake of it, no matter how much the hormones coursed through his young body. Although they would playfully rib him about it, Ed was consistent in turning down the blind dates that his friends arranged for him, maintaining that it was dishonourable to go out with anyone that he had no feelings for.

As yet, Ed hadn't seriously considered the possibility that Kate could be his girlfriend. He was falling in love with her, but he didn't know it. At first, when he had met her, he had assumed that she already had a boyfriend; how couldn't she have, she was gorgeous. Then she told him about her husband and her daughter. Her whole demeanour and her situation automatically made him assume that he lacked the qualities to be taken seriously by her. The thought that they could become romantically involved, seemed ludicrous. She was way out of his league on so many levels. Yet as he walked to work, he found himself speeding up and experiencing a growing sense of expectation that was clearly due to the fact that he would soon be seeing her.

Once again, he arrived early, making sure that he'd be there as soon as Kevin opened the door. He wouldn't risk missing spending even a minute less with Kate. And so Thursday progressed through Friday and into Saturday and the two of them became ever more comfortable in each other's company. Together, they shared stories about their lives, discussed the news in the papers, the merits of the songs playing on Kevin's radio and laughed and joked together, content in each other's company. It was as if their time at work was like one long, unofficial date. In fact, thrown together in this way, there was nothing artificial about their interaction. There was none of the reserve and awkwardness that was typical of couples on their first few dates. The betting shop had brought the two of them together and the challenging working environment created stresses which would determine the depth of their feelings for one another.

Kate was there to greet Ed on the following Monday morning, when she opened the door at ten thirty. It was a pleasant surprise for Ed who quickly learned that Kevin wouldn't be in until later. Quickly, Ed made them both a drink and the two of them sat on their stools, beside their tills, chatting away and telling each other about their respective Sundays. They were interrupted by Sam. He had warmed to Ed as the days had progressed. After Ed's over-ring he'd avoided any further errors and Sam could see that he was a young man who worked hard, unlike the usual lazy and disinterested students who came to the shop in the summer. Approaching Kate, Sam passed over his bet and struck up a conversation with her.

"He's not a bad lad, is he?" asked Sam, talking to Kate as if Ed wasn't there.

"Yes, he's all right," replied Kate.

"Hasn't got much experience about him though, has he Kate? You can tell he's been wrapped up in books. He hasn't seen much of the real world."

"Well, he probably hasn't," said Kate, glancing mischievously at Ed.

"I bet there's a lot out there that he doesn't know about," continued Sam.

This time Sam glanced across at Ed and laughed quietly. Ed sat still, not knowing how to react. He knew that Sam didn't mean anything by his comments, that he was being light-hearted and meant no harm.

"Yes. I definitely think you're right there Sam. Perhaps I should take him under my wing and teach him a few things," said Kate.

Turning to Ed, Kate smiled. Stamping Sam's bet she gave him his ticket. He thanked her and left.

Had she realised what she'd said? It was a question that immediately leapt into Ed's mind. Her words had given him hope, but was Kate being serious? Would she be prepared to go out with him? He looked at her, but her face was giving nothing away. It struck him that her words had actually meant nothing, that she was being light-hearted and friendly with Sam. It was what she was like. Ed couldn't help but feel a sense of disappointment.

Kate noticed Ed's reaction and it was no coincidence that he had gone very quiet, focusing his attention on a copy of the 'Daily Mirror' open on the counter at the side of his till. She looked at him closely, knowing that he was unaware of her attention. He had a long angular face. His nose was perhaps a little too big, but she liked his mouth and his white teeth that showed when he was concentrating and his lips were slightly parted. His black, curly hair needed cutting. She'd have to see to that she thought, if ever she were to go out with him. And there she was again, thinking about the possibility of becoming more intimate with him. She realised that her words to Sam had raised Ed's hopes that she could be something more than a friend. It made her feel guilty. He was clearly sensitive and Kate had no wish to upset him, but suspected that she had. She was now determined to lighten the atmosphere.

"Did you want another drink, Ed?"

Ed looked up from the paper and started to move off his stool.

"No, it's all right. I'll make it," said Kate. "You sit there."

"Thanks," replied Ed, pleased to be talking to Kate again.

"Don't mind me and Sam, we're only being silly Ed."

"No, I don't. I know," replied Ed.

Kate knew that he wasn't being honest but she was determined to cheer him up.

"Anyway, I'm sure you've had lots of experience of life. No doubt you've had a few girlfriends."

"No, I haven't," said Ed, with sincerity.

The answer stunned Kate. She couldn't imagine any other man being prepared to admit to such a fact. They'd lie rather than reveal it.

"You must have had a girlfriend," continued Kate.

"Not really."

"Why?"

Kate was intrigued, she could tell by the way he looked at her that he was certainly attracted to the opposite sex.

"I've never met anyone I really liked enough."

"What. Not just someone you could go out with to the pictures to have fun?"

"No," replied Ed. "If I didn't really like them, then it wouldn't seem right."

"Why not?"

"Well, I think you really have to love someone. If I go out with anyone, I want it to mean something."

"You're a real romantic, aren't you?" said Kate, with obvious approval.

"Well, yes. I suppose I am."

Aware of his sensitivity and feeling increasingly at ease in Ed's company, Kate found herself opening up to him.

"You know Ed, I've had a lot more experience of life than you have. I've grown up in a tough area. I've lost contact with my parents, who I've hardly seen since they divorced and I lost my husband. I've known lots of men and let me tell you, they certainly don't take the attitude towards women that you do. Yet for all that you've had a sheltered life, you're more mature and responsible than any of them. I don't have a boyfriend

Ed. Oh there are lots of men that would like to be, but I fear that they would only want me and not Rosie. And there's no way that I'll have any man telling me what to do. My marriage wasn't always easy, I'll be honest with you and I'm determined that in my home, I'll be the one who makes the decisions. Don't let anyone, any of your friends, change you Ed. Stick to your guns. You'll find the right girl, because you deserve to."

At that point, the front door opened and in came Kevin. It was at the perfect time for Kate. It drew a line under her words, but to Ed it proved frustrating. He'd almost felt as if he could open his heart and ask her if she would be that girl. If she would go out with him. Before he could do that, Kevin had returned and the moment was lost. He felt utterly frustrated. Worse still, Kevin had news for him from Arnold. It would be his last full week at Levenshulme. Sue was returning from her holidays and next Monday, Ed was being sent to Claremont Road in Rusholme and it was unlikely that he would be returning other than on a Saturday. It seemed to Ed that the fates were against him. For all too brief a time, he'd dared to hope that he had a chance to build a relationship with Kate, but now it seemed that the dream was over.

It was with a heavy heart that he went home that night to be alone in his flat. It was the first time that his loneliness had bothered him. Thinking logically, Ed tried to persuade himself to be sensible. After all, he had only known Kate for a few days. He'd got carried away and he'd forget her when he moved to another shop. But deep down, he knew it wasn't true. He now understood that he was utterly in love. He'd spent so much time with her. They had talked for hours, had worked together and he admired everything about her. He knew that it was time to be strong. If he really cared about Kate, then he had to tell her. But could he? The fear of failure gnawed away at him. Perhaps it was better to always dream of what might have been, if he had shown the courage to ask her out, rather than to do so and face the cold reality of rejection.

Chapter 8

Arriving at May's house in Parker Street, Kate was given a warm welcome by Rosie. As she entered the kitchen through the back door, her daughter rushed towards her. Smiling, Kate dropped her bag and swept Rosie up in her arms, giving her a big kiss on both cheeks.

"Have you missed your mam, Rosie?"

"Yes," said Rosie nodding, her curly locks flicking backwards and forwards.

Kate put her daughter down and the two of them sat at the table, where Rosie proceeded to show her mam one of the pictures she had produced in her absence.

"Oh, that's lovely Rosie," said Kate, looking at a series of rough squiggles and odd shapes that had been splashed with the colours of various crayons.

"What is it?" she asked hesitantly, trying not to upset Rosie.

"It's you, me and Nanny May" said Rosie proudly and with more than a hint of surprise that her mam hadn't recognised the three of them.

"She's been waiting to show you that one Kate. She's very proud of it," said May. "Here's some more that she's done. You can have a look through them whilst I make us a brew."

May handed a bundle of pictures to Kate, who could see that her daughter had been busy. Her eyes fixed steadily on her mam, Rosie, kneeling on the chair, excitedly bobbed up and down as Kate looked through them, nodding her approval and praising her for being a clever girl.

"I think Rosie wants me to put the picture of the three of us on the wall," said May, returning with the drinks. "You do, don't you love?" asked May, looking at her great granddaughter.

"Yes, please Nanny," said Rosie, nodding.

"Well, I'm sure I can," replied May. "Why don't you go and sit on the settee and draw your mam another picture whilst I talk to her Rosie."

Obediently, Rosie got off her chair and went over to the settee, watched by her adoring mam. She was such a good girl thought Kate, not a hint of trouble. She was so pleased at how easily Rosie had taken to spending the day with her nan. May had done an excellent job and so had removed all Kate's misgivings about leaving her young daughter to go to work. The extra money that she earned and the opportunity to have a life outside the family home, albeit at work, was beneficial to both her and

Rosie. When Kate was at home with her daughter, she fully appreciated the time they had together. She believed that she had become a better mother, with a heightened sense of her responsibilities and more aware of her daughter's emotional needs.

"Well, how was it at work?" asked May, casually engaging Kate in conversation as they sat together at the table.

"Oh, all right," replied Kate, smiling.

"You seem to have been more cheerful over the last few days," continued May.

"Cheerful?" asked Kate, a surprised look on her face.

"Yes. Just lately, you've seemed pretty content with yourself when you've arrived home from work."

"Oh, have I?" asked Kate, smiling.

"Yes," replied May, pausing. "Are you going to tell me about it then?"

"Tell you about it?" continued Kate, feigning surprise.

"Come on Kitty. I know you better than that. There's got to be something happening at work. You don't go anywhere else, do you?"

Kate smiled.

"You know me better than I know myself."

"Well?" asked May, expectantly.

Kate hesitated, unsure whether she should tell her about Ed. After all, there was nothing really concrete to say. She'd met a nice man at work. She liked him and was well aware that he felt strongly about her too.

"Well," began Kate, "there is a guy who started at the bookies last week."

"I knew it!" said May, triumphantly. "I knew it had to be a man. Nothing else would have brought a smile to your face. If it was some improvement to your job, then you would have told me. When you didn't, I just knew."

Kate had been stopped in her tracks. May did know her all too well and had an unerring ability to sense her feelings and emotions. She couldn't disguise them from her, no matter how hard she tried. If she wanted any peace, she was going to have to tell her about Ed.

"His name's Ed, but there's really nothing to get excited about."

"Isn't there?" asked May, unconvinced by Kate's response and probing for more information.

"It's difficult May. He's a really nice guy. He's finished university and is going to be training to be a teacher. He's just at the bookies to earn some money to help him through the summer."

"Well, he's obviously a worker," said May, approvingly. "He's not one of those layabout students who just live off their parents."

"I don't think his family were particularly well off. He's from Sheffield and was brought up by his grandma."

May nodded approvingly. She hadn't met Ed but what Kate had told her had created an affinity between her and the young man. After all, she too was playing a key role in bringing up her grandchild and Ed came from a background similar to their own.

"He'll not be well off if he's from Sheffield," said May.

A Mancunian, who had only ever been out of the city on day trips to Blackpool, May regarded Sheffield as an archetypal, grimy industrial city, famous for its steelworks and cutlery. No, May was positive that his family couldn't have any money if he came from Sheffield.

"Never mind though," continued May. " He's going to be a teacher you say. He'll do all right then. Its good money that teachers get. You'll be living in Sale or Gatley."

Kate couldn't help but laugh. She'd told May about a new man at work and already she had her married off and living in the suburbs. It wasn't long though, before Kate became more thoughtful.

"You know me May. I'm not too bothered about money. That's the last thing that concerns me about a man. It's his heart, not his bank balance, that I want."

"Believe me Kate, there's nothing wrong in looking for security. Love's overrated. You should know that from our Joe, God rest his soul."

"No May. I won't believe that," said Kate, with conviction. "That's why I wasn't going to mention anything. I have to be sure everything is right before I commit."

"But why do you have to wait? The fact that you're talking about him means you must like him. Surely, you could just go out with him. You are allowed to have some fun you know."

"I do like him May. He's different. He's not all over me. He's not once tried it on. He's quiet, shy really and I have to say that attracts me. He's nice looking, I wouldn't say really handsome, but he's got a good heart and I know that he likes me. I'm finding it hard not to encourage him too much. I love talking to him. He makes me smile, but I'd hate to give him encouragement and then end up not going out with him."

"Oh, Kate. You do worry the life out of me," said May, with a sigh of frustration. "You always have to make everything so complicated, don't you?"

"Well, it is complicated. There isn't just me to think about."

"I know," said May, "but you do know that Rosie won't stay a child forever. She'll grow up, leave home and have a family of her own. You can't give up on the chance of happiness for yourself. You're too pretty, too nice a person to end up like me. This lad could be the one for you.

You have to give it a try. What's the harm in just going on a date with him and seeing how it turns out? Anyway, does he know about Rosie?"

"Yes. I told him about her almost as soon as I met him."

"And, he's still interested in you?"

"Well, yes. More so than ever."

"Kate, you're always saying that other men wouldn't want to take Rosie on; would resent having to care for another man's child. Well, maybe you've got it wrong."

"Perhaps I have May and that's why I'm so uncertain, because for me to be considering going out with him, tells me that I think Ed may be someone that I could learn to love. But it's so difficult."

May could see the anguish on Kate's face. She moved her hand across the table and placed it reassuringly on her arm. May recognised that it had taken a lot for Kate to share her feelings and concerns. She knew that Ed must be a generous and warm-hearted soul. Only such a man could attract Kate. Yet May doubted that Kate would be prepared to enter into a relationship with Ed, no matter how much she encouraged her to do so. Let down badly by her grandson, Kate was afraid of ever putting her faith in any man again. As Kate and Rosie prepared to return home, May was inclined to believe that she would hear little more about Ed.

Chapter 9

Back in work on Tuesday, Kate and Ed's positive relationship continued. It was clear to anyone that the two of them got on like a house on fire. They were like a contented couple, easy in each other's company and with a familiarity that belied the relatively short period of time that they'd spent together. Kevin had noticed their closeness and so had many of the punters, especially Sam who exchanged knowing looks with Kate when he put his bet on that morning.

"So, have you thought about it Kate?"

"About what Sam?"

"About Ed there."

As usual, Sam was talking to Kate about Ed, as if he wasn't actually sat on the stool next to her.

"What about Ed?" asked Kate, raising her eyebrows.

"Well, I think he needs the love of a good woman. Don't you? All this time with his head stuck in a book. What can we do about it, hey?"

Kate laughed.

"Well, we'll just have to wait and see, won't we Sam?"

She winked at him and smiled again. She couldn't help it. She loved little Sam. He could always make her laugh.

"Probably never goes out. Doesn't look the type does he Kate? But he might for the right girl, hey?"

"Well, you never know Sam. Perhaps he might."

Whether or not Sam's aim was to try and help his chances with Kate, Ed didn't know. The conversation had confused him. Kate's responses to Sam's questions, had suggested that she would be prepared to go out with him, but he still had his doubts. Was Kate just being her usual, cheerful self, playing along with Sam, given that she was apt to engage in banter with so many of the punters?

Every contact with Kate was now charged with meaning for him. The touch of her hand when they exchanged money, was electrifying. He couldn't believe how something so basic, could elicit such a response from him. And he was sure that she let her fingers linger, almost as if to tease him. He felt a real intimacy between them and she was so close to him, sat on the stool just a couple of feet away, her hair framing her face, the stray locks that she would brush away from her eyes with her delicate fingers. Her elegant neck and crisp blouse, open at the top and drawing his eyes to the pendant on her necklace and the beautiful, soft skin beneath. And he just knew that she sensed everything about his deepest feelings for her.

Walking home after work, Ed knew that he would have to find the courage to ask her out. He decided that he would do so tomorrow but then realised that he couldn't because it was Wednesday, Kate's day off. So, Thursday. It would be Thursday he told himself. He would ask her for definite. He had to take the risk of suffering her rejection. But when Thursday came, the opportunity looked to have gone. It wasn't Kate who let him into the shop but Kevin and he had some concerning news.

"Kate's not in today, Ed. We've got Sarah coming in from Head Office to cover for her."

"Is she all right? "

Kevin noticed the look of concern on his face and was quick to reassure him.

"Yes. It's her daughter. She's been taken ill in the night and Kate had to take her to the MRI; to Casualty. Obviously, she's only a toddler and she's a little upset, so Kate's taken a couple of days off to look after her."

Ed was relieved. He'd feared the worst. He thought that something terrible had happened. He was just so pleased that everything seemed to be okay. His thoughts about asking Kate out had immediately been forgotten and with Kate not there, it was a while before he realised the implications of her absence. Most importantly though, he felt that he wanted to let her know that he was thinking of her and to give her his best wishes for Rosie, who he knew meant so much to her.

"Is Kate on the telephone Kevin?" asked Ed.

"No. We don't have a phone number for her."

Ed wasn't surprised. There were still lots of homes that didn't have their own phone.

Why do you ask?" continued Kevin.

"I just wanted to let her know that I was thinking about her. It must have been a big shock for her."

Kevin smiled. He knew that Ed had completely fallen for Kate. It had been obvious to him since the day Ed had arrived.

"Well," said Kevin, "I know that Kate's friendly with Sarah. Sarah's been the relief here quite a few times and I know that she often visits Kate. Perhaps she can tell you Kate's address and you can go and see her after work."

His spirits lifted by Kevin's comments, Ed waited eagerly for Sarah to arrive. He didn't have that long to wait. A cheerful and bubbly character, Sarah wasn't much older than Ed and he was delighted to find out that she did indeed know where Kate lived, even to the extent of drawing a little map on the back of a betting slip, so that he could navigate his way through the warren of streets from the bus stop at Devonshire Street, to 17 Bright Avenue where Kate lived.

"You shouldn't find it too difficult Ed. If you walk down Syndall Street, which cuts between Stockport and Hyde Roads, you'll see it branching off to the side."

Appreciative of the help that Sarah had given him, Ed's initial enthusiasm soon began to wane as he started to worry about how Kate would react if he were to just turn up on the doorstep. He soon found that he was expressing his misgivings to Sarah, somehow hoping that she could give him some definitive advice.

"I'm sure everything is all right with Rosie, but I wonder if Kate won't want me intruding. Maybe she'll want to be alone. Not want people coming to mither them."

Sarah's response came as a shock to Ed, but it was a pleasant and surprising one.

"No. It'll be fine Ed. Kate will be pleased to see you. Rosie is ever so friendly and it won't upset her meeting you. Kate will be glad of the company. She's told me all about you. I'm sure that you don't have to worry about intruding."

"Told you all about me?"

Sarah smiled as she saw the confused look on Ed's face.

"Yes. She mentioned you when I went around to see her at the end of last week. You know how we girls are. We like a chat. I know quite a bit about you Ed."

"Oh," said Ed hesitantly, unconsciously averting his eyes.

"Don't worry," continued Sarah, who had noticed his embarrassment. "It was nothing bad."

Sarah laughed and picked up the newspaper from the counter and sat down on her stool to read it, whilst Ed busied himself with filing away the losing bets from yesterday.

Taking a short break to fetch himself a sandwich for his dinner, Ed thought that it would be nice to buy a little present for Rosie, to help her over her illness. He knew that there was a toy shop just down the road, so he made his way there and bought her a small doll; a baby with a bonnet, a dummy and a bottle. Inexperienced when it came to knowing about gifts for young girls, the woman in the shop assured him that his present was suitable for a toddler. Pleased with himself, Ed returned to work only to stop as he reached the door to the bookies. 'Kate,' he thought, 'what about Kate? I can't not buy her something too'. Crossing the road once more, he went into the newsagents and bought Kate a small box of Cadbury's Milk Tray. He was sure that she'd like them.

Back in work, Ed put his presents safely on the side, having shown them to Sarah who was suitably impressed and reassured him that Kate wouldn't be offended by them. She could see that Ed was desperate to make a good impression on Kate; eager to avoid anything that could possibly upset her. She watched him as he worked through the afternoon. He looked tense and on edge. He was clearly unsure about his trip to Bright Avenue. It was such a natural, everyday event to visit someone, but to Ed it was charged with both fear and expectation and Sarah wondered if he would actually go ahead and make the journey to Bright Avenue after all. Inwardly, Sarah couldn't help but feel a rising sense of sentimentality. It was so touching to see Ed's obvious concern for Kate. He was a young man who impressed her as warm and caring and most of all, she could see that he was clearly very much in love with her friend.

Yet Ed certainly wasn't her type. He was too reserved. Sarah liked men who were assertive and confident; who took charge. Yet she could see why Kate was attracted to him. Ed was the perfect antidote to the disappointment she had suffered at the hands of Joe. Kate needed a safe man; steady, predictable and secure. She'd had enough of excitement and uncertainty. That had been fine for her while she was Joe's girlfriend and even when she was first married. Once Rosie had come along, Kate had expected Joe to change, yet it hadn't happened. From the way she'd heard Kate talk about Ed, it was clear that she liked him. From Ed's nervousness and uncertainty that afternoon, it was clear however, that Kate hadn't let him know that. Sarah hoped that Kate could find her way to accepting Ed's affections. However, when she looked at how emotionally confused Ed seemed to be and when she knew the basic distrust that Kate held for men in general, the chances of them getting together seemed, in bookies parlance, a real long shot.

Chapter 10

Fortunately, Ed's resolve didn't let him down. Leaving work, a hearty 'good luck' ringing in his ears from Sarah, Ed made his way over to Errwood Road and set off on the walk back to his flat. 'Good luck'. He turned the words over in his mind. He knew that Sarah was well aware that his visit to Kate was far more than just to show his concern over Rosie. It was to try and let Kate know just how much she had become a huge part of his life and how he wanted to become a part of hers.

Arriving home, Ed had a quick wash and changed his clothes. Gathering up the box of chocolates and Rosie's doll, he left his flat and walked the short distance to the Kingsway to catch the bus down to Ardwick. It was only a few minutes before the bus arrived. Ed was soon sat down watching the scenery rush by. A peculiar feeling began to develop in the pit of his stomach. It was nerves and trying to calm himself, Ed breathed out slowly, expelling the air from his lungs and then following it with a huge intake of breath. The exercise didn't work though. He couldn't ignore the tension that continued to build inside him. All he could do was to continue to gaze out of the window, looking for the familiar landmarks as the bus made its way down Slade Lane and then on to Stockport Road and into Longsight. Ed soon became impatient, his frustration mounting as the bus stopped regularly in order to pick up or drop off its passengers. As the journey seemed to become more protracted, Ed couldn't help but feel nervous. He was desperate to arrive at his destination.

After what seemed like an age, the bus finally reached Devonshire Street, Ed's cue to disembark. Stepping onto the pavement, Ed stood for a moment and watched the bus slowly move off down Stockport Road. Ed took another deep breath. He had feared that his nerve would fail him, but the bus had gone and here he was. Now all he had to do was cross over the road and then there would be no turning back.

With relatively little traffic, crossing the road was easy. On the other side, Ed took the betting slip from his pocket on which Sarah had drawn the map. Looking at it, he then started to follow its directions, walking down Stockport Road. It was only a short distance to the junction with Syndall Street. Ed paused at the corner. The map showed him three roads branching off to the right, the third one being Bright Avenue. With determination, Ed walked briskly up Syndall Street. He was eager to get to Kate's quickly. In that way he would give himself no opportunity to think, for Ed knew that if he were to start to reflect on what he was doing, then he may hesitate and all could be lost.

Reaching Bright Avenue, Ed stopped and turned to look at Horseman's newsagents on the corner, marked clearly on Sarah's map. He looked back down at the map and then again at the shop. He was hesitating, rooted to the spot. It was almost as if he wanted it not to be true; that he hadn't actually found Kate's and could therefore avoid the shattering possibility, that she may respond negatively when he presented himself at the front door. Ed told himself not to be foolish. He had come all this way now and he'd also bought Rosie a present. It was ridiculous not to give it to her. Having mentally chastised himself, Ed advanced purposely down Bright Avenue.

The road contained terraced houses on both sides; two-up two-downs that had been built at the turn of the century. Ed knew that they were probably due for demolition in the not-too-distant future, Manchester Corporation having announced its intention to launch a slum clearance programme that included much of Ardwick. Yet these houses were no slums that Ed could see. It was clear that the families here took pride in their homes and their neighbourhood. As Ed walked down the road, he could see the gleaming windows and neat and tidy curtains. There were small enclosed areas, little gardens with fences and some with small hedges, that set the houses back from the pavement. As Ed looked over them to the numbers on the doors, he could see that the front steps had all been 'brown stoned' and looked spotlessly clean. At the end of the street were groups of young children. Some girls skipping rope and boys on the floor playing marbles. It seemed to Ed a perfect playground with not a car in sight and a dead-end created by the backs of the houses from a nearby street, which meant that Bright Avenue was no thoroughfare.

Reaching number seventeen, Ed walked up to the front door and knocked loudly. He waited, but there was no answer. Uncertainly, Ed knocked again. This time it wasn't long before he heard a movement behind the door and then slowly, it opened. An elderly woman with grey hair and a careworn face, stared out at him.

"Yes?" asked the woman.

"Oh, I'm sorry. I was looking for Kate. I must have been given the wrong address."

The woman, noticing the young man's confusion, smiled.

"No love. You're right. Kate does live here. Who are you?"

"I'm Ed. I work with Kate. I've come to see her. She wasn't at work and I heard about Rosie and I wanted to see if everything was all right."

"Yes, it is. I'm May, Rosie's nan," said the woman. "I've heard about you Ed. Kate has mentioned you."

"Oh," said Ed, sounding surprised.

After a slight hesitation, he continued.

"I've brought a present to help cheer Rosie up. I've got something for Kate too."

Ed lifted up a small holdall in his right hand in which were contained the chocolates and the doll.

May thought it was Ed as soon as he'd spoken. He was unassuming, slightly shy and didn't sound like a Mancunian. The look of disappointment on his face when she appeared at the door, made it clear that he was eager to see Kate instead. Putting all these facts together, it suggested that he could be no one else but Kate's new workmate.

"Well, Ed. Don't be standing out there, come in. Kate has had to go to the chemists to fetch some medicine. She shouldn't be too long. Rosie's here. You can give her the present yourself."

May stood to one side and indicated for Ed to come through the door, as she held it open for him.

"Thank you," replied Ed, as he stepped into the front room.

May closed the door behind him.

"We're in the back," she continued. "You're lucky I heard you. Everyone normally comes to the back door."

"Oh," said Ed, following her through into the kitchen.

As he entered, Ed could see a little girl sat at the table. She was busy crayoning in a picture book. Deep in concentration, it seemed that she hadn't noticed that Ed had come into the room. Looking closely at her, Ed was struck by how cute she looked with her blonde curly hair in which was placed a pale, blue ribbon. She was wearing a pretty blue dress and on top of it a thin, white summer cardigan. On her left hand and wrist was a large bandage.

"Rosie," said May.

Rosie looked up and saw Ed. He smiled at her and she smiled back.

"Mammy's friend, Ed, has come to see us. Say hello."

"Hello Ed," said Rosie, cheerily.

"Hello Rosie," replied Ed.

"Rosie, are you going to show Ed what you've been doing then?" continued May.

"Yes, Nanny."

"Go and sit down at the table Ed and while you're looking at Rosie's colouring book, you can give her your present."

Ed did as he was asked and sat down. Rosie was cheerful and confident; she was a little chatterbox. Ed listened as she told him all about her pictures and May noticed how Ed asked Rosie lots of questions and praised her as he looked at the various pictures that she showed him. May was surprised. He seemed a natural with children, then again Kate had told her that Ed planned to become a teacher. It made her think. Why hadn't her own grandson shown such an interest in his daughter?

"Ed," said May, "you've forgotten about your present."

"Oh, yes. Of course," replied Ed who, fascinated by Kate's little girl, had forgotten the reason for his visit. Picking up the holdall he opened it, took out the doll and handed it to Rosie.

"Look Rosie. It's a little baby. It's yours to play with," said Ed.

Rosie stared at the present in wide-eyed amazement.

"Go on, take it," said Ed, handing it to her.

"What do you say?" said May.

"Thank you," said Rosie, beaming a huge smile at Ed, who couldn't help giving her a broad grin in return.

"Go and sit on the settee Rosie. You can play with your new doll whilst I make Ed a cup of tea. You'd like a drink, wouldn't you?" she asked, turning to Ed.

"Oh, yes please," replied Ed.

Having made the tea, May sat down at the table with Ed.

"Oh, May. I've also brought a box of chocolates, Milk Tray, for Kate. I best give them to you in case I have to go before Kate gets back."

"Thank you," said May, as Ed took them from the holdall and put them on the table.

"Kate likes Milk Tray. You must've known."

With Rosie no longer at the table to distract him, Ed was now conscious that Kate was still absent and as May watched him, he seemed to be getting a little agitated.

"I suspect that Kate has had a problem finding a chemist," said May. "I thought that she would have been back by now. We just wanted some liquid painkiller in case Rosie's hand started hurting her again."

"What happened?" asked Ed.

"Rosie dropped a cup on the floor and it broke, and then she cut her hand badly when she tried to clear it up. Luckily, one of the neighbours has a car and was able to drive her and Kate to the Royal, where she had to have some stitches. She was very brave but Kate was in bits. She blamed herself. I told her not to be so daft. Kids have accidents. It can't be helped."

The conversation put Ed at his ease. He liked May. She was friendly and genuine and it was clear that she cared for Kate and her great granddaughter. She had asked him about his time at university, teaching and about working at the bookies, but never once had she tried to pry into his feelings about Kate. The two had been chatting for some time but there was still no sign of Kate. Looking at the clock, Ed decided that he would need to be making a move in order to catch the bus back to his flat.

"I think that I'd best be going," said Ed and then as an afterthought added, "you don't think that there's anything wrong, do you? Kate does seem to be taking a long time."

May smiled, touched by his concern. She was quick to reassure him.

"No, I'm sure she's fine. She's probably had to go further tracking down an emergency chemist than she expected. Don't worry Ed, Kate's well capable of looking after herself. She'll probably turn up just after you've gone. It's usually the way of things, isn't it?"

"Do you know when she might be back at work? asked Ed. "I know that she isn't coming in tomorrow."

"I'm not sure, but Rosie seems fine, so maybe she'll be back in work on Saturday."

"I hope so," replied Ed. "They're moving me to a new shop next Monday and I wanted to see Kate again before I leave."

May could sense a hint of desperation in Ed's voice. She wished that Kate had been here to see him. She felt sympathy for the young man and so attempted to hold out some hope for him as far as Kate was concerned.

"There's no reason why you can't come back here to see Kate, if she's not in on Saturday. I know she'd be more than happy to see you Ed. You know where we are now, so you'll be very welcome."

"Yes, that would be nice," said Ed, politely. His words however, were somewhat unconvincing.

Saying goodbye to Rosie and May, Ed left seventeen Bright Avenue. His visit was over. It had been nice to meet Rosie and he had enjoyed spending time with her and May. However, Kate hadn't been there and he realised that his great enterprise was incomplete. Not seeing her had left a huge gap in what he had hoped to achieve. Furthermore, it had taken a great deal of effort for him to summon up the courage to come out that night. That nervous energy had now been spent. Ed had suffered a huge disappointment and what's more, despite May's offer to him, he was unsure whether he would have the resolve to come and visit Kate again.

Chapter 11

Making his way down Bright Avenue, Ed noticed a group of young men stood at the corner outside Horseman's newsagents. Thinking nothing of it, he walked towards them ready to turn into Syndall Street and off down to the bus stop. It was still light, but the street lamps had come on, which gave the impression that it was becoming a little gloomy. As Ed approached the men, he could see that they had turned to watch him and he began to feel slightly uneasy, concerned that they were perhaps paying him a little too much attention. Nevertheless, he didn't hesitate. Ed believed that if he walked confidently and looked straight ahead, he would appear far less of a potential victim. It seemed to have worked. There were five of them and the first two had moved aside to let him pass but as he walked on, he heard a voice call out to him.

"Hey. Where've you been then?"

Ed thought quickly. He couldn't ignore the voice. If they thought he was afraid to engage in conversation with them, they'd surely turn on him. He knew that he wasn't a fast runner. He couldn't outpace them and if he tried, it would simply show them his weakness. Stopping, he turned around. A young man stepped forward. Leather jacket and jeans and a white tee shirt, sneering at him like Elvis. Taking their cue, the other lads crowded around Ed, who was now covered on three sides. Ed tried his hardest not to look flustered, but inwardly he couldn't lie to himself. He was worried. As calmly as he could, Ed responded.

"I've been visiting a friend, but unfortunately they weren't in. I'm off home now."

"Oh, unfortunately," said one of the others with a smirk. He was a weaselly, thin and sour looking individual. Ed, not normally violent, felt contempt for him. He knew that he could easily take this lad out. It was obvious that he hid behind his bigger and probably tougher, mates.

"I say, doesn't he talk all posh," said one of the others, ridiculing Ed by trying to mimic an upper-class accent.

"Yes, what ho!" added another.

The gang moved in closer. Now Ed had no chance to run. A lad with brown hair and an Eddie Cochran quiff, stepped right up towards him. He seemed to be the leader and looked fiercely at Ed.

"Well, if you want to visit around here, then there's a charge. What do you think he should pay boys?"

His face broke into a wicked smile as he looked around him. To his side, the scrawny 'weasel' reached into his jacket pocket and extracted a flick knife. Ed didn't know what to do, what to think. It had all happened so quickly. There was a pause that seemed to last for ages. It was if the young men were expecting him to respond but he couldn't; no words would come out of his mouth. It seemed to Ed that his mind and body were shutting down, accepting the inevitability of the pain to come.

"Hey, what's going on?"

It was a voice from far away, or so it seemed, seeping into Ed's consciousness. It got louder, waking him out of his stupor.

"Freddie, Paul. What do you think you're doing?"

The gang stepped back and then moved away from Ed. And suddenly there she was in front of him. It was Kate, his guardian angel.

"Is this how you lot carry on?" she asked, sternly addressing the lads. "And you Freddie," she continued, turning towards 'Cochran', "I thought more of you."

Freddie looked at the floor. The others looked embarrassed.

"We were only having a laugh, Kate. Honest. We didn't mean anything by it. Sorry mate," he added, looking at Ed.

"It's okay," said Ed.

"No, it's not okay," said Kate.

She was forceful and in control, just like she was with the awkward punters in the bookies. But this was far more dangerous than that. A gang with knives who Ed felt sure, if Kate hadn't turned up, would have taken great pleasure in inflicting some serious damage on him. She clearly knew them but still, she was taking a huge chance in terms of her own safety. Furthermore, the way in which she'd responded to Ed's comment and then looked reproachfully back at him, meant that he wasn't sure whether or not he was being told off too.

"This is Ed," continued Kate. "He's my friend and he'll come to see me whenever he wants and without any stupidity from you lot. Is that clear?"

She looked fiercely at the young men and with that look, she was even more beautiful. And at that point Ed knew exactly why the gang would do what she said. How could they not be captivated by this powerful, gorgeous and exciting woman.

"We're sorry Kate," said the 'weasel'.

"Yes, sorry," mumbled the others.

"It won't happen again," said Freddie. "You're welcome here anytime pal."

Freddie walked forward and held out his hand for Ed to shake. Ed took hold of it firmly.

"No hard feelings, hey?"

Ed nodded affirmatively. With that the gang slowly moved off up Syndall Street towards Hyde Road. It wasn't long before they were larking around, swinging on the lamp posts and play fighting with one another along the pavement. Kate turned to Ed.

"Come on Ed, I'll take you down to the bus stop so you can get home. What are you doing here anyway?"

Ed hesitated. He felt embarrassed. She'd had to save him and was now providing him with 'safe passage' to the bus stop.

"Ed?" prompted Kate. "Are you all right?"

"Yes," said Ed. "I'm fine."

He didn't sound convincing and Kate patted the top of his arm.

"Come on Ed. We need to make a move. I need to get back home and so do you."

Kate led Ed down Syndall Street on towards Stockport Road and the bus stop.

"You still haven't told me why you're here Ed."

"I'd come to see that everything was all right Kate. Kevin at work said that Rosie wasn't well and that you weren't able to come in for a couple of days."

Hearing those words, Kate felt a warm, pleasant feeling inside. A wave of emotion swept over her as she looked at Ed, the signs of bewilderment still evident on his face after the unpleasant experience outside Horseman's. She was impressed. By coming, Ed had shown a real sensitivity, recognising how much Rosie meant to her. Such a genuine concern wasn't usual in a man; well certainly not in the men that Kate had experience of.

"Rosie should be okay Ed. She's tough. I think she was more upset when she cut herself because I was in a panic. She was very brave having stitches and, touch wood, she seems to have come through it all very well."

They had now reached the bus stop and Ed, feeling calmer, was savouring the time he was sharing with Kate. The two of them were together and it seemed to him as if he had her all to himself. He was getting her undivided attention, unlike at work where there were so many distractions. Ed looked fondly at her as she continued to tell him about Rosie. He wished that these moments could last forever, but he knew that inevitably the bus would come and he would have to leave Kate and return home. He was desperate to let her know how much he cared about her. But he dithered. The moment didn't seem right. Besides, he felt slightly foolish due to the fact that Kate had been forced to come to his rescue.

"Kate, I'm sorry that you had to get involved back there. I didn't want to put you in a dangerous position like that."

Kate smiled. It was ironic that he was thinking of protecting her, when quite clearly, she knew that he couldn't have. And she wasn't bothered. Kate had no wish to go out with someone physically tough. Joe had been something of a hard man, but he was weak in those areas that really concerned her. Being a man meant loving your wife and family and being responsible for keeping a roof over their heads. That wouldn't be served by posturing on street corners, in pubs and clubs and being able to 'batter' everyone else in Ardwick. No, what Ed perceived as his weakness, Kate saw as a strength; real compassion and concern, that was the type of man that she wanted.

"Ed. It wasn't at all difficult. I know all those lads. There's no way that they would have caused any trouble with me there. They saw you as an outsider and an easy target. They're just foolish. Once they knew you were with me, it was all over."

Ed wasn't convinced that it was quite that simple. He felt that Kate was trying to make him feel better. In a sense that pleased him, but the night hadn't turned out how he had hoped.

"It's here Ed."

Ed looked down the road and saw his bus approaching. Kate put out her hand to request the driver to stop and the bus had soon slowed down and drawn to a halt alongside them. It was all too quick, no time for proper goodbyes.

"I'll see you on Saturday Ed," said Kate, as he stepped on to the bus. "Rosie should have recovered enough for me to leave her by then. Thanks for coming. It was very thoughtful of you."

"Bye Kate. See you Saturday."

The conductor pressed the bell and the bus slowly pulled away, Ed standing to wave to Kate as she slowly disappeared into the distance. Turning, he went and sat down, taking out his money to pay for his ticket from the conductor, a middle-aged, balding man who was talkative and cheerful.

"Have you just been to see your girlfriend then?" the conductor asked.

"I wish she was," replied Ed, with a sigh.

The conductor looked at him sympathetically.

"Yes, I can see why," he replied, after a pause. "She's very pretty, isn't she?"

"Yes, she certainly is," said Ed.

"Well. You never know. If you play your cards right."

The conductor winked and having given Ed his ticket and his change, moved back down the bus.

It would soon be Saturday, the end of Ed's last day at Levenshulme. It would be his final chance. Tonight, had passed him by. He had to draw on all his courage and be brave enough to ask her out. He couldn't risk spending the rest of his life wondering what might have been. Somehow, he would do it and so overcome the crippling fear of the consequences of failure.

Chapter 12

Returning home to Bright Avenue, Kate entered the kitchen through the back door. She was greeted by May who, given that it was now nine thirty, was starting to be slightly concerned about the length of time she had been away.

"Oh, Kate," she said, with obvious relief, "I was starting to get worried."

Kate smiled.

"Has Rosie gone to bed?" she asked, not seeing her daughter in the kitchen.

"Yes, she got tired. I took her up to your room. She wanted to be there when you got back. We both had a nice surprise whilst you were out," she continued.

"I know," said Kate, interrupting. "Ed came to see us, didn't he?"

May was taken aback.

"How did you know that?" she asked.

"I saw him after he'd left you."

"But that was ages ago," said May, slightly confused.

"Well, Ed got into a spot of bother. Freddie Morris and some of his mates tried to rough him up. It was lucky I came along when I did. He wouldn't have stood a chance if it had turned nasty."

"I hope you didn't put yourself in any danger," said May, clearly concerned.

"No. It all calmed down quickly enough. I get on well with Freddie. He wouldn't want to upset me. He was full of apologies as soon as he realised that I knew Ed."

"Oh," said May, seemingly satisfied.

"Sit down love," continued May, "I'll make us a brew. I've got time for a drink before I go home."

Kate sat at the table whilst May busied herself with the mugs, teapot and kettle.

"I managed to get some painkiller for Rosie. I don't know how I could have lost the other bottle. I'll probably find it again tomorrow after going to all this trouble. The notice on the chemist's door was wrong. I had a wasted journey going to the chemist in Rusholme. It was closed and I ended up having to go all the way to 'Boots' in town. I knew they'd be open."

"Well, Rosie seems fine Kate. You might not need it. At least you've got it in now."

"Yes, I suppose so."

May finished making the tea and brought the mugs over to the table and sat down opposite Kate.

"He's a nice lad Ed, isn't he?" asked May.

"Yes," replied Kate.

"I hope Freddie and his mates haven't put him off," said May. "I told him that he'd be welcome to come back at any time."

"Oh, you did, did you?" said Kate, feigning mild disapproval before breaking into a smile. "You're quite the little matchmaker, aren't you?"

"No, seriously Kate. He seems a sensible, quiet lad. It was good of him to bring the presents, wasn't it?"

"What presents?" asked Kate, surprised.

"Oh, didn't he tell you? He bought a doll for Rosie and a box of Milk Tray for you."

May got up and walked over to the cupboard. She opened it and returned with a box of chocolates. Kate was surprised. She hadn't expected them and certainly not a present for Rosie.

"Where's the doll?" asked Kate.

"Oh, Rosie's taken it to bed with her. With it being new, she doesn't want to lose sight of it," replied May.

Kate sighed. She was surprised that Ed hadn't mentioned anything about the presents.

"Well, that's strange May. I walked with him to the bus stop and we stood talking whilst we waited for the bus, but he never told me."

"He was ever so good with Rosie," continued May. "Surprising for such a young man. He was laughing and playing with her at the table and praising her drawings. She really liked him, Kate. He seems genuine enough and not bad looking too."

Kate was fascinated. She sat silently after May had finished speaking and looked down at her mug, deep in thought. May had given her an independent insight into Ed's character and what she had heard pleased her. Despite her absence, it seemed clear that Ed had genuinely taken an interest in Rosie.

May watched Kate from across the table. She was quiet, deep in contemplation. May knew that what she had told her, had clearly given her much food for thought.

"So?" said May, after what had been a lengthy silence.

Kate continued to look down, seemingly unaware of May's question.

"Kate," repeated May, trying to prompt a response from her.

Slowly, Kate picked her head up and looked across at May.

"Yes?" she asked.

"Well, what do you think?"

"About what?" said Kate, finding it difficult to focus on the question.

"About Ed."

"I told you. I think he's a nice guy."

"No, silly," said May, frustrated at Kate's lack of a coherent response. "Don't ignore the question. What are you going to do about him? It's quite obvious from talking to him that he's really struck on you."

"Yes, I suppose so. Then again," said Kate, "it could just be infatuation. He's told me himself that he's not had a proper girlfriend, so if that's the case, his feelings probably won't last."

"It's not infatuation. Believe me," said May, firmly. "No, that lads already spent a lot of time with you. All those days together in work. You already know so much about each other and if you still get on so well after the stresses of working in the bookies, then you must both think a lot of one another. Why don't you just give it a chance Kitty? Go out with him. You've got nothing to lose. I've already told you. If you want to go out, I'll have Rosie for the night. You won't have to worry about coming home early, you can relax and enjoy yourself. You deserve it Kate and I like Ed. He seems worth a try."

"I'll think about it," said Kate, quietly.

May was moving too quickly for her. Kate needed more time to consider what she should do.

"Well, I've got to be going love," said May. "You will think about it won't you?"

"Yes," replied Kate.

May stood up and Kate rose with her. The two women embraced and May kissed Kate on the cheek.

"I'll come round with Rosie about dinner time May and we'll go out to the shops. I need a few things for Rosie."

"Okay," said May. "I'll expect you then."

Opening the back door, May was gone.

Sitting at the table, with the radio on quietly in the background, Kate thought about the events of the evening and what May had told her about Ed's visit. All her instincts about him seemed to have been borne out. He was quiet, sensitive and considerate. Although not physically strong, she had witnessed his courage at first hand. Outnumbered, he had not tried to run from the gang and he was no quivering wreck when she arrived just in time to save him. She wanted a man who thought first and acted rationally. Joe had been far too eager to wade into difficult situations with his fists flying. Furthermore, Ed had accepted the fact that Kate had a young daughter and May had been adamant that he'd shown genuine enthusiasm when he'd been playing with Rosie. There was a definite chance, that given the opportunity, Ed would be prepared to become part of her family.

Kate therefore decided that she would take a chance and go out with Ed. His natural shyness however, would mean that in all probability, she would have to give him some encouragement if she were to get him to ask her out. Normally, this would have been unthinkable for her; she would not feed any man's ego in such a way. With Ed however, it seemed different. There wasn't an arrogant bone in his body.

Clearing away the mugs, washing them quickly and placing them on to the draining board, Kate made sure that the back door was secure, then turned off the radio and the downstairs lights and went upstairs. Rosie was asleep in her mam's bed, breathing softly on the pillow. Beside her was the doll that Ed had bought, upon which she still had her little hand. It was a lovely scene. Rosie was content and Kate could see that it was possible for her to take the chance. It was a big step she was about to make. She hadn't been out with anyone since Joe's passing but now, having met Ed, she felt ready to move on. As May had told her, why couldn't she have another shot at personal happiness and perhaps, Ed would prove to be the man to give it to her.

Chapter 13

It was early on Saturday morning. Ed was tired. He'd not slept much during the night. Different scenarios kept going through his head as he tried to imagine just how he would ask Kate the question; would she go out with him? He had tried to work out when would be the best time. It was the busiest day of the week and it started early with the morning greyhounds at White City. Not at work, punters came in to put on a few bets before the pubs opened at dinner. The racing was on the television and that encouraged many of the occasional gamblers to come in and place a bet too. As the new football season hadn't started, men gravitated towards the betting shop for entertainment. Ed knew it would be a frantic day and it would therefore be difficult for him to steal a quiet moment with Kate. He regretted not asking her on Thursday night. It had been the ideal opportunity. They had been alone together and there had been no distractions.

Yet, it was too late. Ed knew that he had to ignore what might have been and concentrate fully on what could be. After today, there would be no second chances. The opportunity would never come around again and he wouldn't forgive himself if he failed to summon up the courage to ask her. Shaking off his tiredness, Ed strode briskly down Errwood Road, feeling very much like a man on a mission.

Arriving at work, the door had already been opened and so in he went. As he looked over the counter from the shop floor, he was surprised. There was no sign of Kate. Ed felt a sinking feeling. Kate wasn't going to be in. His chance was gone. He'd paid the ultimate price for his hesitancy. Unlocking the door from behind the counter, Kevin could see the concerned look on Ed's face. It wasn't any time at all before he understood the reason why. Hanging up his coat, Ed turned towards him.

"Isn't Kate coming in?" he asked. "Is everything all right?"

Kevin smiled. He remembered when he'd been Ed's age and how much he too had once been in love. Older now and to some degree more cynical, his instinct was to poke fun at Ed, yet he could see how much Kate meant to him. He was a good lad, hard-working, far more amenable than the students he usually had to put up with. Most were far too arrogant for their own good and did as little as possible for the money they collected. Ed had thrown himself fully into the job and was eager to learn all aspects of the bookmaking business. He was keen to engage with the punters and showed respect for those he worked with. Kevin liked Ed. He just couldn't bring himself to upset him.

"No, everything's all right," replied Kevin. "Kate rang yesterday to tell me that she would definitely be in, although she may be a little delayed."

"Oh, good," replied Ed, unable to hide his satisfaction.

"Good?" asked Kevin, with a smile.

"Er, yes," said Ed. "Rosie must be fine."

"And Kate too?" asked Kevin, lifting his eyebrows and continuing to smile.

"Well, yes," said Ed. "Do you need me to file yesterday's losers?" he asked, obviously keen to change the subject.

"Yes. Thanks Ed. They're on the side."

Grateful that he had curtailed Kevin's line of questioning, Ed got down to filing the bets. He felt awkward. He realised that Kevin could see his obvious concern for Kate and knew just how much he liked her. Yet until he'd asked Kate out and she had hopefully accepted, he wasn't about to acknowledge his feelings to anyone.

It wasn't long before Kate arrived. Ed noticed her immediately as she came in through the door and moved gracefully across the floor. As usual she looked lovely; a simple brown skirt and blouse, open toed heels and smart jacket, her hair immaculate. As she approached the counter, she gave him a huge smile.

"Come on Eddie," she said, playfully. "Let me in and get a brew on."

Ed quickly moved over to the door and unlocked it to let her in.

"Hi Kate. Is everything all right? Is Rosie okay? "

"Yes, thanks Ed. She's fine."

Having shut the door behind her. Ed turned. He was motionless, admiring her as she took off her coat.

"Well?" said Kate.

Ed didn't respond. He seemed in a daze, mesmerised by the sight of her.

"Are you going to make us a drink?"

"Oh, yes. Yes, of course."

"Well go on then. It won't make itself, will it?" said Kate, laughing. "It only needs me on the till at the moment."

Having made Kate a drink, Ed was soon busy at his till. Kate looked at him closely. She noted his angular face, his curly hair, his brown eyes, white teeth and the slight dimple in his chin. His nose, although slightly prominent, had a cute quality to it. At first, she hadn't regarded him as particularly handsome, yet his kind and considerate personality had gradually won her over. Looking at Ed now, Kate could acknowledge that he was certainly attractive; both May and Sarah had commented on the fact. What had really changed her perception of him though, was his concern for both her and Rosie. To Kate, there was an attractiveness to his character that seemed to shine through his features, so transforming his place in her own feelings and sensibilities.

As the day wore on Kate, having decided that she would respond positively when Ed asked her for a date, realised that her prospective lover was finding it hard to broach the subject. Like Ed, she knew that he would be at the Claremont Road office on Monday, so his inactivity was providing her with a growing sense of frustration. She'd thought that as he'd had the conviction to come to Bright Avenue, he would eventually summon up the courage to ask her out. But it was taking him too long. After Ed had fetched her a sandwich for dinner and before the horse racing got underway, she decided that as Ed wasn't forthcoming, she was going to have to force the issue herself. Sat together at the tills, Kate took the initiative.

"Do you like going to the pictures Ed?"

"Yes, I do."

"Oh. I've not been for a while," continued Kate. "It would be nice to go again sometime."

Ed, his mind partly occupied with thoughts about choosing the correct moment to ask Kate out, ironically hadn't recognised the direction in which the conversation was going. As such, his response wasn't what Kate had hoped for.

"Yes, you'll enjoy it. I actually go quite a lot myself."

"Oh," replied Kate, feigning surprise. "So, you go a lot, do you?"

"Yes," confirmed Ed, still slow on the uptake.

"Well, perhaps I could go with you sometime."

"Yes, that would be nice," replied Ed, clearly not realising the significance of what Kate was saying.

Kate looked at him. She felt like throwing her arms around him and giving him a huge hug. He seemed so innocent, so naïve, so lacking in the ways of the world. She'd never pursued a man like this before, yet in Ed's case it didn't seem to matter. She was going to have to leave him in no doubt about exactly what she was saying.

"So, how about us going to the pictures tonight then?" asked Kate.

Her words cut Ed to the quick. They seemed to come out of the blue. Was she being serious? He hesitated and looked closely at her. There was no suggestion that she was joking with him. She clearly meant what she had said. Flustered, he attempted to reply.

"Ah. Tonight. Oh, I'm not sure if I can. What about another night?"

Immediately, Ed felt the floor opening up beneath him. He couldn't believe what he'd just said. He wished he could take it back. He didn't mean it. What had he done? He'd thrown away his chance. How stupid was he?

"Well," said Kate, surprised by his response. "It's either tonight or you can forget it!"

Ed's spirits rose. Her firm and insistent words had saved him. She had given him another chance and there was no way that he would turn it down.

"Tonight! I'd love to go tonight! Of course, I can go. I want to go," said Ed, almost falling over the words, so eager was he to get them out.

Kate smiled. Ed was a bundle of enthusiasm now. She realised just how nervous and uncertain he had been, terrified of saying the wrong thing.

"Okay, I'll let you off. Go over to the newsagents and fetch the 'Evening News,' so I can have a look at what films are on."

"Right" said Ed, finding it hard to contain his excitement.

Yet he felt that he needed to. He wanted Kate to see him in control, believing that it would make him appear more mature. He was too conscious now of his lack of experience and didn't want to appear foolish and perhaps encourage Kate to reconsider their evening out. As a result, emerging from behind the counter, he walked steadily across the floor of the shop, only to race over to the newsagents once he'd got outside.

In no time at all, Ed had returned with the newspaper and handed it to Kate who opened it at the entertainments page.

"'The Naked Edge.' We'll go and see that at the ABC," declared Kate, satisfied with her choice. "It's a mystery; a thriller. Sarah's seen it and said it's good".

Ed didn't know the film, but Kate's choice of a thriller wasn't necessarily because she enjoyed the genre, but because she knew that it would allow her, should she choose, to hold Ed's hand during the 'scary' bits. Kate was surprising herself, already going far further in her mind than she had anticipated. Yet having forced the issue of their date with Ed, she felt comfortable and in control. She knew that anything that was going to develop, would be because she wanted it to. She would be able to enjoy the evening without any sense of trepidation and with everything on her terms. After Joe, that was just what she needed.

Chapter 14

For both Ed and Kate, the hastily arranged date was to prove something of a mad rush. Ed had to be at Bright Avenue for just after seven, so they could get to the ABC in plenty of time for the start of the supporting feature. Ed had a quick wash and prepared to get changed. However, the only fresh shirt that he had was still wet on the cuffs and no matter how much he ran the iron over them, they just wouldn't dry. But there was no time, he had to get going and so racing out of the door, he made his way quickly across to the Kingsway and caught the bus down to Kate's.

Meanwhile, Kate herself was similarly challenged. Arriving home, she quickly collected together Rosie's pyjamas and a change of clothes and took her daughter to her nan's. May was delighted that Rosie would be staying and couldn't hide her satisfaction at the news that Kate was going out with Ed, a young man she clearly approved of. Rosie was happy to be with her nanny, so much so that she continued colouring at the table after Kate told her that she wouldn't see her again until the morning. Returning home, Kate barely had time to get changed herself before there was a knock on the front door. There, out of breath, was her eager young suitor.

"I've made it!" exclaimed Ed.

Kate looked at him. His face was red and sweating. He was stooping forward slightly and breathing hard as he leaned on his arm, which he'd rested on the door casing. Waiting to recover, he began to talk hesitantly, his words punctuated by deep breaths.

"I thought I was late, so I ran as quickly as I could from the bus stop. I took a wrong turn and ended up on Devonshire Street."

Kate was touched. His desperation to go out with her was obvious. She could still see a look of panic on his face, a result of him getting lost she assumed.

"You daft thing," she said. "We've still got half an hour. Come in and sit down. It's only down the road."

"Are you sure?" said Ed.

"Well, I don't want to walk down to the pictures with you gasping and wheezing like an old man," replied Kate, with a smile.

"I suppose not," said Ed, walking through the front door and following Kate into the kitchen.

"I'm sorry that I didn't come to the back door, but I don't know how to get to it," said Ed. "That's why I came to the front door."

"There's an alley off Syndall Street. It brings you to the backyards of the houses on both Bright Avenue and Richmond Street," replied Kate. "We'll be going out that way."

"Oh," replied Ed.

Kate could see that Ed was nervous, another indication of just how much the night meant to him. Normally, at work, he was at ease with her, but since Thursday night's encounter he had been tense, desperate not to say the wrong thing and so damage his chances with her. Tonight, his utterances had become almost mechanical. It was as if Ed had forgotten the numerous and varied conversations that they had shared together, many of which had covered personal and to some degree, intimate details.

"Do you want a cold drink before we go?" asked Kate, thinking it may help him to relax. "All that running, you must be thirsty."

"No, it's okay. I'm fine now."

"Are you sure?"

"Yes, honestly," replied Ed who, having sat down, had rediscovered his physical equilibrium, but whose emotions were still very much in turmoil.

"Come on then," said Kate, picking up her handbag from the table. "Let's get off."

Ed sprang to his feet and followed her out of the kitchen. Kate locked the door behind her and they walked out of the backyard, into the alley and down towards Syndall Street. From there they walked down Apsley Grove, past the Apsley House pub and had soon reached Stockport Road and the ABC.

As they walked, Kate chatted away, trying to make Ed feel more at ease. Although she hadn't been on a date, a proper date, since before she'd married Joe, Kate felt comfortable. Ed was no amorous Romeo whose attentions she would have to fight off. In fact, he hadn't even attempted to hold her hand as, side by side, they made their way to the cinema. Kate was unsure whether this was because he had, in the circumstances of the evening, become even more reserved, or whether it was because he feared that if he did try to hold her hand, she may consider him as being too 'forward'. It was thus clear to Kate that if their date were to have a romantic ingredient, she would have to be the one to create it.

Surprisingly, there wasn't much of a queue when they arrived at the ABC and they were quickly at the ticket booth. Before Ed could react, Kate had taken out her purse from her handbag and was asking for two seats for the stalls. Ed was surprised, assuming that he would be paying for their night out. After all, he was a man. It was the convention that he paid.

"Kate, it's okay. I'll get the tickets."

The woman in the booth looked at Ed and then back at Kate. Ed had the uncomfortable feeling that she would consider him a cheapskate. Noting the concern on his face and looking at the woman, Kate acted to save his reputation.

"Don't worry Ed. You can give it to me later. I'm not used to being taken out to the pictures. I always have to pay for myself."

The woman smiled, nodded her head and took the money from Kate's hand. Passing her the two tickets and her change, the woman turned and spoke to Ed.

"Don't forget to give it her back love."

She gave him a concentrated stare and Ed nodded back in acknowledgement.

"Remember, it's not a proper date otherwise, is it?" she added, looking back at Kate for confirmation.

"Don't worry, I'll make sure he does," replied Kate.

Kate's independent nature had come to the fore. The thought of any man paying for her was inconceivable. She had bought the tickets without thinking; it didn't concern her. She wanted to spend the evening with Ed and she was happy to pay for him. What the incident had achieved however, was to underline to Ed just how different Kate was. She wasn't one to stand on convention. She lived life on her own terms. She would never be the 'little woman'; the girlfriend or wife hanging on the words and whims of their man. Her decisiveness and her independence excited Ed. He was the perfect foil for Kate, a man without an ego, content to accept that in so many ways she was his superior. Furthermore, she knew it. Not once had Ed been unhappy to act on her instructions at work; he constantly sought her advice and guidance. He respected her abilities without any signs of resentment.

Entering the auditorium, the couple settled into their seats and got ready for the film. There was an arm rest between them upon which Kate placed her hand. Ed looked down. Where should he put his? He wanted to place it against hers but decided to keep his hands on his knees, still unsure as to how she would react. It wasn't as if he hadn't touched her before. He knew that he'd done it many times. Every day they passed items to one another and their hands often made contact. But this was a different situation.

So that was how the two of them sat throughout the first feature. There was no physical contact between them but Ed felt content, happy to be there. It was still early and perhaps they would become closer once the next film began. As the first film ended and the lights came on, Ed turned towards Kate.

"Would you like an ice cream?" he asked. "I still haven't paid you yet for my ticket."

"Go on then," said Kate, smiling.

Kate understood that Ed was eager to please her. As he made his way to the back of the theatre, she watched him closely. She suspected that once he overcame his nervousness; his fear that he may make a wrong move and upset her, that he would prove to be a passionate lover. He needed to be encouraged; he just wasn't going to take the initiative. After all, she had put her hand on the arm rest between them and, even in the dark of the theatre, unobserved by others, he hadn't shown the nerve to take hold of it. She was disappointed and began to feel that Ed was becoming something of a challenge. She felt determined that once the main picture did start, she would take hold of his hand.

Returning with the ice cream, Ed handed it to Kate.

"Thanks Ed. What did you think of the first film?"

Ed hadn't really thought about it. He'd been content to just sit there with Kate.

"It wasn't very scary, was it?" continued Kate.

"No, not really."

"Never mind, the next one should be okay. It's got Deborah Kerr in it."

"Yes. Gary Cooper's in it too, so it should be good," replied Ed.

Soon, the lights dimmed, the darkness descended, the music boomed out and the opening titles for the 'Naked Edge' were beamed onto the screen. The two of them settled back into their seats, Kate's hand once again placed on the rest between them, Ed's hands on his knees in front of him. Trying, this time, to concentrate on the film, after about ten minutes, Ed felt the touch of Kate's hand on his. His chest rose as unconsciously he drew in a deep intake of breath and his heart beat faster. Her fingers played softly on his palm and then moved towards his wrist. It should have enabled him to relax, but instead it led him to panic. Afraid of making the wrong impression, he withdrew his hand slightly from hers, conscious that his shirt was still wet and dreading the thought that if she discovered it, she would think him foolish. Turning slightly towards Kate he could see, in the reflected light of the screen, that she was looking towards him. She tightened her grip on his hand. Moving her mouth close to his ear, she whispered softly.

"You don't need to pull your hand away."

"I'm sorry. I didn't want to," said Ed. "It's just that my shirt's a bit wet. I didn't have enough time to dry it before I came out."

He wished he hadn't said it. Now he would look foolish after all, but at least he had let Kate know that he wanted to hold her hand.

"It's all right Ed," said Kate, chuckling softly. "What are you like, hey?"

Kate gave him a reassuring squeeze and felt his fingers wrap themselves around hers in response. She felt just like a fourteen years old girl again, giddy and excited by the pleasure of holding hands. It was refreshing. It seemed like starting out all over again.

Kate shifted in her seat and leaned her head against Ed's shoulder. Gently, he squeezed her hand. She'd shown him signs of affection and he'd responded, the two of them could now enjoy the film together. Yet, holding Kate's hand, Ed's intention to watch the movie evaporated. Just like in the first feature, it was all a blur. He could never have imagined how, by just holding hands with a woman he'd fallen deeply in love with, he could feel so alive. His senses were heightened to a level he had never known before. His body tingled, he felt electrified and he could think of nothing but Kate. A movie was unfolding before his eyes, but he wasn't registering what was happening. When the end titles finally rolled and the lights came up Ed, so indecisive at first in taking hold of Kate's hand, now found it hard to release it.

"Come on Ed," said Kate, finally. "It's time we made a move."

Withdrawing his hand from hers, Ed slowly stood up and followed Kate out of the auditorium. As they left the cinema Ed, for the first time, took the initiative and took hold of Kate's hand. But he walked slowly as they stepped on to the pavement, not sure of where they were going. Would he be walking Kate home, or would she be taking him to the bus stop? He was unsure. As they walked the short distance to the bottom of Apsley Grove, Kate resolved the issue for him.

"Come on Ed, let's go back home and I can make us both a drink."

It was nearly eleven o'clock, quite late thought Ed, but he knew that the buses ran well into the night. Even if they hadn't, he didn't want the evening to end just yet and eager to spend more time with Kate, was happy to walk back to Burnage if he had to. Walking hand in hand, within a few minutes they were back at Bright Avenue. Opening the back door, Kate told Ed to sit at the kitchen table while she made them a drink.

"Have you enjoyed the film?" asked Ed.

"Yes, have you?"

"Yes, I have Kate. It was a nice evening."

"I think so," said Kate.

"So, Rosie's staying at her nan's," said Ed

"Yes, I wasn't sure what time I would get back," said Kate. "I didn't want May to have to stay up too long and then go back home."

"I suppose they'll both be asleep by now," said Ed.

"Yes, I'm sure they will be."

Kate could tell that Ed was nervous. It was understandable. She knew that he'd never been alone with a woman in such circumstances before. It had been an enjoyable evening for him. They had walked home hand in hand and now they were alone together in her home. Hoping to make Ed feel more relaxed, Kate cheerfully continued their conversation, asking Ed about the films he'd enjoyed and the actors he admired.

As Ed listened to Kate, he thought of how beautiful she was; far too special for someone like him. He still couldn't believe that he was sat there with her. Yet, he was and furthermore he had begun to consider that perhaps tonight would become even more special. They had held hands and perhaps they would kiss and then what? Inexperienced, Ed began to feel afraid. Afraid of being inadequate, of not knowing what to do or if and when to do it. Ed suddenly understood that whatever happened, it would be down to Kate. He would have to put himself in her hands completely, for only in that way could they emerge from the night with their relationship strengthened and intact.

Having made the drinks, Kate suggested that they take them into the front room. Going through, Kate turned on the lamp and shut the curtains. She sat down at one end of the sofa, Ed moving to the other. They placed their mugs on a small coffee table in front of them. Standing up, Kate walked over to the radiogram.

"There should still be some music on," said Kate. "Let's see."

There was. Kate turned the volume down low, so that the strains of the music together with the soft glow of the lamp, created a pleasant ambience that wouldn't intrude upon their conversation. Ed saw a clock on the fireplace in front of them. It was now almost eleven thirty. For just a moment he considered the lateness of the hour, of whether he should still be there, but he had absolutely no desire to go. For all his nervousness, he had no wish for the evening to end. He felt an almost overwhelming desire to tell Kate just how much he loved her, but still he hesitated.

Putting her drink back down on the table, Kate moved along the sofa. She was now sat beside Ed, leaving little distance between them. She felt in control and most importantly, the moment felt right. She turned towards him, put her left hand on his and with the fingers of her right hand gently touched his cheek. She felt Ed's hand become tense and saw his face redden.

"Don't worry," she said, softly. "I won't bite."

Moving closer towards him, she gently pulled his face towards her. She rested her lips against his and kissed him. She felt his lips respond, but not completely. He really was an inexperienced lover. His vulnerability, his lack of confidence was genuine. Convinced that she could trust Ed completely, Kate acted in a way that she would have found unbelievable just a few hours before. Standing up, she moved over and then sat back down on Ed's knee. As he moved forward, she put her arms around him and kissed him again, fully on the lips. This time she felt him relax, responding to her completely, surrendering to his passion as he kissed her fully and deeply in return. Putting his own arms around her, he pulled her body towards him. He was excited, his emotions racing out of control and sat on his knee, Kate could feel his arousal, fully aware of just how much he wanted her.

Disengaging from his embrace, Kate got back to her feet. Ed looked at her. He was excited but uncertain whether he'd gone too far. Kate looked at him. She smiled and tenderly touched his hand.

"Wait here Ed. I'm going to slip into something more comfortable, as they say in the movies."

She smiled again, a smile that removed all his doubts and that told him that what was about to happen would be so very, very special. But as she left the room and went upstairs, his heart began to flutter and his doubts returned. He stared in front of him. He still felt vulnerable. He was inexperienced. He'd never been intimate with a woman. What would he do? He had never, ever, even in his wildest dreams, expected to be in this situation. In fact, he respected and loved Kate so much, that he hadn't allowed himself to think of her in that way. She was too special for that. Yet now, here, it seemed that they were going to make love and he was so desperate for it to be as wonderful as it could be. He knew that he would have to submit to her completely but then, after all, hadn't she been guiding all the events that evening anyway? Sat on the sofa, Ed stared in front of him. He was still, rooted to the spot, unable to focus his eyes on the objects on the fireplace on the wall opposite. He heard Kate's footsteps coming down the stairs and her push the front room door open. He turned. She looked beautiful. She was wearing a pretty, silk red nightie and with its thin straps, he could see the top of her arms, chest and shoulders. Her skin appeared so soft and delicate. She walked over to him and held out her hand.

"Come on Ed. Let's go upstairs," she said, quietly, but insistently.

Taking his hand, she pulled it ever so gently, raised him to his feet and led him over to the door and to the bottom of the stairs.

"Up you go," she said, quietly.

Ed obediently climbed the stairs with Kate following behind him.

"It's on the right," said Kate, directing him towards the front bedroom.

Ed went through the door. His heart was pounding, he felt his throat tighten and he breathed heavily. He was excited, yet tense, afraid that somehow, he would let Kate down.

Yet Kate was determined that wouldn't happen. Calm and sensitive, she knew what a special moment this was, not just for Ed but for her too. Her actions weren't taken lightly. She had grown close to Ed over the time she'd known him and she wanted this. She wasn't completely sure yet, if she loved him, although she understood instinctively that he loved her. Somehow, what she was doing seemed right. She was a passionate young woman. She wanted to enjoy once more the feelings of making love to a man she cared for. It had been a long time, but most importantly, her actions had real meaning. Taking Ed's hand, she spoke quietly, but insistently.

"Sit down on the bed."

Ed did as he was asked. Kate sat beside him and turned to face him.

"Don't worry Ed. Just relax."

Kate moved her lips towards his and kissed him. The two lovers wrapped their arms around one another, their bodies tingling with expectation. Ed felt almost overwhelmed by emotion. He couldn't believe how it was possible to love someone so much; how he could feel so connected to another human being. How wonderful it was that Kate would be the chosen one; his first experience of full intimacy with a woman. And it was happening because he truly loved her. It had a depth of meaning that meant so much to him. He'd been ridiculed for his old-fashioned ideas. Yet he knew what others didn't; without love, true love, sex was merely a physical act without any lasting meaning. Surrendering to Kate's will, Ed prepared to be in complete union with the woman he adored.

"Come on Ed. Stand up. You need to take your clothes off."

The request was so natural, made with a calm assurance and Ed quickly and eagerly did as he was told.

"Lay down Ed," said Kate, her voice silky and sultry.

He moved along the side of the bed, lay his head on the pillow and stretched his body out on the bedspread. For a moment he wondered if he should have got under the covers, but the thought soon passed as Kate looked down at him. She was a vision of loveliness with her beautiful face and her hair lay across the top of her shoulders. As she leaned forward towards him, he looked down her nightie to the top of her breasts. Overwhelmed, Ed's heart began to pound.

"Move over," whispered Kate.

Ed realised that naked on the bed there was no hiding his desperation for her. But he felt no embarrassment, just a longing for Kate, now his lover, to make their relationship complete. Moving alongside him, Kate lay on the bed. Lifting her head, she kissed him on the forehead, then on his lips and the top of his chest. Ed felt Kate move over and astride him.

He looked up at her on top of him, excited by her dominance and eager to submit. As he lay expectantly, she moved her hand, guiding him towards her, joining them completely. Moving rhythmically together, the young lovers were wild and ecstatic, their shared experience climaxing in an explosion of pleasure. Lying together, their energy spent, the two of them shared a succession of long, soft and heartfelt kisses. It was a perfect expression of their feelings for one another and their recognition that what they had just shared was so special.

Ed would have lay there forever if he could. He was so in love. How could anything make him feel better than he did at this particular moment? He didn't want it to end and he would never, ever forget one detail of this wonderful night. Kate too had been deeply moved. She felt a sense of wonder. She had never experienced anything like this with Joe. Neither her passions or her feelings had ever been aroused to this extent. She was satisfied; spent. She had doubted that it was the right thing to do, but she had trusted her instincts and she now realised that she did in fact love him.

Finally, getting up, Kate straightened her nightie and looked down at Ed. He was still lying motionless on the bed.

"Come on Ed, I'll get you some pyjamas and we'll go down and have a drink. You'll have to stay the night now, won't you?" she added, with a smile.

Ed got up and put on a pair of pyjamas that Kate had taken from a drawer in the chest under the window.

"Don't worry Ed, they've never been worn. They're a new pair that I bought a couple of years ago. Just fold up your clothes and put them on the chest there."

Going downstairs, the two went to sit in the kitchen. It was half past one.

"You're probably hungry now Ed, with all that exertion" she said, smiling. "Do you want me to make you a sandwich?"

"Yes, that would be nice. Thank you," said Ed.

Sat with a drink of tea and a sandwich at the table in Kate's kitchen, listening to Kate telling him about her childhood, Ed began to imagine himself there permanently as Kate's husband. As the night wore on the two continued to talk, finding out even more about one another. Ed felt so alive, nothing else now mattered other than Kate. He knew that she was the meaning of his life. She was the one. She had been sent to him. It was no coincidence; no chance or fortune. It was meant to be. Everything that had happened was meant to lead him to her: choosing to come to Manchester; deciding to work at the bookies; being sent to Levenshulme, when he could have been sent to any of the other shops;

Kate working there and effectively single at the point that he had met her. Everything had come together to create this moment; this opportunity. He mustn't let it go.

Finally, at four o'clock, Kate suggested that they should get some sleep.

"Come on Ed, let's go to bed."

It was said so naturally. It told Ed that she accepted him, that she was going to allow him to sleep with her. Getting under the covers he cuddled into her; the first time that evening that he had taken the initiative. She responded warmly to him and he fell asleep with his arm around her. He felt safe, but protective too. He would never, ever let her go. She was so precious to him and he knew that his love for her would last for eternity.

Chapter 15

"Come on Ed. Time to get up."

Ed felt a hand on his shoulder.

He was already awake. As soon as Kate had moved free of his embrace, he had stirred. He'd felt her sliding across the bed and slipping her legs out from under the covers. He could still sense her touch and her warm, fragrant body. It was something deep and inexplicable. He no longer felt like an individual. He had forged a connection with Kate that was both physical and spiritual.

Ed opened his eyes and looked up at Kate. She looked beautiful, framed in the light penetrating through the net curtains and playing on the top of her shoulders, bare but for the thin straps of her nightie.

Ed quickly got out of bed, eager to respond. He took off his pyjamas and then realised that he wasn't dressed. So relaxed had he become in Kate's company, that he felt no need to go diving across to the chest of drawers to grab his clothes. Kate looked at him with a broad smile on her face.

"My, you're getting very forward. What a fine figure of a man you are," she said, playfully.

"Oh, sorry," said Ed.

Slightly embarrassed he crouched forward, his arms in front of him to cover himself the best that he could.

"It's nothing I didn't see last night," said Kate, smiling.

Once more at ease. Ed stood upright again. Moving over to the cupboard in the corner of the room, Kate opened the door and pulled out a large bath towel and gave it to Ed.

"Here, wrap this around you. We'll go down, get a stripped wash and have some breakfast."

Ed looked at his watch. It was eight o'clock. They had only had about four hours sleep but he felt completely alert, his mind and body invigorated by his experiences since arriving to take Kate to the pictures yesterday.

Yesterday. So much seemed to have happened since then, that it seemed a lifetime ago when he had left Kate at work to get ready for their date. What had taken place between the two of them had made him into a different person. He was now embarking on a new life and he supposed that what had happened was like a rite of passage; he had become a complete human being. Yet Ed instinctively understood that if the night were to have lasting significance, it could only be through the fulfilment of his relationship with Kate.

Downstairs in the kitchen, Kate turned on the Ascot boiler which was mounted on the wall above the sink and filled a plastic bowl with hot water. In it, she placed soap and a flannel. She called Ed over to her and told him to stand on the mat in front of the sink.

"Take off the towel" said Kate, softly.

Ed, stood in front of her, removed it from around his waist.

Kate looked at him, running her eyes up and down his body from head to toe. Briefly, he glanced back at her and she could still see the look of innocence in his eyes. He had made love to her but it hadn't altered the dynamic between them. If anything, he appeared even more devoted to her. What attracted her to him, hadn't changed. He was unassuming, quiet and kind. There was no hint of arrogance about him. No suggestion that he would take anything about her for granted. She had given him the greatest prize of all and he had responded by loving her all the more. Kate felt a tenderness towards him that she had never felt for Joe and their lovemaking had shocked her. It had aroused feelings and emotions that she hadn't experienced before and that she felt so eager to enjoy again. Taking the flannel, Kate rubbed the soap into it and proceeded to wash Ed all over. Trying to ensure that neither of them became too aroused, she carried out her task with gentle humour.

"No getting fruity Ed. Stop it!"

She laughed gently, enjoying the sight of Ed's face which was red with embarrassment. Try as he might to control it, his body was clearly responding to the strokes of her hand inside the flannel.

"Right. That's it. You're done," said Kate, playfully patting him. "Calm down and get yourself dry."

The two of them having washed and dressed, Kate made them some tea and toast and they sat together, a contented and happy couple, at the kitchen table. They knew in their hearts how special the night had been, but the pressing question for both of them was, where would they go from here? To Ed, it was simple. He was absolutely certain that Kate was the woman he wished to marry. He knew that he wanted to spend his entire life with her. Yet he feared that Kate may not want to take that step. She would probably be far less certain about her feelings and he knew that he would have to give her time.

Ed was right. Kate had surprised herself by her actions, yet she had no regrets. Nevertheless, she had Rosie to think about and Ed still had much to prove. Furthermore, she now felt a sense of responsibility for him and had to be certain that whatever she decided would be the right thing for Ed too. He had real prospects in life and she wasn't going to let him sacrifice them. She knew that she couldn't live with herself if that was the case. It was up to her to ensure that Ed took the right path, so that he could obtain emotional fulfilment without sacrificing material security.

"I need to go and see Rosie, Ed. Pick her up from May's."

"Yes, of course," said Ed. "She'll be getting worried about where you are. Can I come too?"

"Of course, you can."

Kate was pleased. She could see that Ed had no desire to leave her and most importantly, he was comfortable with the fact that Rosie's needs came first.

The two of them cleared away the breakfast pots, Ed volunteering to wash them whilst Kate fixed her hair. As she stared into the mirror on the back wall, Kate could see Ed working busily in the background, going through the drawers and cupboards to find the tea towels and the places for the cups, plates and cutlery. Without being aware of it, Ed was endearing himself to her even more. He was a new type of man, happy to help carry out the household chores. Kate could see that he would be a partner for her in every sense of the word.

Satisfied with her appearance, Kate finally declared herself ready. Shutting the back door behind them, she and Ed made their way the short distance to Parker Street.

Rosie was sat colouring at the table as May opened the door. Looking up to see Kate, she put down her crayon and quickly got off her chair. She ran the few steps over to her mam with her hands held out before her.

"Mammy! Mammy!"

Kate crouched down and Rosie flung her arms around her neck and kissed her on the cheek. Getting to her feet, Kate picked up her daughter, clutching her tight against her chest.

"Well, you're certainly happy to see me," said Kate. "Have you been a good girl for Nanny?"

"Yes," said Rosie, nodding her head up and down.

"Very good," said Kate, a broad smile covering her face.

"Has she Nanny?" asked Kate, turning to May.

"Yes, she's been as good as gold. Haven't you Rosie?"

Rosie nodded her head in agreement.

"Okay then, let me put you down."

Kate lowered Rosie to the floor. Content, Rosie went back to her chair and once more sat down to get on with colouring her pictures. Since their arrival, Ed had carefully watched the interaction of mother and daughter. He realised how utterly dependent Rosie was upon her mam and he knew that it must be a heavy responsibility upon Kate's shoulders, but one she assumed willingly. He admired her so much. Her determination to go out to work in order to create a better life for her daughter. It must have been very tough for her to leave Rosie in the early days, but Ed knew for himself how independently minded she was. Kate was determined to overcome any obstacle that stood before her.

Sitting down at the table next to Rosie, Ed asked her if he could do some colouring too. Rosie nodded appreciatively. It was clear that she liked him and accepted his company.

"Shall I use this book Rosie?" asked Ed, putting his finger on another colouring book at the side of the table. "Then we can both colour at the same time."

Rosie nodded and turned back to her picture, her little hand showing great dexterity as she filled in the various shapes and objects. It was perhaps fortunate that she hadn't cut her right hand, thought Ed. She would have found it difficult to colour or draw with that large bandage around her favoured hand and wrist.

Kate and May watched Rosie and Ed at the table. Ed seemed a natural where children were concerned. Kate could see, as May had already told her, that his interest in Rosie was genuine. He was nothing like the many young fathers who showed so little interest in their children. Those, like Joe, who were eager to abandon them to the care of their mothers, whilst they went out to the pubs and clubs.

"Whilst you're here Kate," said May, drawing her attention away from the table, "let me show you the bedspread I've bought Rosie for the winter. I've put it away in the back bedroom."

May looked knowingly at Kate, who understood immediately that May was eager to find out what had happened between her and Ed.

"Okay," replied Kate. "Ed", she continued, "I'm just going to look at the new bedspread. I'll only be a minute. You'll be okay with Rosie, won't you?"

"What?" replied Ed, unsure of what Kate had said, given that he was so engrossed in his colouring.

"I'm just nipping upstairs for a minute."

"Oh, fine. Okay."

The two women went out to the stairs and up to the back bedroom. Kate hardly had the chance to close the bedroom door behind her, before the inevitable question came.

"Well?" asked May, expectantly.

"What?" replied Kate, taking pleasure in making her wait for an answer.

"You know what!"

Kate couldn't help but break out into a huge smile. It was now obvious to May.

"You spent the night with him, didn't you? He never went home, that's obvious, but you spent the night with him."

May smiled. She was no prude. She knew Kate and that she would never have foolishly compromised herself in any way. She trusted her judgement. Nevertheless, she was surprised. Ed must certainly have made a huge impression on her, for it to have happened.

"Well? What are you going to do?"

Kate looked back at May. She was full of questions. Kate showed no signs of resentment or irritation however. She understood why May was concerned. She was aware of just how much May cared for her and Rosie.

"Don't worry May. He's a lovely guy. He's surprised me so much. So caring and considerate and I know that he idolises me. He seems to be a big hit with Rosie too."

"Yes, I told you, didn't I?" said May.

"I'm not getting carried away" continued Kate, "things have a habit of going wrong."

May looked disappointed.

"Kate, I've told you before, forget your mam and dad and our Joe, not everyone's let you down. I hope you don't think that I have."

"No, of course not," replied Kate, quickly.

"Well promise me that you'll give this lad a proper chance. You must trust him or you wouldn't have spent the night with him. You're a sensible young woman. Have faith in your instincts."

May looked into Kate's eyes, determined to let her know that she trusted her judgement and wanted to see her happy.

"Come on May," said Kate, after a short pause. "We're being rude. We can't leave Ed on his own any longer. Let's go downstairs."

"Okay," said May, "but think on what I've said."

The two women went back downstairs. Entering the kitchen, they could see Rosie and Ed with their heads down, colouring away in their respective books. It was a lovely picture and one that Kate would remember for a long time. She felt optimistic but also a little afraid. She was well aware that her feelings for Ed were serious; that this could really be love. Yet committing herself was such a serious step to take and one that would require her to put real trust in Ed; a leap of faith that was huge following the experience of her marriage to Joe.

Chapter 16

It was time for them to leave.

"Come on Ed, Rosie. Put your crayons and books away, it's time we were going."

Kate passed them a small shopping bag and the two of them filled it.

"Don't forget your doll," said Kate.

Rosie went over to the settee, picked up Ed's present and returned to deposit it in the bag.

"I think we'll take a walk to Ardwick Green. We can sit and look at the flowers, can't we Rosie?" asked Kate.

Rosie nodded and smiled. She loved going to the park.

"Well, you'll need to get your sandals on then," continued her mam.

Rosie fetched her brown summer sandals from beside the kitchen door. They had a strap and a buckle and were Rosie's favourite footwear. She took great pride in being able to fasten them herself, finding it easier than getting the hang of tying her shoelaces. Yet, sat on the settee, Rosie was struggling. She was just too excited at the prospect of going to the park to be able to get the end of the buckle through the hole in the strap. Ed watched her. She looked comical. All fingers and thumbs and a look of intense concentration, mixed with frustration, as she kept failing to secure the strap. Wrinkling up her little nose and frowning, Rosie continued to struggle until Ed felt that he should step in to help her.

"Do you want me to do it Rosie?" he asked, kneeling down on the floor in front of her.

Rosie looked at him and relaxed her fingers on the strap. She sighed out loud.

"I can't do it."

"I know Rosie," said Ed. "It's only because you're excited. Let me try."

Rosie was unresponsive. She seemed unsure. She wasn't happy that she hadn't succeeded in doing it herself.

"I know," continued Ed. "Let me have a go and you can tell me if I've done it properly. What about that?"

Rosie thought for a few seconds, a quizzical look on her face. She was weighing up Ed's suggestion.

"All right," said Rosie, finally.

Rosie moved her hands away from the sandals and Ed quickly fastened one and then the other. Getting to his feet, Ed took a step back to give Rosie some room.

"Stand up Rosie. Make sure that they're not too tight."

Rosie stood up. In an exaggerated fashion, she picked up both her feet in turn and planted them heavily back down on the floor.

"Are they comfortable?" asked Ed, desperately trying not to burst out laughing after her comical antics.

"Yes!" said Rosie, nodding her head for additional emphasis.

"Well," said Ed, "you're all set to go then."

"Are you coming Ed?" asked Rosie.

"Of course, he is. That's if he wants to," said Kate.

Ed turned round and realised that Kate and May had been watching him the whole time. His natural and spontaneous desire to assist Rosie had impressed them. It was yet another instance of his genuine, caring qualities. He had been willing to give Rosie his full attention and quickly she had come to like and accept him.

"I'd love to come," said Ed. "I always enjoy going to the park."

"Ed can carry the bag," said Rosie.

Kate and May burst out laughing. Rosie's comment had put Ed in his place. He had been designated as nothing more than the hired help. Ed smiled. It reinforced to him how much his relationship with Kate involved responsibilities to Rosie too. And it was something that he happily accepted.

"Come on then, let's get going," said Kate. "Rosie, give your nanny a kiss."

Rosie walked over to May who had crouched down. She flung her arms around her, planting a big kiss on her lips.

"Oh, that was lovely Rosie," said her nan, standing back up. "Nanny will see you again tomorrow. Have a nice time in the park."

Rosie walked towards the back door.

"You two enjoy yourselves as well," continued May, looking at Kate and Ed. "I'll see you again soon I hope Ed."

Ed nodded and May smiled. Kate opened the door and they descended down the steps into the backyard and out into the ginnel to make their way to Syndall Street. Although their progress to Ardwick Green was slow, given the pace at which Rosie could walk, it felt to Ed as if they had reached the Park in no time at all. Talking to both Kate and Rosie, the time seemed to fly by. Crossing Hyde Road at the side of the ABC and then over Higher Ardwick, they were at the gates to Ardwick Green and were walking into the park. Finding a bench, the three of them sat down. It was a beautiful summer's day and here, among the trees, flower beds and open spaces and with the sun shining down, it almost felt as if they were out of the city. Even the noise of the traffic, coming to and from the centre of Manchester and making its way past the southern side of the park, was subdued. Less of it, as it was a Sunday, the noise seemed to melt away into the background. Getting off the bench, Rosie walked a few steps towards the nearest flowerbed to examine the vibrant red and yellow roses that had caught her eye.

"Be careful Rosie," warned her mam. "Don't touch them, they've got sharp thorns. They'll prick you."

Rosie pulled her arms down by her side and stood completely still.

"It's all right Rosie," continued Kate. "They won't bite! Just be careful."

"Yes Mammy," said Rosie, who carefully walked a couple of tiny steps closer towards the flowers.

Kate and Ed looked at one another and laughed. Their eyes met and Ed took her hand in his. Kate smiled. She felt happy and content. It was a feeling that she hadn't known for so long and one that she had despaired of ever feeling again. Yet Kate couldn't ignore the practicalities that inevitably imposed themselves upon their developing relationship. At the centre of everything was Rosie and Kate had to be certain that Ed understood the nature of the commitment he was taking on. Furthermore, she didn't want her growing love for him to prove detrimental to Ed's future. It was important that she made him question just exactly what his hopes and expectations should be. He must understand that despite their night of passion, she hadn't placed him under any kind of obligation. Sitting quietly on the bench had helped to clear her head and breaking the silence, she began to talk.

"Ed."

"Yes."

"We need to talk."

"Oh?"

Ed looked surprised. Could it be that he was fearing rejection?

Kate squeezed his hand and smiled, looking straight into his eyes. She realised that she would have to choose her words carefully.

"You know Ed, there's lots of nice girls out there. You're young, a decent guy. You should find out more about yourself. Women will like you. You're kind and considerate. It's what many of them want."

Ed looked at her. What was she saying? It seemed as if she was having second thoughts about him.

"But I'm with you Kate. I'm not interested in anyone else."

"Ed. You're still young."

"But so are you," replied Ed quickly, not allowing Kate to continue.

Kate put a hand on his knee.

"No Ed, listen to me. We may be similar ages, but I've been married. I've got a child. I've experienced far more of life then you have. You need to do the same."

"But I can do that with you."

Ed's response was immediate and delivered with a firm sense of conviction.

"I know that I love you, Kate. I'm absolutely certain. I've never felt like this about anyone."

"I know," replied Kate, "but you have to be sure. I'm your first love. I may be just an infatuation. You have to be certain. Infatuation can last for a period of time. You don't always see someone's faults and I've got lots. You're blinded to them at the moment."

"You're telling me that I don't know my own mind."

Ed couldn't hide his obvious sense of frustration, but Kate was determined to continue.

"I'm not sure that you do Ed and no doubt others will tell you the same. What we shared last night was wonderful, but there's more to a relationship than just making love."

"I've had the experience you talk about," insisted Ed. "Experience gained through having to make choices. I chose to wait. Last night, I knew that it was right. Everything about you is right. I sensed it on the first day that I met you. I don't want other women. Sex has no meaning unless you love someone and I know that I love you. For me, you are the one."

Kate was moved. Never had anyone spoken to her with such feeling and emotion. But she had to challenge him. She had to give him every chance to walk away, without feelings of guilt or regret. If their relationship were to continue, she had to be sure that their future together would stand every chance of success.

"But Ed, I've got Rosie. I'm a widow with commitments. You need to find someone single; have your own children and build a life together. It wouldn't be right for you to take on Rosie. She's not your daughter. Not your responsibility."

"But she's part of you Kate. I know that. I accept that. It's part of why I love you so much. It's because you're so giving and you care. Not only about Rosie, but about everybody. About me now. You're so concerned that you might not be doing what's best for me. Don't you see? I understand all your concerns. But please give me some credit. Experience of life doesn't give you wisdom. I may not have had it tough as a kid, like you, and I haven't lost a partner like you lost Joe, but I do understand how difficult life can be. But I know that together, you, me and Rosie, we can build a happy life."

It had been a dramatic plea and when he had made it, Ed's energies were spent. Kate looked at him. How could she continue to argue? He had answered all her concerns and most importantly, he talked about the three of them. He understood implicitly. A relationship with her brought with it a ready-made family and Ed was clearly willing to assume that responsibility. She glanced at Rosie who had now sat down on the bench beside them and was busy drawing flowers in a sketchbook that she had taken from the shopping bag. She was happy and content, not at all disturbed by the conversation between her mam and Ed. It seemed that she had already accepted Ed's continued presence with them.

"Okay Ed. You've got to understand that I have to be certain. We'll take it steady, see how we go. It'll give us both the chance to reconsider."

Kate saw the relief on Ed's face. He moved towards her, put his arm around her shoulders and pulled her slowly towards him, kissing her softly on the cheek. Moving away slightly, Kate moved her lips against his and kissed him long and lovingly, feeling his body and his embrace tighten. It was a wonderful moment for the two of them and it sealed their immediate future together.

"Mammy! Mammy! Look at the birdie!"

Breaking their embrace, Kate and Ed turned to look at Rosie who, standing in front of them, was pointing at a couple of pigeons on the grass by the flowers.

"Yes," said Ed. "Aren't they nice?"

"We should've brought some bread to feed them," said Kate. "You'll have to remind me next time we come Rosie."

"Yes, Mammy."

"Anyway, come on it's time we were going. Put your book back in the bag and Ed can carry it back to the house. It is his job after all!"

Kate looked at Ed and the two of them laughed. With Rosie walking slowly between them, her outstretched hands holding one of theirs, they made their way back to Bright Avenue, a happy and contented little family.

Chapter 17

Having returned to Bright Avenue, Ed knew that at some point he was going to have to return to his flat. Yet, he really didn't want to. He felt that the life he had led until yesterday, had ceased to have any meaning for him. He couldn't face the thought of going back to Burnage where, once again, he would be on his own. Furthermore, Ed knew that he wouldn't even see Kate at work until Saturday, as for the rest of the week he would be at Claremont Road. Sat with him at the kitchen table, Kate could see that Ed looked distant and concerned. The happy mood that he had been in whilst they were out, had slowly disappeared.

"What's wrong Ed?" she asked, moving her hand across the table and placing it gently on his.

"Oh, nothing," said Ed, hesitantly.

His eyes were staring down at the table, seemingly unable to engage hers. Kate knew that something was bothering him.

"Ed. Look at me."

Kate's words, soothing and reassuring, encouraged Ed to lift his head. He could see Kate's piercing green eyes looking directly at him. She looked so beautiful.

"Come on. I know you well enough now. You're worried about something, aren't you?"

Kate hesitated, waiting for a response. But it was difficult for Ed. How could he explain how he felt and then, if he did, would she think that he was trying to put pressure on her? After all, they had agreed and Kate had made clear, that they were going to take their relationship slowly.

"Well, Ed?" asked Kate. "You've got to talk to me now that we're going out together."

Kate's words gave Ed the confidence he needed.

"I was just thinking that I'll soon be going back to my flat and that I might not see you again until next Saturday."

"Why won't you?" asked Kate, surprised.

"Well, I'll be working in Rusholme and perhaps you'll be busy in the evenings and won't be able to see me."

"Ed," replied Kate, smiling reassuringly. "You really are puddled. Do you think that you're not welcome here? Of course, you are. You can stay over too. After all, the more time we spend together, the more chance we have to see how we all get on. I wouldn't be very impressed if you didn't want to spend your evenings with me, would I?"

Having worried about putting too much pressure on her, Ed was now determined to reassure Kate that he wanted to spend as much time with her and Rosie as possible.

"I want nothing more than to share my evenings with you. I'd love to stay overnight and not have to go back to my flat. It'd be great if we could all live as a real family."

Ed was energised, passionate. It was the side to him that Kate suspected he had only ever shown to her. She thought of the saying, 'still waters run deep'. It seemed to sum up Ed perfectly. Usually so quiet and unassuming, once he was with her, a completely different side to his character emerged. One of eagerness, excitement, ardour. In their conversation in the park, she had challenged him to evaluate his feelings towards the life he would have with her and Rosie. He had done more than reassure her. It seemed to Kate, that she had been too hesitant. Ed had told her that for him, she was the one. Now it was time for her to find out if she felt the same. Yet there was only one way to establish whether she did. As such, Kate found herself making Ed an offer.

"Ed."

"Yes."

"Why don't you go and fetch some clothes and whatever you need for the next couple of days and you can move in with us. We can go and get the rest of your things one night in the week."

Ed was stunned. It was what he wanted, but he had never expected that events would move so quickly. Yet he was concerned for Kate. Was she sure? Was it best for her?

"Are you certain Kate?" he asked. "Will it be all right with Rosie? And what about May too? What will she think?"

"Ed. I'm an adult," said Kate, firmly. "I make my own decisions and I already know that Rosie likes you and accepts you being with us."

"What about your neighbours? Shouldn't we be married before we live together?"

Kate was touched by his concern. It was the product of his sheltered background. He didn't understand that among the working classes, 'living over the brush' was more acceptable. It still meant commitment, but not necessarily, marriage.

"No, Ed," replied Kate. "You don't have to worry about that, but one thing you mustn't do, is give up your flat."

"I won't Kate. I wouldn't want you feeling that you have to put up with me because I have nowhere else to go. I know how kind you are, but it wouldn't be fair for me to stay if you felt that our relationship wasn't right for you."

Kate stood up and walked around the table to Ed. She bent down and kissed him. She had advised him to keep his flat in case he was the one who wanted to leave, yet typically, he'd only thought of her.

"Go on then Ed. Catch the bus down to Burnage and get some clothes," said Kate. "Rosie and I will get the tea on ready for you coming back and then you can wash the pots up afterwards," she added, with a smile.

"Right," said Ed. "I'll be as quick as I can."

Smiling broadly, he grabbed his jacket and almost raced to the door.

"Hang on!" said Kate, loudly.

Ed stopped and looked back towards her.

"Haven't you forgotten something?"

Ed looked bemused.

"What?" he asked, quietly.

"A kiss," said Kate, smiling.

Ed walked back towards her and pecked her on the cheek.

"That's not a kiss," said Kate. "Give me a proper one please."

Ed moved back towards her and placed his lips on hers. The two of them shared a long, lingering kiss, Ed placing his arms around Kate, pulled her towards him. He felt an electric sensation coursing through his body, a sense of excitement and joy fuelled by the knowledge that they would soon be together. It was all like a dream. The best dream he'd ever had.

Pulling away, Kate breathed out softly. She too had felt the affinity between them; the excitement in their kiss. Their passions had once more been aroused and they both needed to calm down.

"Go on then, off you go," said Kate, finally.

"Okay," replied Ed, slightly embarrassed by the intensity of their embrace.

All the while, little Rosie had been colouring away in her books on the settee. Hearing the door open, she looked up and saw Ed leaving.

"Where's Ed going Mammy?" she asked.

"He's gone to fetch his clothes love. He's going to be staying with us."

"Oh, good," said Rosie. "He can do some colouring with me."

"Yes darling, he can," said Kate, smiling as Ed closed the door behind him.

It was the seal of approval that Kate had been looking for and it was unsolicited. With Rosie's acceptance of Ed, Kate was sure that her new family would have every chance of success.

Chapter 18

It had all gone so well. Kate looked back over their first three months together and realised how Ed had almost seamlessly become an integral part of their lives. She couldn't but wonder at how well the two of them got on together; such a contrast to her relationship with Joe. Of course, the characters of the two men were so different and now, rather than conflict, there was true consensus. Kate had always sensed that after Rosie's birth, Joe was harbouring a feeling of resentment. She believed that he felt trapped; that he had lost his sense of freedom. Kate now realised that it was simply because he was too young to be married and was unable to assume the responsibilities of a husband and father.

Kate saw many young husbands with similar attitudes and wondered if it was perhaps a natural consequence of their environment. The social expectations which created working class men, who felt that the home and family were the domain of the wife and mother. She wondered how many of them would eventually grow out of such ideas. Very few, if the experiences of the older women on Bright Avenue were anything to go by. Furthermore, the new 'freedoms' of the early sixties hadn't made a great difference to the lot of women. In fact, it had made things worse. The growing affluence brought by slowly increasing wages, the emergence of teenage fashions and music, had led to a new generation of young men who sought pleasure and possessions; individual fulfilment. Loyalty to their wives and girlfriends was seen as inconsequential. Such attitudes had been all too evident with Joe. He refused to allow Kate to see his wage packet, grudgingly contributing small amounts of money that weren't sufficient to meet the bills. Yet he had a growing collection of suits, shirts and jackets and trendy shoes that he had bought in town. All of these to impress when he went out to watch the new groups at clubs like the 'Three coins' and the 'Oasis'.

For Kate, Ed was like a breath of fresh air. He was unassuming, deferential to her needs and enthusiastically assumed the duties of a father. There wasn't anything he wouldn't do for little Rosie and within a very short space of time they were 'pals'; inseparable. In fact, the three of them were a family in all but the legal sense of the word and Kate knew that Ed was eager to take that final step, after just a few months of living together. Yet Ed respected her wishes. He didn't press her about getting married and he kept his flat in Burnage to reassure Kate that, if things weren't working out, she could ask him to leave. But that was the last thing on Kate's mind and as she began to prepare for Christmas, she considered that perhaps the festive season would provide the opportunity to become engaged and so formally acknowledge their commitment to one another.

Circumstances soon conspired to undermine Kate's plan however. Suffering bouts of dizziness and sickness, Kate knew that it could only mean one thing. She was pregnant. They hadn't intended this to happen, but it had. With some difficulty, she had managed to hide her concerns from Ed. Inexperienced in such matters, he was unable to read the tell-tale signs. Kate knew that if she had told him, he would be eager for them to get married. But that wasn't what she had wanted. She felt guilty. She had no wish to trap Ed into marriage. She was determined to give him as long as possible to focus on his qualification as a teacher. Kate therefore decided that she would say nothing. Yet it was a difficult burden for her to bear and it was clear that at some stage, as the baby began to grow inside her, that she would no longer be able to keep her condition a secret.

Whilst Ed and May were unaware of Kate's condition, her best friend was about to find out. In early November, Sarah was covering at the Levenshulme office and had arranged to meet Kate in the morning so that they could travel to work together. Kate had already taken Rosie to her nan, so the two women had time for a chat before they set off. After a few minutes, Kate rushed to the back door and the outside toilet. Concerned, Sarah had followed her, hearing the unmistakable sounds of Kate being sick. Once Kate had recovered and they had come back into the house, Sarah playfully asked her if she was pregnant. Met by tears, Sarah was stunned.

"Oh, Kate. You are, aren't you?"

She threw her arms around Kate and pulled her close, comforting her friend who was sobbing quietly. Waiting for Kate to calm down, Sarah tenderly patted her shoulder. Eventually Kate straightened up and took a deep breath, dabbing her eyes with a tissue. Sarah led her over to the settee and the two young women sat down.

"Does Ed know?" asked Sarah.

"No. I've not told him."

"Shouldn't he know?"

"No. Not yet."

"Why?" asked Sarah. "Are you having second thoughts about the baby?"

"No!" said Kate, shocked by Sarah's words. She would never, ever want to lose her baby, although she was aware that there were many suggested remedies and those you could go to, if you wanted to terminate an unwanted pregnancy.

"I'm sorry Kitty. I didn't mean it in that way. It didn't come out right," said Sarah, hurriedly. "What I meant to say was, are you concerned about Ed?"

"No, that's not it. I know Ed would be over the moon. He loves Rosie and he'd definitely be happy for us to have another addition to the family."

"So, what's the problem?"

"It's not how I wanted it. It's too soon. I'm worried that if Ed finds out, he'll want to give up his course. He'll be going down to Piccadilly to see Arnold for a manager's job. Arnold likes him, that's why he gives him holiday work and the Saturday job at Levenshulme. But it would be such a waste. I want him to be a teacher and he does too. But I know that he'll think that by giving up teaching, he'll be putting us first."

"Is it only that though?" asked Sarah, looking at her friend intently.

"No, it isn't Sarah. I don't want to feel like I've trapped him. I want him to be able to walk away from me and Rosie, if he were to meet someone else. This way, he can't."

"I don't believe it!" said Sarah, in amazement. "How can you say that you've trapped him? You're all but married now. It seems to me that he's already enjoying all the benefits of being a husband. He sleeps with you, doesn't he? Ed's not stupid. He knows the risks in doing that. Besides, what are you worrying about? Anyone can see that he adores you. He isn't my type, but even I get a bit jealous of how he hangs on your every word and will do anything you ask of him. You're not trapping him. If anything, he's trapping you! He's the one who's desperate to get married."

Still feeling a little dizzy, Sarah's stern words about Ed had jolted Kate and she responded fiercely to her friend's perceived criticisms. She was determined to defend him.

"No, Sarah! He's good and kind. He still pays rent on his flat so that I can ask him to go at any time I choose. He knows that our relationship is in my hands, not his. No, I won't accept anything bad about him. I want his commitment to me to be without any pressure at all."

"Yes, okay. Perhaps I was a bit hard on him" said Sarah, not wishing to fall out with her friend, "but you're going to have to tell him Kitty. You're keeping the baby and it's his. He does have a right to know."

"Yes. But I want to leave it as long as I can."

"What about the baby though? Surely you don't want to be unmarried? You know how the doctors and the hospital will treat you."

"Don't you think I've been through all that? I don't think of anything else Sarah. The thought of a child of mine being called a bastard. Well …"

"Well, tell him. Don't leave it any longer."

Sarah was insistent. She felt that she had to make her friend see sense. She genuinely believed that Kate was being far too considerate towards Ed. Delaying telling him could create a host of additional problems.

"No, Sarah. I'll get Christmas out of the way first. I want it to be a really happy time for the three of us and then I'll let him know."

"I think you're wrong Kitty. I know you don't want to hear it, but I'm your friend, I care about you. You shouldn't leave it any longer, if only to find out what he feels about the news. You never know. You may be wrong about him."

"It doesn't matter. I've told you Sarah. There's no way that I'm not having this baby."

The two of them sat quietly for a time, both taking in the magnitude of their conversation. Finally, Kate looked across at her friend and put her hand on hers.

"Come on Sarah, it's time we were off. First though, you must promise me that you won't say a word of this to Ed."

Sarah was silent. Kate looked directly into her eyes.

"I mean it Sarah. I told you in confidence. You're not to tell Ed anything."

Seeing the look of determination on Kate's face and hearing the insistent tone of her words, Sarah reluctantly agreed.

"Okay. I promise. I won't. But I've not changed my mind. You should tell him Kate."

The subject now closed, the two of them set off to work.

Chapter 19

Sarah had certainly intended to honour her promise, but events were to unfold differently and she was to become the instrument by which Ed discovered the news of Kate's pregnancy.

It was the second Saturday before Christmas and that morning Ed had awoken to find that Kate wasn't asleep beside him. It surprised him that he hadn't been disturbed by her getting out of bed. Asleep, he was always in contact with her, his hand on her body or lay beside her, feeling her reassuring presence. Her movement away from him would normally have roused him from his slumber. He must have been very tired he thought. Getting out of bed, he pulled on his clothes and quickly made his way downstairs. About to push open the kitchen door, he heard the unmistakable sound of someone being sick. He knew that it had to be Kate and as he entered the room, he could see her bent over the sink in obvious discomfort.

"Kate!" exclaimed Ed, as he rushed over to her. "Are you all right?"

It was a stupid question and he knew it. He patted her on the top of her arm, trying to demonstrate his concern for her condition.

"No, stop," said Kate, weakly. "Leave me."

She waved her arm behind her as if to emphasise the point.

Reluctantly, Ed stepped back. He wanted to hold her, to help, but finally realised that there was very little he could actually do but wait. Yet it wasn't easy as he saw Kate's body tighten and then heave forward as once again, she was violently sick. He wondered what had caused her to be so ill. Was it something that she had eaten? Or perhaps, she had picked up a bug. Whatever it was, it had made her very ill.

Gradually, the heaving stopped and Kate's body relaxed. Slowly, she began to stand upright again but she seemed dizzy and weak, placing both her hands on the edge of the sink in an attempt to find some stability.

"Ed," said Kate, quietly.

"Yes," replied Ed, stepping back towards her.

"Can you help me over to the table please?"

Ed put his right arm around her back and under her shoulders and supporting her, walked the few steps over to the kitchen table. He pulled out a chair and slowly she sat down. He could see her face now. It was pale and drawn. Her eyes were moist with tears. She had been in real pain.

"You need to see a doctor," said Ed.

"No," said Kate quietly, but insistently. "I'll be all right in a minute."

Ed was unconvinced. She seemed short of breath, but he knew that there was no point in arguing with her.

"I just feel a little dizzy. I'll be fine soon."

Kate looked up at him, grabbed his hand and smiled weakly.

"Sit down Ed."

Ed pulled a chair alongside her and sat down. He held her hand and then patted her knee. Kate could see the signs of concern on his face. She'd hoped that he'd stay asleep long enough for her to recover, but she should have known, he always seemed to sense when she wasn't well or worrying about something. He was bound to wake up. Now the most important thing, as far as she was concerned, was to reassure him before he started to ask any awkward questions.

"I'm going to be fine Ed, don't worry. It must've been the sandwich I had at work. It was probably off. I do feel a bit dizzy though, but I'm sure it'll pass."

"What about work?" asked Ed. "You don't look well enough to go in. Shall I ring Arnold at nine and tell him?"

"No. Let's wait and see. I might feel okay by then."

Ed looked at her. She appeared so pale and shaken and he seriously doubted that she would be.

"Had I best wake Rosie, just in case she needs to get ready to go to May's?"

"No, leave her for a bit Ed. Just sit with me for ten minutes."

"Do you want a drink of tea?" asked Ed.

"Oh, no thanks" said Kate, shuddering.

"Sorry Kitty. I didn't think."

"It's okay. It's not your fault" said Kate, squeezing his hand.

Sat there quietly, just for a moment Kate thought of telling Ed exactly why she was being sick. But she still felt dizzy and queasy and in no condition to answer his inevitable barrage of questions.

Ten minutes had soon stretched to twenty and looking at the clock, Ed saw that it was now eight thirty. It was obvious that Kate wasn't going to recover sufficiently to be able to go into work. Arnold would have to be told and Ed would also need to go and fetch May.

"Do you think that I should get washed and ready to go to the phone box Kitty?"

Kate looked at him. Reluctantly she knew that she was going to have to admit defeat. She felt frustrated, given that she hadn't suffered much with morning sickness when she had been pregnant on Rosie. Well at least Ed would be paid for his Saturday work, so the loss of her day's wage wasn't quite so bad.

"Yes, I suppose you'd better" said Kate, with a sigh. "Go and let May know once you've been to the phone box. Ask her if she can come here, instead of Rosie going there."

Getting washed and changed, Ed went to the phone and left a message for Arnold that Kate was ill. He then went to see May who, collecting a few things, walked back to Bright Avenue with him. The pair of them were reassured to see that Kate, having got washed and changed, had perked up a little. Giving Kate a kiss and a large dose of sympathy, May took off her coat and sat down with Rosie, who had now made her way downstairs and was playing with her dolls on the settee. Ed felt a sense of relief. He realised just how lucky they were that they could call on May to help in situations such as this. Not only would she be caring for Rosie, as she usually did, but she could also keep an eye on Kate too. Soon, it was time for Ed to go. Giving both Kate and Rosie a kiss, he set off for the bus stop and on to work.

Arriving at the bookies, Ed was greeted by a concerned looking Kevin.

"Is Kate all right Ed?"

"Yes, I think she's going to be. She's perked up a little bit, but she's still not up to coming in."

"Arnold said that she's been sick. Is that right?"

"Yes," replied Ed.

"She needs to get to the doctors. That's twice now. She wasn't well in the week," continued Kevin.

"Oh?" said Ed, unaware of what Kevin was talking about.

"Didn't you know?" asked Kevin. "She was feeling sick on Tuesday. She was all pale and had to sit in my chair for a while, because she felt dizzy on the stool."

Taken by surprise, Ed didn't know what to say.

"She probably didn't want to worry you Ed. You know what she's like," said Kevin, trying to reassure him.

"Yes, probably," said Ed, still feeling a little confused.

"Sarah should be here soon," said Kevin, changing the subject. "Arnold's sending her down to cover for Kate."

"That's good," said Ed.

Both he and Kevin were pleased by the news. Sarah worked hard, unlike many of the relief staff who stayed rooted to their stools and did little other than take the bets. That was fine during the week but on Saturdays, when everyone was rushed off their feet, they needed all hands to the pumps if the day were to run as smoothly as possible. It wasn't that long before Sarah arrived and as it was still relatively early, she and Ed weren't that busy. As a result, they were able to sit on their stools and talk. Aware that Kate was ill, Sarah immediately asked how she was.

"She seemed a little better when I left," replied Ed, "but she was really sick this morning. I got fairly worried but you know Kate, she wouldn't let me make a fuss."

Sarah nodded.

"But I'm a bit worried now Sarah. Kevin told me that she felt sick and dizzy on Tuesday. She never told me though."

Ed noticed that as he spoke to Sarah, it seemed as if she was trying to avoid any kind of eye contact with him. He couldn't help thinking that she seemed a little uncomfortable, but quickly dismissing the thought, he continued.

"Perhaps I should try and get her to go and see the doctor. What do you think Sarah?"

Sarah sat thoughtfully on her stool. She could see that Ed was worried. She knew how aware he was of Kate's lack of concern for her own well-being. As she was Kate's friend, perhaps he thought that she may be able to suggest a way of getting her to go. It was an awkward situation for Sarah and she wished it was later when the dogs were well underway. Then the punters would be arriving in larger numbers and the two of them would be too busy for conversation. But it wasn't. She felt torn between her promise to her friend not to say anything and the need to let Ed know just exactly what Kate's condition was. Listening to him, she felt that it was only fair that he knew the truth. After all he should know and, for all she'd presented Kate with a worst-case scenario, she too believed that Ed would embrace his additional responsibilities with enthusiasm. Besides, she reasoned, just how long could Kate wait before she would have to tell him and surely it was best to give themselves more time to plan before the baby was born. It was better for them and certainly, better for Rosie and the baby. She thought that Kate was trying too hard to please everyone and in the process was putting an intolerable burden upon herself. She was carrying a secret that must be hurting her emotionally and probably wasn't helping to combat her bouts of morning sickness. She knew that Kate had been sick twice that week as did Kevin and perhaps, several of the staff at Head Office. People loved to gossip and it wouldn't take long before someone suggested that Kate might be pregnant. How long would it then be before it was mentioned to Ed. Surely Kate didn't want that to happen. Therefore, Sarah decided that she was going to tell Ed herself and face her friend's displeasure. More accurately, she would almost tell him, leaving Ed to work out the rest of the details for himself.

"Ed," said Sarah, quietly. "Listen carefully. I don't want anyone else to hear, but I need to tell you about Kate."

Fearing the worst, Ed's face displayed a look of panic.

"No, don't worry Ed," said Sarah, quickly trying to reassure him. "Kate's okay. But she's probably going to be suffering from sickness for a few weeks yet."

Ed looked at her wide-eyed and amazed. Sarah could see that he didn't have a clue about what she was trying to tell him.

"Ed. You need to talk to Kate," she continued. "Tell her that you've spoken to me and ask her to tell you why she keeps being sick."

Ed stared at her. He was silent. Sarah realised that he simply couldn't connect up the clues that she was giving him. Having come this far however, she knew that she couldn't let the matter rest. She would have to take a new approach.

"Look Ed, I'll come back with you to Kate's when we get off the bus after work. I'll talk to her, before you go in."

She patted Ed on the leg reassuringly.

"Right", she continued. "I'm going to get a sandwich for dinner. Do you want one?"

Ed was still silent, pondering on what she had told him.

"I'll just get you one, you can give me the money when I get back. Come on Ed, you're needed on the pay out."

Ed looked up and could see little Sam waiting with a winning bet at the counter. He got off his stool and walked over to him.

"Kate not here this morning?" asked Sam.

"No, Sam. She's not very well," replied Ed.

"Oh," Sam replied. "I hope you're treating her right."

Sam and the other regulars knew that Ed and Kate were going out together.

"Yes. She just been a bit sick, that's all. She'll be back on Monday."

"I hope so," said Sam. "Never get any luck when Kate's not here."

"Oh. I'm sure you do Sam."

"No. I don't," said Sam, as he took his winnings and wandered off to finalise his selections for the day.

Over the course of the next hour, Ed found himself fielding a succession of enquiries from a whole host of punters concerned at Kate's absence. Reassuring them and seeing the satisfied looks on their faces, Ed felt blessed. How lucky he was to be living with his wonderful Kitty. She was a real ray of sunshine. Her friendly nature, her winning smile, her sense of humour and pretty face, making the world a far more pleasant place for so many.

Busy for the rest of the afternoon, Ed didn't have time to reflect on what Sarah had told him, but inevitably the day's racing drew to a close, they cashed up and Kevin indicated that he and Sarah could set off home. On the bus, the two of them made small talk. Sarah was unwilling to say anything more and Ed was well aware that he had no way of convincing her to do so. Having got off the bus, the two of them walked quietly up Syndall Street. Reaching the ginnel that gave access to the backyards behind Bright Avenue, they were soon at Kate's back door.

"Wait outside Ed. Let me speak to Kate first," said Sarah.

"May might still be there," said Ed.

"Don't worry. If she is, I won't say anything in front of her."

Sarah's answer reinforced Ed's realisation that what he was about to learn was of real consequence. He stood back and Sarah went up the steps to the back door and knocked. She then pushed the door open and went inside. As he waited, he kept going over what she had said to him earlier in the day, but he still couldn't work out what she had been trying to tell him. It was all such a mystery. He didn't have a clue what to think. What on earth was the matter with Kate?

It seemed ages before the door opened once more, although in reality it was very little time at all. Sarah seemed in good spirits. She stepped down from the back door and walked over to Ed. She smiled and told him to go in; that everything was fine. Saying goodbye, she walked out of the backyard and was off home. Ed made his way to the back door and went into the house. He felt nervous, a sense of trepidation. He didn't like uncertainty and given that it involved Kate's health, he found himself silently praying that everything would be fine. Kate was sat at the table; Rosie playing with her dolls on the settee. May had obviously already gone home. Getting up, Kate walked over and threw her arms around him. She looked up and he bent his head down to kiss her. He could see tears in her eyes.

"Kitty. Are you all right?" he asked, quietly.

"Yes. I'm fine," she whispered. "Hold me Ed."

Ed needed no invitation. His heart had melted the moment he had seen her tears and she had shown him her vulnerability. It was so rare that he ever saw her showing any signs of emotional distress. She was the strong one. The Rock of Gibraltar for all of them. To see tears in her eyes was distressing to him, yet at the same time it gave him the opportunity to comfort and protect her and so feel useful and satisfied at the fact that she needed him. Holding on to her tightly and feeling her body moving against his, as she breathed slowly, yet rhythmically, he felt at one with the world. He just wished that they could hold on to this moment for ever. It was pure and beautiful. It was love. Kissing her softly on the top of her head, Kate looked up towards him once more and he moved down to kiss her on the forehead and then briefly, on her lips. Looking into Ed's eyes, Kate recognised once again the strength of his feelings for her. How silly she had been. It was wrong to have hesitated about telling him. She pulled herself together, stepped away from Ed and wiped her eyes.

"Sit down Ed. I've got something to tell you."

Relieved that he would finally know, but still worried about how serious it could be, Ed sat down next to Kate at the kitchen table.

"Look at me Ed. Give me your hand."

Kate put out her hand on the table top and Ed carefully took hold of it.

"Have you worked out what's wrong with me?" she asked.

"No. What?"

"Well, you know that I was sick at work and now I've been sick this morning. That I've been feeling dizzy. Don't you know?"

Kate looked at him, waiting expectantly for him to respond.

"No," said Ed, eventually.

Serious as the moment was, Kate couldn't help but smile. She gently stroked his hand.

"You really are behind the door, aren't you Ed?"

"What?" said Ed, by now totally confused.

"Morning sickness?" asked Kate.

Suddenly, it seemed as if the penny had dropped. Kate watched as slowly a look of recognition crossed Ed's face. He looked at her, his eyes and mouth wide open, but it was as if he couldn't say anything.

"Do I have to spell it out?" asked Kate.

Still. Silence.

"I'm pregnant!"

Kate watched as a huge smile broke out over Ed's face. She felt him grip her hand tightly, hardly able to contain himself. Suddenly he was all a fluster.

"Oh, oh. Are you okay? Shouldn't you be lying down? Should you be working? Shouldn't you be at the hospital?"

A series of questions came out of Ed's mouth in quick succession. It seemed to Kate that Ed didn't know what he was saying; that her words had simply triggered a hasty and confused response.

"Whoa! Hold on! Calm down!" said Kate, firmly.

She squeezed his hand and looked him in the eyes. Ed paused, but she could see that he was breathing deeply, his chest rising and falling in quick succession. She wasn't sure whether it was fear or excitement. Most likely, she thought, it was a combination of both.

"Oh, Kate. I do love you."

Kate's heart leapt with joy. Ed's words confirmed everything. He was no reluctant father. Deep down, she had always known that her condition would bring them even closer together.

"When. When will the baby be born?" asked Ed.

"Not yet! I'm only around four months, there's plenty of time yet."

"Am I all right to give you a hug Kitty?" asked Ed, looking concerned.

"Of course, you are. You just have, haven't you?"

"Oh, yes," said Ed, feeling rather foolish.

"I'm only pregnant. I won't break," said Kate, laughing.

"Well… It's just…"

"Shut up and don't be potty! Come here."

Kate stood up and held out her arms to Ed. He rose from the table and she threw them around him. She felt him holding her carefully and tenderly, as if she were a china doll. So different to Joe she thought. Finally, pulling away from him, she noticed that Rosie had stopped playing with her dolls and was on the settee looking at the two of them, mesmerised by the scene she had just witnessed. Although very young, Rosie was aware that the two adults were discussing something of great importance.

"Come here Rosie," said Kate.

Bending down, she opened her arms and gave her daughter a huge cuddle, kissing her on the cheek.

"Do you love your mam?" she asked.

"Yes Mammy," said Rosie.

"How much?"

"To the top of the sky and all the way back down," said Rosie, with a real sense of certainty.

Looking on, Ed smiled. He knew that little Rosie was as much a part of what lay ahead as the two of them. With a baby on the way, Ed would now have to become Rosie's real father and it was a role that he welcomed.

"Kate, we have to get married now. It's best for you and for Rosie. Please, would you marry me?"

Kate and Rosie turned to look at him. Rosie, having heard Ed mention her name was wide-eyed, but not really sure what he was talking about. Kate saw a deep and earnest look on Ed's face. He was deadly serious and looking directly at her.

"I thought it might be a bit more romantic than this," said Kate, with a smile. "Never mind, it's not the ideal circumstances for a proposal, is it?"

Ed was nervously expectant, waiting almost in desperation for her answer. She could see that he was hanging on her every word. It was clearly an agonising wait for him.

"Yes, of course I'll marry you Ed. Only I didn't expect that I would be in this position so soon."

Ed looked at her. He was delighted; overjoyed that she had agreed. Yet he was surprised that she had only told him about her pregnancy now and that after Sarah's intervention. He had to know why she had delayed telling him.

"Why wouldn't you tell me before Kitty?" he asked.

Kate looked down at Rosie.

"Rosie, are you going to sit at the table and do some colouring, whilst Ed and Mammy sit talking on the settee?"

Rosie nodded, picked up her books and crayons off the settee and settled down at the table.

"Let's sit down Ed," said Kate.

The two of them moved over to the settee and sat down next to one another. More comfortable, Kate began to talk.

"I had to be sure that I was doing the right thing for you Ed. I didn't intend to get caught and I didn't think it was fair to you. I knew the baby wouldn't show for a while, so I chose to wait."

"But you knew that I wanted to marry you. You and Rosie mean the world to me. I've told you before. I know my own mind and I know how much I love you."

"Yes Ed, but having a baby is different."

"Why? I already help you to look after Rosie. If I didn't like children, I couldn't do that, could I?"

"I know Ed, but this baby will be your responsibility. Rosie isn't. It's different."

Ed thought he could understand what she was saying and although there had never been a chance that he wouldn't stand by Kate, he wondered what she would have felt if he hadn't wanted the responsibility.

"You should have told me Kate," he said, as gently as he could. "It was too important for you to know how I felt. God forbid, but what if I'd not wanted to stand by you and the baby. What then?"

Kate knew he was speaking in earnest. Since they had lived together, he had called her Kitty, just like all her friends. He only used her full name when he was being serious.

"It wouldn't have mattered Ed. I would have had two children, rather than just one."

"But then people would have talked about you if you'd not been married. You were prepared to do that?"

"Yes, if necessary, Ed."

"You would have said nothing if I'd wanted to walk away?"

"No," replied Kate. "A relationship can't survive unless both of you are totally committed to one another. I learned that from my marriage to Joe."

"But you stayed with Joe," said Ed, looking confused.

"Yes, I did for Rosie's sake. It was so she would have a dad, but all the love I'd had for Joe was gone when he used to go out with his friends and leave me and Rosie on our own. I didn't want to take your life away from you Ed and have you feeling resentful, just like Joe did. You needed to know that, if you wanted, you could still be single and fancy free."

Ed was surprised. Kate hadn't talked to him much about Joe. He had suspected that Kate's marriage had been less than perfect, but he had never heard her talk so critically about him before.

"It wasn't just that," continued Kate, "I really had to think about whether you marrying me and having responsibilities so quickly, was fair on you."

"But I'm a lot older than you and Joe were when you first got married and had Rosie."

"But Ed," replied Kate, "you're not like we were. You've been to university. Your road is a different one. It would break my heart if I felt that I'd ruined your future by becoming pregnant."

Ed wasn't surprised by her response. It was Kate all over. Sometimes Ed became exasperated by her constant concern for others. He often told her, like May did, that she should think more about herself. Then he realised, that her generosity of spirit was one of the main reasons why he loved her so much. And he knew, that whatever his frustrations, he would never want her to change.

"But I won't ruin my future, why will I?" said Ed, after due consideration. "I'm going to get a job and support us properly. You'll need to stop working now and I can't provide enough for us all on a grant. I'll go and see Arnold. I know that they're looking for trainee managers."

Kate laughed.

"Why are you laughing?" asked Ed, upset that she didn't appear to be taking him seriously.

"I'll do it first thing on Monday," he continued, with a clear note of determination in his voice.

"I know you will," said Kate. "It's just what I told Sarah and why I hesitated to tell you about my condition."

She spoke fiercely, almost dismissively it seemed to Ed. He sensed that they were having their first argument and what a time it was to have it.

"What do you mean?" asked Ed, looking confused.

"You. Being stupid. Giving up your teacher training and for what? Working in the bookies! You won't go very far doing that, will you? A manager, that's all. It's the owners that make the money. And then what happens if you get fed up and begin to regret giving up teaching? That creates resentment and how do you think that will affect our marriage? I've told you. There's no way that I'm going to hold you back."

Kate grabbed his hands once more and looked him straight in the eyes. She was determined to get through to him.

"I'm telling you Ed how it's going to be. You are staying on and you're going to qualify as a teacher. And you'd better, or you'll have me to answer to. You'll have a job by next September and I'm sure that we can get by until then. I can keep working right up until the baby is born."

"How can you?" asked Ed. "You're not well enough."

"Of course, I can. It's only morning sickness. It'll pass."

"Only!" said Ed. "I've seen you. This morning you were terrible!"

Kate looked at him. Although his desire to make a personal sacrifice of his future had angered her, she was still touched by his concern. Nevertheless, she wasn't going to relent on him just yet.

"It does pass Ed. I worked when I was pregnant on Rosie and there's no way that I'm not doing it now. You'll do as I say Ed, or I'm not getting married. It's up to you."

Kate's eyes shone fiercely, her gaze pierced right through him and into the distance. When she was like this, Ed couldn't help but feel a tremor of excitement. She stirred something deep and inexplicable inside of him. It was a thrilling sensation. He would never have admitted it, but he loved her being in charge. When she was, she seemed even more beautiful. Meekly, his eyes averted like a naughty child, he responded.

"Okay, Kitty."

"That's final then," said Kate, firmly. "We're going to carry on, just as normal. That's the end of it."

"What about getting married?" asked Ed, quietly.

Although having been firmly dealt with, Ed was determined that he wasn't going to let her forget her earlier acceptance of his proposal.

"When will we? Shouldn't it be soon?" continued Ed.

"Well, it should be sooner, rather than later, if I'm not going to be showing at the Register Office," said Kate. "We'll go down to All Saints when I'm off work on Wednesday and get it arranged."

Ed was pleased. Reassured and satisfied. His life had changed so much in just a few short months and with Kate now by his side, he felt almost invincible. He could never say she was his, she was far too independent for that, but he knew beyond a doubt that he was totally hers; his character, his very essence submerged in her. Ed accepted that in their relationship she would be the dominant force and it was a factor that Kate herself appreciated and ultimately, the reason why she was prepared to marry him. Ed would be no Joe. He would be a true husband and father and with her guidance, they would build a happy future for their family together.

Chapter 20

Events moved quickly for Kate and Ed. They both realised that they had to. Visiting the registry office early on Wednesday, they had made their application to get married in a month's time. The New Year would see them as man and wife. Rosie and May had of course to be told and both approved. They had informed them the following day after their decision had been reached. May was pleased, she liked Ed and believed that he would eventually give Kate and Rosie more stability and security. Rosie, still too young to really understand what was happening, was excited to know that Ed would be staying with them 'forever'. Kate knew that her daughter was at a tender age and had no real recollection of Joe. It seemed natural that Ed could become her father. Rosie would have no hesitation in accepting the fact and her mam decided that, once she and Ed were married, Rosie would call him 'Dad'.

Setting the date for their marriage brought home, in no uncertain terms, the responsibilities Ed now had to face. Yes, he knew that he had already accepted a commitment, alongside Kate, to care and provide for their family, but there had always been a sense on Kate's part that their relationship may not be permanent. She had made clear to him that he was free to leave at any time he chose. Consequently, Ed always felt a degree of insecurity about his condition. It was reinforced by Kate's insistence that Ed keep his flat, regardless of the fact that the money spent in rent would have proved very useful in supplementing the family finances. Ed had accepted her reasoning, yet continued to harbour hopes that she would tell him to give it up. It would indicate that she no longer had any doubts about the strength of their relationship. Finally, now that they were getting married, Kate made the decision that signified to Ed that his life was about to change forever.

It happened on Christmas Day. They had tidied away after the day's festivities. Rosie had gone to bed. She was delighted with the new pram that May had bought for her and the dolls, paints and crayons that she had received from Kate and Ed. May, a little tipsy, had been taken home by Ed and now the lovers were alone. Snuggled up together in front of the fire in the front room, the two of them were listening to the radio, which was on softly in the background. Ed was sat up, Kate leaning her head against his shoulder, whilst his right arm held her towards him. He felt relaxed and content. It was then that Kate had spoken the unforgettable words.

"Ed," said Kate, quietly.

"Yes," mumbled Ed in reply.

He felt Kate lift her head from his shoulder and turned his face towards her.

"I think that it's time for you to give up your flat. We'll need the money and there's no need to wait until we're married."

"I'll get on to it right away."

Suddenly alert, Ed began to rise from the settee.

"Not right now!" exclaimed Kate, laughing. "Tomorrow will do. You can call on the landlord after the racing."

Settling back down, Ed stroked Kate's arm.

"Yes. I can do that. It would have been nice to have had another day at home though, just like everyone else."

"I know, but remember Boxing Day is a bank holiday. It's triple time for both of us. The extra money will come in useful."

Ed smiled. In reality tomorrow wouldn't prove to be difficult. After all, he and Kate would be working together and now, giving up his flat, he was definitely looking forward to spending the rest of his life with her.

Looking at him, Kate couldn't fail to notice that the smile on his face had just got broader.

"What are you made up about? You're grinning like a Cheshire cat."

"It's giving up my flat. I finally feel as if I really belong here."

"Of course, you belong here," said Kate, surprised.

"No, Kitty. Still having the flat meant that part of me was somewhere else and I wanted to be one hundred percent yours."

Kate looked at him. He looked back, an intense expression on his face. She shook her head slowly and sighed.

"I'm afraid you're too deep for me Ed. You're being daft again, aren't you?"

Smiling, Kate leaned forward and kissed him. The two embraced and held each other tightly. Ed knew that Kate understood implicitly what he had meant. However, it was her way. She wasn't going to acknowledge it.

At work the next day, Kate had announced that the two of them were to be married. The reaction was one of surprise. It was clear that no one except Sarah, who had closely guarded their secret, had seen it coming. The two of them seemed such an unlikely couple. Such very different characters. Eventually though, everyone had said their congratulations and with that, the matter was closed. In the days that followed however, when Ed wasn't present, there were suggestions that Kate didn't really understand what she was doing. Kevin questioned Ed's suitability. He knew that they were going out together, but Ed was nothing like Kate.

Yet the most serious examination of Kate, came from Sarah. She was clearly worried for her friend. Sharing knowledge of Kate's condition, Sarah thought that she understood why she was marrying Ed, but still wasn't convinced that they were a match made in heaven and found it hard to understand why Kate seemed to have no misgivings about marrying him. Sarah herself, had recently broken up with her boyfriend Len, feeling that their relationship lacked excitement.

"He's just not like you Kitty. Are you certain that you'll truly be happy with him?"

"Well," replied Kate, "they do say that opposites attract and you have to say that in a lot of ways we are different."

"That's what I mean Kitty. I'm sorry, I don't want to upset you, but I do worry."

"No, it's fine Sarah. It's good that you're making me justify what I'm doing. But I can tell you that I've already given it lots of thought and I do love him. Yes, he's quiet and reserved, but not with me or Rosie. He's so dependable Sarah. You've recognised that yourself. I've had the dashing, exciting husband that all my friends fancied and were envious of and I can tell you now, I'd never want another man like Joe. Men like that don't really love anyone but themselves. They're totally unreliable."

"But Ed's boring in comparison. I can't imagine him ever showing you a good time. Joe did," continued Sarah.

"And all the others as well. You forget Sarah. You've never been married. If you end up with someone like Joe, then you'll understand. And I hope, for your sake, that you never do."

"Surely, you're being too harsh on Joe," said Sarah, unable to accept what Kate was telling her.

"No. Take a look around Sarah. Open your eyes. All the married women in the streets of Ardwick. How many of them are truly happy? How many simply pretend, desperate to turn back the clock to when they were young like us, with their lives ahead of them but with the experience to avoid making the same mistakes? We women are stupid. We're too emotional. We let men like Joe sweep us off our feet with their looks, their cheeky smiles and the patter. Oh yes, they really want us, they really love us, then once they get a ring on our finger, it's all quickly gone. We're the homemaker, the baby minder, whilst they carry on as normal, out at the pub seven days a week whilst the 'little woman' stays in to mind the kids. And if you should complain, at best it's a blazing row, at worst a kick or a punch. And why do we put up with it? Because there's nowhere we can go. Joe was a Catholic. I went to see Father Brennan at the Holy Name because Joe wanted me to convert and I'd had Rosie baptised a Catholic. When he found out about Joe's drinking and that he went out every night, not appearing until the early hours of the morning, do you know what he said?"

Animated, Kate looked intensely at Sarah.

"No," replied Sarah, quietly.

"He told me that it was a woman's duty to stand by her husband regardless and that he was sure that in time, Joe would settle down. He didn't even offer to talk to him. Not that I would have let him, because Joe would have really kicked off then."

"I didn't know that Joe could be violent" said Sarah, clearly shocked.

"I didn't want anyone to and I tried hard to make sure that Rosie never saw it," continued Kate. "But just like with Father Brennan, it's the same with we women. We all know how many around us are suffering just the same as we are, but it's almost a golden rule. You just have to get on with it. What do they always say? 'You've made your bed, so now you've got to lie in it.' But none of us expected to get treated like that. I vowed to myself, after Joe, that no man would ever treat me like that again. It's my name that's in the rent book now and Ed knows it's my house. He accepts that I'm in charge of our family. He respects me and Rosie and welcomes the responsibility. And that's why I love him. And, it might surprise you to know, that I find him attractive and for me, he's a great lover."

"Kate!"

Sarah smiled. Kate's final statement had shocked her. It was a comment that was so unlike her friend but, she realised, it was clear that Kate wished to defend Ed in every way possible. It proved to Sarah, beyond any doubt, that Kate really did love him.

Kate laughed. She'd even surprised herself.

"Well, he is. But don't you go telling anyone."

They both laughed. It was a pleasant end to what could have been a difficult episode in terms of their continued friendship. It had been good for Kate though. She had certainly been tested, but she had justified and confirmed her belief that in marrying Ed, she had done the right thing.

Chapter 21

It wasn't going to be a traditional wedding. Then again, neither had her first one been. The Register Office at All Saints had been sufficient for that and now, it would be so again. Kate had never thought about having a church wedding and reception. In any case, it was far too expensive. With no doting parents to meet the cost and no chance of raising the money herself, it wasn't a practical option. Kate also knew how little the splendour of the occasion would influence the success of her marriage. It couldn't guarantee a loving and lasting relationship. Trust and devotion, those were the qualities that counted and ones that were priceless. As Kate contemplated the state of her relationship with Ed, she was pleased that they had lived together first. Although there were many who condemned 'living over the brush,' Kate knew that the experience had meant that married life with Ed, would bring no surprises. With Joe, the pair had been madly in love, or at least Kate had thought they were, but once they were spending twenty-four hours a day together, the flaws in their relationship soon began to appear. Kate had watched Ed very carefully over the last few months, long enough for any misgivings or second thoughts to surface. Ed had been a stalwart partner. He'd told her that he loved her and wanted to spend his life with her from the start and he'd never wavered in that belief. Selfless, he always put her and Rosie first. She knew that she could depend on him.

Yet, as Kate lay in bed listening to the sound of the milk float making its way down Bright Avenue, she was nervous. She hadn't slept well. It was her wedding day; Wednesday January 17th, 1963 and now she couldn't help but ask herself if she was doing the right thing. She had her independence; her freedom. She'd lost that married to Joe and she naturally worried that she would lose it again. She turned her head on the pillow and saw Ed sleeping peacefully beside her. He looked content, blissfully ignorant of the doubts that were now coursing through her mind. She wondered if she should back out; call it off. After all, perhaps it was for the best. Her heart was pounding, she felt it difficult to breathe. She just didn't know what to do. She wanted to get up and go downstairs, so that she could think alone in the kitchen, free from Ed's presence. She knew how much today meant to him and it simply added to the pressure to see him lay there beside her. Carefully, she moved towards the edge of the bed. There was no response from Ed. Relieved, she slipped out from under the covers, put on her slippers and walked quietly to the door.

Putting on her dressing gown, she went out on to the landing and tip toed quietly down the stairs.

Reaching the bottom, she stopped. She couldn't believe what she had just done and felt an overwhelming desire to laugh. She quickly pushed open the kitchen door and went in. Closing the door behind her, she stifled a chuckle. It was pure comedy. The way she had tiptoed away from Ed, skulking down the stairs like a naughty child. She smiled. Strange she thought, how such silly things put everything into perspective. It was normal to have doubts. Especially in her case. But she had already considered every possible scenario concerning their marriage and she had decided that it was the right thing to do. What could be different now? It was time to commit herself to a man once more and she knew that in Ed, she had found the right one.

Inevitably it wasn't long before she heard footsteps at the top of the stairs. Kate smiled. It was Ed. She already knew that once he couldn't touch or sense her in bed, he would be awake and coming downstairs to see that she was all right. Kate went to the sink and filled the kettle. She lit the gas ring on the cooker as Ed came through the kitchen door.

"Morning Ed. Are you going to give me a kiss?"

Kate turned towards him and held out her arms. Quickly, he moved forward and embraced her, kissing her on her cheek and then lingering softly on her lips.

"Ooh!" exclaimed Kate, playfully. "Your last embrace before you make an honest woman of me. I hope you still get as excited when I've got a ring on my finger."

Ed pulled her towards him and kissed her fully on the lips. She was gorgeous. He pressed his body against hers, his ardour now aroused.

Kate pushed him gently away.

"There's no time for that now Ed. We've got a wedding to get to."

She looked directly into his eyes and then saw the disappointed look on his face. He clearly wanted their embrace to lead on to something more. She laughed gently at him.

"I don't know," said Kate, tutting and shaking her head. "Sometimes you've got a one-track mind, haven't you?"

Ed blushed.

"I'm sorry Kitty. I can't help it. You know how I get when you start teasing."

"Oh, and how's that?" asked Kate, playfully.

"You know!"

Ed looked at the floor and Kate burst out laughing. She knew that she shouldn't be leading him on, especially when nothing could come of it. But then again, she liked to see how much he wanted her. He had a hunger and a passion that made her feel needed, desired and importantly, secure and in control.

"Sit down Ed. I'll finish making us a drink."

Ed sat down, watching Kate whilst she made the tea. She brought it over and sat down.

"May's coming at eight thirty to help get Rosie ready. You're sure that you've booked the taxi, aren't you Ed?"

"Yes."

"And the weather isn't going to stop them getting to us on time?

"No. The taxi firm told me that the driver will set off earlier, if they think that the roads are going to be a problem. But they don't expect them to be."

The couple's wedding was taking place during the worst winter in living memory. The freezing cold conditions had set in at Christmas and the continued presence of snow and ice, had brought many parts of the country to a standstill.

"And Sarah and Chris will be here for nine thirty," continued Ed, "so you can get on with doing your hair."

Unlike Kate, Ed had no nerves. He was keen, eager to get on with the day and no aspect of the wedding's organisation had been left to chance. He had all the paperwork present, money for the taxi and his suit laid out ready for him to put on. Kate looked at how calm he was and envied him. Whilst he seemed so relaxed, all she could think of, was that something was bound to go wrong.

At seven thirty Ed went upstairs to wake Rosie. He looked at her fast asleep, her little head on the pillow. Her long blonde hair contained the 'rags' that her mam had carefully placed last night, in order to make her hair even more curly.

"Come on sleepy head. Time to get up."

Ed gently tapped Rosie on the shoulder and watched as she slowly opened her eyes. Recognising him, Rosie smiled and sat up.

"We need to get ready Rosie. Nanny's coming in a bit to help you get dressed. Your mam and I are getting married."

Rosie's eyes opened wide and a broad smile broke out on her face. It was so exciting for the little girl. She had been wishing for this day for what seemed like forever. She couldn't wait to put on her new blue and white dress, with its white collar and ribbons and her new coat. With the cold weather, she would have to keep her coat on until they reached the register office, but once there, she would look lovely with her attractive new dress and her long, blonde curly hair, framing her angelic face.

"Ed?" asked Rosie.

"Yes."

"When do I call you Daddy?"
Rosie looked up at him, an inquisitive look on her face.
"When we come home, afterwards," replied Ed.
"Oh," said Rosie, clearly disappointed that it couldn't be sooner.
"Why?" she continued.

It was a difficult question for Ed to answer. He knew that it might prove embarrassing if she were calling him Daddy during the ceremony. What would the Registrar think? That they'd had Rosie out of wedlock? That would be seen as scandalous and Ed wanted Kate to avoid any kind of potential embarrassment. But how could he explain that to Rosie? At four years of age, she couldn't possibly understand. Ed gave her what he thought, was the simplest of replies.

"Because we have to wait until the Registrar …"
Rosie looked blankly at Ed.

"The man who marries your mam and I," continued Ed in more simple language, "tells us that we are husband and wife. Then you can call me Daddy."

"Oh," said Rosie, with obvious disappointment. She clearly didn't understand at all why that should be the case.

"Come on, let's go down and get some breakfast" said Ed, quickly changing the subject. "I'm having some cornflakes and some toast," said Ed, eagerly. "Do you want some?"

"Yes please," replied Rosie, nodding.
"I'm having some strawberry jam on my toast. Are you going to?"
"Oh, yes. I love strawberry jam!" said Rosie, excitedly.
"Come on then," said Ed.
Taking Rosie's hand, he walked with her to the top of the stairs.
"Let me go down first," said Ed.

Ed descended the first couple of stairs and then turned back to watch Rosie grab hold of the handrail and carefully and deliberately, make her way down towards him. The stairs were steep and although Rosie could handle them well, neither Kate or Ed would allow her to go up or down them unaccompanied. Reaching the bottom, they went into the kitchen and Ed set about making the cereals and toast. As they sat eating their breakfast at the kitchen table, Ed watched Kate as she carefully put the final touches to her hair in the large mirror mounted on the back wall. Applying a small amount of eye make-up, she declared herself ready. She looked beautiful; radiant. Ed had watched her face in the mirror as she had worked, her back towards him. He felt as if he was intruding, almost as if he were taking secret, forbidden glances at her. He loved what he saw. How lucky he was to have experienced this beautiful woman. To have held her close and made love to her. They had already shared so many intimate moments together. Ed smiled contentedly. He felt so happy.

Mirrors though, reflect both ways and what Ed didn't realise, was that whilst he was watching Kate, she too could see every expression of love and admiration on his face. Continually, she was confronted by signs of his love for her. His devotion, especially on this day, threatened to overwhelm her, but she fought off her emotions, knowing that today there were far too many practical matters to attend to.

Stepping back from the mirror, Kate turned towards Ed and Rosie.

"Right, you two. Once you've got your breakfast finished, you need to get weaving. Rosie, you can sit quietly and crayon until Nanny May arrives and Ed, you need to get your suit sorted out and get dressed."

"Yes Mammy," said Rosie.

"Yes Kitty," said Ed, giving her a playful salute.

Kate wasn't amused and looked sternly at Ed. The day had now become very serious for her.

"I don't want any slip ups Ed. There's lots of things still to do."

"Yes. Sorry Kitty," said Ed, suitably chastened.

Ed realised that Kate was becoming tense, far less relaxed about the day than he was. He resolved to avoid any more flippant remarks until the ceremony was over. Fortunately, the events of the morning seemed to run like clockwork. May had arrived just before eight thirty. She had already been to the florists and picked up their sprays of carnations. Quickly, she set about getting Rosie ready, whilst Ed and Kate put on their wedding clothes in the front room. Both were wearing simple, inexpensive outfits. Ed, a plain black suit, white shirt and dark blue tie. Kate, a light blue, two-piece suit. Unusually, she had worn a decorative white necklace that nestled in the gap between the lapels of her jacket and rested against the soft bare skin at the base of her neck. Her only concession to glamour had been the purchase of a fashionable white hat, with matching gloves and handbag, that she had bought from 'Pauldens.'

Once dressed, the couple made their way back into the kitchen. Looking at Kate, May was filled with a sense of pride.

"Ahh, Kitty, you look lovely. Doesn't she Ed?"

"Yes. Beautiful. I've already told her. I'm so lucky, aren't I?"

"You're both lucky," replied May, quietly. She swallowed and took in a deep breath. They could both see that there were tears in her eyes. She was starting to get emotional. May genuinely believed that this was the best thing that could ever happen to the pair of them and she felt so grateful that Rosie, her beautiful great granddaughter, would now have two loving parents. Pretending not to notice, Kate changed the subject, so giving May a chance to compose herself.

"Oh, you've done a wonderful job on Rosie. She looks lovely," said Kate, switching attention to her daughter, who was sat playing with her dolls on the settee.

Rosie did indeed look cute. Her new dress fitted her perfectly and May had placed blue and white ribbons in her hair. Kate was sure that Rosie would take the limelight once they arrived at the register office. She felt pleased and proud, realising that she had so much to be thankful for.

At nine thirty, Sarah and Chris duly arrived. Sarah had changed her day off work in order to be one of the witnesses. She had gradually come around to the idea that perhaps, after all, Kate and Ed really were suited to one another. Looking at them, she could see how much they were in love and in the confident and assured way that Ed was approaching the day, with absolutely no sign of any nerves, she was witnessing a side to him that she had never seen before. It was clear that where Kate was concerned, Ed could act decisively.

It wasn't long before the taxi arrived, a black cab driven by a friend of May's, who lived on Parker Street. Quickly, they all got into the car and set off to All Saints. The journey seemed to take no time at all and soon the party was being deposited on the pavement close to the register office. Going in, Ed reported to reception and they were soon in the waiting area. Sitting down, they were ready for their turn. It was now that Kate's nerves returned. May grabbed her hand and squeezed it gently.

"You'll be fine," said May, quietly. "You're bound to be nervous. Everyone is."

Kate glanced to the other side of her where Ed was talking to Chris.

"Ed's not nervous," said Kate, turning back towards May.

"Well, he knows he's on to a good thing and he's so in love with you Kitty. My Joe, God bless him, never realised what he'd got."

Kate was surprised at her comments. But May's words had strengthened her. She still found it strange though that May was praising Ed over her own grandson, although it hadn't been the first time that she had done it.

Suddenly, the doors to the Registrar's room opened and a happy couple emerged kissing and smiling, followed by their cheerful friends and relations. Their party was far bigger than Ed and Kate's and it was some time before they had dispersed. Meanwhile, the doors to the Registrar had closed as the paperwork was sorted out and the room straightened ready for Ed and Kate. It was only a short delay but for Kate, trying to contain her nerves, it was one that she didn't need. She breathed out slowly and then back in again, trying her hardest to relax. Her mind began to race and the thought entered her head that she could run away and not go through with it.

Turning towards her, Ed could see the blood draining from her face. For the first time that day, the thought crossed his mind that perhaps it could all go wrong. But the idea had no chance to linger as he steeled himself to the task in hand. He wasn't about to let his beautiful Kitty escape from his grasp. He wouldn't lose the woman of his dreams. Gently, but decisively, he took hold of Kate's hand and kissed her tenderly on the cheek. Then carefully, with his finger, Ed moved back a lock of hair that had strayed close to her eye. Kate looked at him, his soft touch so reassuring. It reminded her of how he would sit for ages, drawing softly on her back when she returned from work, tired or feeling stressed. It never failed to relax her and now his soft, gentle caress, had once more calmed her.

"Edward. Kate."

The couple looked up. It was the voice of the Registrar. He was stood at the open door.

"I'm ready for you," he added, motioning them towards him.

Holding on to Ed's arm, Kate stood up. She felt the strength return to her legs and her breathing become more even. With Ed and Kate leading the way, the small party went into the room.

"You'll all fit on the front row," said the Registrar, pointing to the first line of several rows of chairs that filled the room.

"Edward. You sit there. Kate, you to the left of him. The two witnesses need to be either side of you."

Sarah walked around to the side of Kate, whilst Chris moved next to Ed. May and Rosie sat at the side of Sarah.

"Oh, don't you look lovely!" said the Registrar's Assistant, a pleasant middle-aged lady with a huge smile, who admired Rosie as she walked to her seat.

Rosie, who had suddenly become very shy, looked down at the floor. The formal surroundings were rather daunting for the little girl and she wasn't as lively as usual.

"Ah, poor little thing," continued the assistant to Kate. "It's a lot for her to take in, isn't it? She looks ever so pretty, doesn't she? She's done you both proud."

"Yes, she has," replied Kate, smiling.

With everyone settled, it was time to begin. The Registrar asked the couple and their witnesses to stand up and the two young lovers prepared to commit their futures to one another. It was Ed's turn first and he confidently repeated the words of the Registrar, dedicating himself, in the eyes of the law, to his new wife. Ed's forthright response had strengthened Kate's resolve, but she still felt herself shaking as she spoke the words of dedication to him. Taking Kate's left hand in his, Ed placed the wedding ring on her third finger. The Registrar declared that they were now man and wife and the two lovers shared a lingering kiss.

There now came the inevitable hugs and handshakes.

Overcome with emotion, May found it hard to hold back the tears. She wiped her eyes and dabbed her nose with a tissue. Observing her closely, Rosie expressed concern.

"Nanny, you're crying."

"I'm all right," said May. "It's because I'm happy darling. That's all. Your nanny's just being daft."

Rosie was confused, but content once May had given her a quick cuddle. Looking at her mam and Ed, Rosie walked towards them and pulled on Ed's sleeve in order to get his attention.

"Can I call you Daddy now?" she asked.

"Of course, you can," said Kate, smiling at her daughter. "He is your daddy now."

"For ever?" asked Rosie.

"Yes darling," said Kate, bending down to give her daughter a kiss.

Signing the register, the couple were given a copy of the wedding certificate and then they were gone.

Making their way outside on to the Register Office steps, Kate and Ed paused to kiss, as Rosie gleefully showered them with confetti. It was then time for the photos, the resident photographer taking pictures of Kate and Ed and then the whole wedding party together. There could be no official reception, as the young couple had no money to spend on such things. May had however, arranged for some sandwiches and cake and a little alcohol, to toast the newlyweds with, to be there for them when they got back to Bright Avenue.

It was a strange feeling for Ed, returning in the taxi. Sat by the window, he was deep in thought as he watched the people, shops and houses go by. He had lived with Kate for over five months, but now it was different. She was officially his wife and he was finally assured that he would be given the family responsibilities he craved. Kate had accepted him unconditionally, showing that she really loved him. Today was a confirmation of his new life. He looked at Kate. Sat by his side, with Rosie on her knee, she was deep in conversation with Sarah. Leaning towards her, Ed kissed Kate softly on the cheek. Surprised, she stopped talking and turned to face him.

"Steady on Ed. There's plenty of time for that later on," said Sarah, smiling.

Ed blushed as May and Chris, watching on, laughed.

"You've gone and embarrassed him now Sarah," said May, "and Kitty too."

It was a touching scene; two young lovers who regarded their intimacy as personal and special.

"Mammy, why is your face red?" asked Rosie, looking intently at Kate.

"Out of the mouths of babes," said May, her words causing further merriment among the three adults.

Kate and Ed remained quiet, holding hands and looking contentedly at one another.

Shortly after, the taxi had arrived, drawing up outside the house in Bright Avenue. May got out and opened the front door. She, Rosie, Sarah and Chris, stood waiting to the side.

"Are you going to carry Kate over the threshold, Ed?" asked May, expectantly.

"Yes, if she'll let me."

"Of course, I will. But you'd better not drop me!" said Kate, laughing.

"I won't," said Ed, with an air of confidence that quickly turned to concern, as he thought about the possibility that he might. After all, he was accident prone and Kate often stopped him from doing difficult jobs in the house, given that he could be such a 'calamity'.

Passing her handbag to May, Kate waited for Ed to lift her up. Carefully, he cradled her in his arms and advanced steadily towards the door. She felt as light as a feather and looking into her eyes, he just knew that there was no chance that he would drop her. Carefully, he turned sideways, negotiated his way over the front step and had Kate safely in the front room. He could feel her arms around his neck and then their lips come together, as they enjoyed a long, lingering kiss.

"I love you Mrs Deane," said Ed, quietly. "Thank you for marrying me."

Ed kissed Kate once more and then he carefully placed her back down on the floor, as the others came into the house.

"Well done Ed," said Chris. "We were all betting on whether you'd drop Kate or not."

Chris laughed as did Sarah and May.

"Come on," said May. "Let's have something to eat. It's all ready for us in the kitchen."

As they walked through, they saw plates of sandwiches, sausage rolls, pork pies and cakes, which May had collected from home prior to them leaving. In addition, there were some bottles of beer, sherry and Babycham for the adults and pop for Rosie.

It was a small but happy celebration. The happy couple needed no grand occasion to remind them of the importance of the commitment that they had made to each other. By mid-afternoon, it was time for Sarah and

Chris to drift away. Rosie was exhausted. It had been a long and exciting day for her. May had arranged for her great granddaughter to go home and spend the night with her. As such, the young couple would be alone on their wedding night.

"It's not exactly a honeymoon," remarked May, "but at least you'll have some time to yourselves. It is a special day, after all."

Collecting some dolls, colouring books and crayons, May and Rosie duly departed. Rosie however, had insisted that she give both her mammy and new daddy a big kiss before she left. On their own at last, the young couple snuggled up to one another on the settee in the front room. May had earlier set the fire going and as they lay together, listening to the radio, Ed and Kate felt warm and relaxed as they stared into the glowing embers of the fire.

"You look beautiful Kitty," said Ed, breaking the silence. "Really beautiful. I'm so lucky."

Kate lifted her head, which was lay across his chest.

"You're not so bad yourself," she said, smiling.

Laying her head back down again, she felt Ed's hand move slowly down her side and then stop to gently squeeze the top of her leg.

"That's nice," said Kate, appreciatively.

Encouraged by Kate's response, Ed drew softly on her hips and ever so slowly moved his hand towards the inside of her thigh. Lay against him, she could feel that he had become aroused. She too felt the desire to consummate their union; the first time that they would make love as man and wife.

"Come on Ed," she whispered, "let's go upstairs."

Getting up off the settee she looked down at him. She could see that he had lost none of his ardour for her. There was little evidence now of the signs of embarrassment and uncertainty that she had seen in him on that first night they had spent together. Yet for Ed, she remained the one who was very much in charge. They had made love so many times and she excited him so much. And now he could hardly manage to restrain himself. He wanted her so badly and she knew it. He looked at her. Her beautiful, long hair; her lovely dress that showed off her glorious figure and her sleek calves and delicate ankles. She was his fantasy; but also, his reality.

Taking Ed by the hand, Kate took him up the stairs and into the bedroom.

"Lie down," she ordered, pointing to the top of the bed.

Slowly, Ed did as he was told. He was aroused. Excited, expectant, almost ready to explode.

Kate stood at the side of the bed. Very slowly she removed her dress and revealed her white slip; a satin, silky white material that clung seductively to her breasts. Getting on to the bed she knelt astride him. Looking down at him she saw Ed's eyes glaze over and watched as he took in a series of deep breaths. He reached out towards her.

"No. Not yet," she said, firmly.

She was teasing him. He was hers completely and she knew that she held him in the palm of her hand. He looked up, imploring her to fulfil his desire.

"Oh, Kitty. Please, I can't wait!"

"You'll just have to," she replied. "It'll be worth it."

Kate's voice was charged. It was powerful and he felt as though she were reprimanding him.

Ed breathed hard once more, positive that he couldn't wait. His feelings were intense; his heart started to flutter. How could she do this to him? Yet, how exciting it was.

Slowly, Kate lifted the hem of her slip and lifted it slowly up her body and over her head, revealing the brilliant white underwear beneath. Ed could see the top of her breasts and her soft, inviting body. Getting back off the bed, she walked alongside him and, ever so delicately, removed her stockings as she placed each leg in turn on the side of the bed.

"Get under the covers Ed."

Ed, as if in a trance, fumbled unsuccessfully with the sheets, unable to get under them.

"Here. Leave it to me," she said, seductively.

She pulled the eiderdown, sheets and blankets from around him and drew them back, allowing Ed to lie down.

"Move over," said Kate, firmly.

Doing as he was told, Ed made room for Kate as she too slipped into the bed and covered them both up. Straddling him, he was hers unconditionally and eagerly she took everything he had to offer. It was wild and passionate as they made love again and again. Kate knew that in marrying Ed, she had done the right thing. He was a man who could satisfy every one of her needs. Eventually, exhausted, the two lovers fell asleep in one another's arms, their destinies entwined forever.

Chapter 22

Having lived together for five months, Kate and Ed settled easily into the routine of married life. It seemed little different from what they were used to. In practical terms, there wasn't much that had changed. Life was still a struggle financially, although as Ed had given up his flat, it meant that they had a little extra money available to them. They both knew however, that when their baby arrived in June and Kate was no longer working, they would face a tough, but hopefully short period of time, until Ed found a teaching post for the start of the new school year. On that front, it looked promising. Ed's training college had made it clear that there was a shortage of teachers in Manchester, Salford and all of the other surrounding authorities, the post-war baby boom having started to impact on the secondary education sector. So, although they would initially face some difficult times, the young couple felt optimistic about their future.

For Kate, austerity was a way of life and with her new husband so selfless, her existence seemed far more acceptable. It was still a surprise to her however, when Ed suggested that they get a television set. He'd read that by the end of 1962, three quarters of all British homes had one. Kate had no difficulty in believing him. Over the last year, she had noticed that increasing numbers of their neighbours had been getting aerials erected on their roofs and renting a television off companies such as Radio Rentals, Rediffusion and Granada. Yet, she wasn't too keen on the idea.

"No Ed, we don't need one. Rosie isn't bothered and I'm happy listening to the radio."

"I know Kitty, but there's lots of interesting programmes for Rosie to watch. It will help to fire her imagination."

"Are you sure it's not you who wants it?" asked Kate, giving Ed a stern look.

"No," replied Ed, taken aback.

"Really?"

Kate was clearly unconvinced by Ed's response and he knew it.

"Yes, really," replied Ed. "I'll be honest," he continued, "I would probably enjoy watching it, but my main thought was for you and Rosie. You see, I know you all too well. You'll say you're not bothered about having one, because as usual, you're thinking about the money that it will cost. That's true isn't it? Now it's your turn to be honest," he concluded, a satisfied look on his face.

Kate looked at him and sighed. What could she do with him?

"Don't tell me that Kevin and Sarah haven't told you about the programmes that are on and that you wouldn't like to see them for yourself," continued Ed. "We spend nothing on you Kitty and this is one thing that I know you'll enjoy. So, I really do want it for Rosie, but I want it for you too."

Reluctantly, Kate had agreed and within a week they had a new aerial on the roof and a rental television set in the front room, paid for by a sixpenny slot meter on the side. Rosie was absolutely fascinated by her first sight of 'Watch with Mother', the screen slowly coming to life after what seemed like an age waiting for the valves to warm up after the set had been switched on. She had been fascinated as she listened to the story and watched the action. Soon she was a big fan of 'Sooty' and 'Rag, Tag and Bobtail.' Best of all, Rosie became even more inspired with her drawing and colouring, eager to produce pictures of all the new things that she had seen. Kate too was pleased. She had felt left out of the conversations about 'Coronation Street' and 'Z Cars' at work and now felt she could share in the new media that had taken the country by storm. Furthermore, she loved being able to sit down and cuddle up with Ed on the settee, watching the television after he had finished his writing and marking and little Rosie was in bed.

Yet, for both of them, the television remained only a limited part of their life and separated during the week by their different places of work, their time together in the evenings was considered by both to be precious. They loved talking to one another about anything and everything and at weekends, they would take Rosie out to the park together. May had been impressed by the growing strength of their relationship and had commented on it to Kate one morning, when she had taken Rosie to her nan's just before Easter.

"You know Kitty, you're a fortunate girl."

It was the term she invariably used to address Kate. For May, she would always be seen as the young teenager her grandson had first gone out with.

"Ed really loves you. People will say it's the joy and excitement of being newlyweds, but for me, it's far more than that. You two lived together before you were married. You've had long enough to become familiar with one another and for the early enthusiasm to fade, yet Ed absolutely idolises you."

"I know," replied Kate, unconsciously nodding in agreement.

"Don't get me wrong though," May continued. "So, he should. You're a beautiful, kind and loving girl. He's lucky, just like you. I'm so pleased that you've found happiness Kitty."

Kate could see that there were tears in May's eyes. She was becoming emotional.

"Just why my Joe was so, so foolish, is beyond me," she continued. "He just couldn't see what was in front of him."

"Come on May. Joe wasn't that bad," said Kate, trying to cheer her up a little bit.

May sighed and shook her head.

"Come on now Kate. It's you all over. You don't need to defend my grandson to make me feel better. I don't not love him. I always have and I always will. But he didn't treat you and Rosie right."

As Kate walked down to the bus stop on her way to work, she thought about May's words and yes, she was lucky to have found happiness with Ed. But as May had also said, he too was lucky to have her. She had given Ed a strength that he hadn't possessed alone. He now had a real purpose in life; a determination to do his best for her and Rosie. Importantly, she had provided him with love and not just a sentimental type of love, but an unconditional love that, whatever difficulties he faced, he knew that she would always be beside him. Their relationship was not one of equals. It would never be and only on rare occasions would Kate show her vulnerable side and let Ed take the initiative. For Kate, after her fractious marriage to Joe, she now felt liberated. She was in a marriage where there was harmony and cooperation, where she, as a woman, was respected and in control.

Kate's situation was unusual in the context of marital relationships in the homes of Ardwick. The rent book was symbolic of the new relationship that the couple had. It was in Kate's name and that was how it remained. After their marriage, the landlord had come with a new rent book, to put in Ed's name. He was astonished to be told by Kate that the old one was satisfactory and that no changes were necessary. Ed had agreed, declaring his desire for his wife to have security under the law. It was to remain her home. The landlord had accepted their decision, although declared that the arrangement was highly unusual. Nevertheless, as the rent was always paid on time and Kate maintained the property to the highest standards, the issue was quickly forgotten.

The landlord did however, fully understood the couple's sentiments. Often, when he visited his other properties, he was met by the sight of a bruised and battered wife who, when they handed over the rent at the kitchen table, seemed almost apologetic that the sight of their misfortune may cause embarrassment to their visitor. Such women were without protection, subject to their 'master', the 'king of the castle'. The husband whose name was on the front of the rent book and who, in consequence, could simply throw them out with their children at any moment they pleased. For such women, a 'battering' had to be taken, for they simply had nowhere else to go.

It was a reality that deeply concerned Kate. She saw the injustice around her. It was ignorance; simply down to the way that things had always been. Working class women, downtrodden and exploited. Yet it angered her so much that so many of her own generation were simply prepared to accept it. Then she would stop and consider. What else could they do? Where could they and their children go? To parents without the room to take them, or who would tell them that they must stand by their husband; it was their duty to take the rough with the smooth. It was impossible to rent somewhere themselves. What landlord would let out a property to a separated woman with kids? The council too, also demanded that it was the husband's name in the rent book and battered wives who harboured hopes of getting on to the council housing list and taking their children to a new home, were simply overlooked. In any case, there were few houses available to those not directly involved in the slum clearance programme. Kate therefore realised that she had been too harsh. So many wives had become victims of their circumstances and of a society that didn't care. That didn't really acknowledge their existence. There was, she knew, little chance of escape. In fact, when she looked at her own future, she felt a sense of guilt that she too would be turning her back on the problem. She was going to be a teacher's wife and would, no doubt, end up moving to the suburbs. Life would then be so different and it would be easy to forget her past. She and Ed would share in the growing affluence of early Sixties Britain, yet there were so many who were unable to do so. It concerned her and one Sunday spring afternoon, walking with Rosie and Ed in Ardwick Green Park, Kate expressed her feelings to her husband.

"Ed, I know that after you qualify, it will be great to have the chance to move into a nicer house with a garden. Rosie and the baby will love it. It's cleaner and healthier, but I can't help having misgivings about it."

"Why Kitty?" asked Ed. "I'm sure that Sarah and all your other friends would jump at the chance to move if they had the opportunity."

"Yes, they would, but they're not like me. I don't feel it's right. I see so much injustice, so much hardship and struggle. It shouldn't be like that. I know that you'll think I'm being daft, but I'd feel like I was running away. I want to make a stand, do something about it and now that I'm married to you, I hope I'll have a chance to do so. But then I get frustrated. I look at you Ed. You finished school, you've been to university, have got an education and now you can use it to make a difference. I don't have that advantage and if I leave here, I probably won't be able to do much anyway."

Ed saw the concerned expression on Kate's face. His heart went out to her at such times. She simply cared too much, but it was one of the reasons that he adored her.

"Not too many so-called clever and educated people want to make a difference Kitty, unless it's for themselves. Trust me, I've met so many of them at university. And in terms of being intelligent, you're the most sensible and perceptive person that I've ever met."

Kate looked at him. She had a sense that he was simply trying to placate her.

"Don't try to be patronising Ed," said Kate, quietly.

"I'm not. I wouldn't dare," said Ed, with sincerity. "You've opened worlds up to me that I never knew existed. You taught me how to love; about what's really important in life. You have true wisdom Kitty and you've got the biggest heart that I've ever seen."

"But I look around me Ed and I want to see things change," continued Kate.

"But they will Kitty. They'll make conditions better. The Corporation are going to address the problem of housing in Ardwick, Chorlton-on-Medlock, West Gorton and elsewhere. They'll provide better homes with indoor toilets, bathrooms and proper heating."

"When?" said Kate, dismissively. "They're supposed to have been doing it since before the War."

"They will Kitty. It's just going to take a few years longer."

"And in the meantime?" she asked.

"Education Kitty. That will bring change. New attitudes, new rights for women. Even equality. It has to come."

"No, it doesn't Ed. I should know. It won't unless people keep fighting. Keep struggling for change and you should be doing it as well. Every day in your classroom. Change the attitudes."

"I try," said Ed, clearly on the defensive.

"Well make sure that you do. And why don't you think about standing for the council. You could really help people around here."

"Me?" said Ed, surprised.

"Yes, you!" replied Kate, staring intently into his eyes.

"No one around here would want me to represent them Kitty. Have you forgotten Freddie and his mates?"

"You get on alright with them now, don't you?"

"Well, yes," replied Ed. "But it's only because of you. None of the neighbours speak to me. Well, nothing more than a quick hello. I'm afraid that I don't think they're really keen on me."

"No, that's not true Ed. It's because they're suspicious of you. It's the way that you talk, the fact that you've been to university and that you're not from around here. You just have to win them over. You could do it in time."

"Well. I'm not convinced," said Ed, hesitantly.

"I was won over, wasn't I?" asked Kate.

"Well, yes. Then again, you're so different. You give everyone a chance. You judge everyone by their character. Not many people do that."

"I still want you to think about it," said Kate, firmly.

"I will," replied Ed.

The conversation over, they turned their attention to Rosie, the three of them enjoying the rest of the pleasant, spring day.

Chapter 23

The wider and loftier ambitions that Kate had suggested to Ed during their walk around Ardwick Green Park, were soon to be reduced to insignificance. It was Tuesday morning, June 5th 1963 and Kate was preparing for another day at work. She had insisted on working until the last possible moment. After all, she told Ed, she had done so when pregnant with Rosie and it had produced no adverse effects on either of them. She had reminded him that they needed the money. There were to be no arguments; she was going to do it again. Although Ed felt uneasy about the situation, he knew very well that once Kate had made up her mind about something, there was no altering it.

That morning, just before Ed left for school, Kate had seemed in good spirits. He had held his wife tenderly, sharing a long, loving kiss with her. He had been reluctant to break off from the embrace and Kate finally had to pull herself away.

"Come on Ed. There's no time for any of that. You need to get off."

"Any of what?" asked Ed.

"You know what" said Kate, looking sternly, but playfully at him.

Kate noticed Ed's face starting to go red with embarrassment. She laughed but was still touched by his reaction. After all this time, he was still prone to bouts of shyness when matters of intimacy were raised between them.

"Looking like this," she said, pointing to her swollen tummy under her smock, "I don't know how you can."

Ed looked at her with admiration.

"You look beautiful Kitty. Absolutely gorgeous."

It was now Kate's turn to blush. Throughout her pregnancy, Ed had been resolute in displaying his affection for her and most importantly, he made it clear that he still genuinely desired her. His passion gave Kate a sense of well-being, as did the practical support he provided as he increasingly took over many of the household chores.

"Go on, off you go" said Kate, playfully pushing Ed towards the back door. "Do you know Ed, every morning I breathe a sigh of relief when you've gone," she joked. "It's only then that I know that I'll finally get some peace. I'll see you again after work."

It was the last words that she had spoken to him before the fateful telephone call. His morning at school had gone well. He had been given a placement in a boys' secondary modern and he had settled quickly into the role. The school had been more than generous to him. He was lucky, as they had been prepared to give him every chance to show his potential. They wanted to help him become a good teacher, so only one of the classes that they asked him to take, had a reputation among the staff for being difficult. It meant that as long as he was well organised and could confidently provide direction and fairness in the classroom, the majority of students would happily cooperate with him. As a result, his lessons had impressed the observers from his college, who had informed him that as long as he completed his written assignments on time, he would successfully qualify as a teacher. This was now the final week of his practice and with his future in teaching almost secured, he and Kate had much cause for optimism.

After dinner, Ed was registering his first form history group when one of the school secretaries came into the classroom. Walking in behind her was the deputy head. Momentarily surprised, Ed began to feel a sense of trepidation as he saw a worried expression on the secretary's face.

"Mr Deane," said the deputy. "Would you go with Mrs Foster to the office please. I'll take over the class. There's a telephone call for you."

Ed followed Mrs Foster out into the corridor.

"Don't panic Ed. It's St Mary's. Your wife's been taken in. They wanted to let you know."

Reaching the school office, Ed picked up the phone. It was Sarah.

Chapter 24

Kate had felt fine when she got off the bus and walked into work that morning. May had already commented on how well she looked when she had dropped Rosie off to her earlier. Yet, sat on her stool towards the end of the morning, Kate began to feel a little dizzy. Kevin, who for the last couple of weeks had been watching over her somewhat nervously, had quickly noticed.

"Are you all right Kate?" he asked, calling across to her.

"Yes," replied Kate. "I just feel a little light headed. Don't worry. It's nothing serious."

Kevin looked at her. She had gone pale and she seemed a little distant.

"I'd rather you came over here and sat in my chair."

"No… I'm okay … honest," replied Kate, with some difficulty.

Kevin saw Kate put her hand up to her brow before slowly dropping her head. He suspected that she was in some discomfort. Getting out of his seat, he walked over to her. It was clear to him that, despite what she had claimed, Kate was anything but 'okay'.

"Come on Kate. You're not well. Let me help you," he said, insistently.

Kevin put his arm gently on her shoulder and encouraged her off the stool. As Kate put her foot on the floor, he could feel her slipping forward and sensed that she was about to faint. Quickly, but carefully, he hooked his left arm around the back of her waist to ensure that he could support her and keep her on her feet. Sarah, sat at the next till, jumped up to help him. Together, the two of them managed to sit Kate down on Kevin's chair.

"Keep your head down Kitty," suggested Sarah. "It'll make you feel better."

Kate however, wasn't responding. Her breathing had become more rapid. Sarah took hold of her hand and felt Kate's fingernails press firmly into her palm.

"It's the baby," said Kate, quietly.

Sarah could see the lines of pain etched into her friend's face as she gritted her teeth in an attempt to fight off her discomfort.

"Kevin. Phone for an ambulance," said Sarah. She was thankful that Kate was at work and not at home, where a telephone wasn't readily to hand.

Kevin quickly rang 999, the operator responding almost immediately. Soon he was giving Kate's details to her.

"Kevin. Tell them that Kate's waters have broken," interrupted Sarah. "We need the ambulance quickly."

Sarah had seen the tell-tale signs on the bottom of Kate's smock. Clearly in pain, Kate had been unable to communicate the fact to her.

"They're coming Kate," said Kevin, trying to reassure her, but getting little response.

Putting the phone down, Kevin felt helpless, unsure of what he could do to alleviate Kate's distress. Looking up he could see several punters had gathered around the pay out, clearly concerned about what was happening. Kevin had been shocked by what he had just experienced. It had occurred so quickly. Yet he realised that he had to pull himself together. As calmly as possible, he walked over to the pay out to speak to the punters.

"It's okay. Kate's going to be fine. We've sent for an ambulance. She just needs to be quiet lads. If you can just bear with us for a bit."

He tried to sound confident, to be as reassuring as he could. Yet in reality, he was more than just a little concerned about Kate's condition. The punters having slowly dispersed away from the window, Kevin turned to Sarah.

"Sarah, you're going to have to go to the hospital with Kate. I'll ring Arnold now and tell him to send me some cover."

Quickly, Kevin was on the phone. Expecting Arnold to show signs of irritation, he was surprised. Arnold's only concern was that Kate would be all right and he fully agreed that Sarah should stay with her. It took the ambulance no more than ten minutes to arrive, yet for Sarah and Kevin, worried about Kate, it seemed like forever. Fortunately, the ambulancemen were experienced and professional. Sarah and Kevin were relieved; reassured that there were now medical personnel present to take the burden of responsibility off their shoulders. They had soon brought in a wheelchair and were taking Kate, accompanied by Sarah, into the back of the ambulance that was parked outside.

"We're going to have to lie you down love," said the younger of the men to Kate, who was still breathing sharply and in pain. Helping her out of the chair, the two men managed to get Kate sat on the side of the stretcher and then carefully laid her on her side, pulling up the restraint to make sure that she was safe and secure for the journey.

Whilst the elder man, the driver, got into the front of the vehicle, his colleague secured the back doors and sat down with Kate and Sarah. Soon they were off, moving quickly down Stockport Road and then along Plymouth Grove and Upper Brook Street towards town, their destination

St Mary's. Sarah looked down at Kate. She was being brave, determined that she wouldn't cry out. Kate had never been 'mard' and she wasn't about to start now, whatever the circumstances. Nevertheless, Sarah could clearly see the signs of distress on her face. Holding Kate's hand, Sarah stroked it gently with her fingers. Suddenly she felt Kate's hand tighten around hers. Quietly, almost in a whisper, her friend called out to her.

"Sarah."

"What Kitty?" asked Sarah, moving towards Kate so that she was able to hear her over the noise of the warning bell of the ambulance.

"Tell Ed … Ring his school … I want him at St Mary's."

"Okay Kitty. Don't worry. I will."

Sarah looked into Kate's eyes and smiled reassuringly.

"It won't be much longer Kitty. They'll soon be taking care of you. There's nowhere better than St Mary's."

"She's right love," said the ambulanceman to Kate. "Your friend can phone when we get there. The receptionist will let her make the call and then she can come back and sit with you."

Weakly, Kate nodded and made an attempt at a smile. She was becoming accustomed to the pain, determined that it wouldn't get the better of her. But it was difficult and she was worried. Nothing like this had happened when she was carrying Rosie and her mind was now working overtime, wondering about what was wrong with her and increasingly afraid that her baby was in real danger.

As soon as they arrived at St Mary's, there was a doctor waiting for them, the ambulance having radioed ahead. As they went into the building, Sarah went to the reception and soon was on the telephone to Ed's school.

Whilst she had stood waiting for the school secretary to fetch Ed, Sarah tried to maintain her self-control. She had no wish to put Ed in a panic, but she knew that she had to let him know the seriousness of the situation. Therefore, trying to remain as calm as possible, she told him that Kate's waters had broken and that she had been brought in to St. Mary's by ambulance to have the baby.

"You have to order a taxi Ed and get here quickly. Kate needs you. I don't think it will be too long now before she has the baby."

Saying goodbye to Ed, Sarah thanked the receptionist and made her way back to Kate, who had now been moved to a delivery room and was being spoken to by the doctor. Noting Sarah's arrival, the doctor made his apologies to Kate and turned and walked towards her.

"Are you related to Mrs Deane?" he asked, quietly.

"No, but I've been her friend for years," replied Sarah.

The doctor looked at her. Sarah suspected that he may have some bad news, but as she wasn't a relative, he wouldn't be able to tell her anything.

"I've just been on the telephone to her husband at work. He's getting a taxi and should be here soon," said Sarah.

"Good," said the doctor, nodding. "Are you all right to stay with Kate, whilst we prepare her for the delivery? She's being very brave and I'm sure you can help to keep her spirits up."

"Of course," replied Sarah.

Sarah could see that Kate was in a bad way. She was finding it hard to talk; her breathing was rapid and shallow. It didn't seem as if the medical team were able to give her anything for her pain yet. Sarah pulled up a chair next to the bed in which Kate was lay. A couple of nurses had taken off her clothes and had replaced them with a simple gown. Sarah held her friend's hand and stroked it softly, hoping and silently praying that Kate was going to be all right.

Chapter 25

Arriving at the hospital, Ed quickly paid the taxi driver and rushed inside. Flustered, he approached the reception desk. The receptionist, seeing the signs of worry etched into his face, gave him a sympathetic look. It wasn't enough to calm him but did suggest that she wasn't ignorant of his concerns.

"Can I help you?" she asked.

"Yes. Mrs Deane. I'm here to see Mrs Deane."

Ed spoke slowly, hesitantly. He'd rushed in from outside and was trying to catch his breath. To the receptionist, he looked on the verge of panic.

"I'm afraid I have to ask," said the receptionist calmly, "but who are you?"

"Mr Deane. Kate's husband."

The woman looked down carefully at some papers on the desk in front of her.

"She's having a baby," said Ed. "She was brought in by ambulance."

"Ah, yes," said the receptionist. "She's gone to the delivery suite. You can make your way there along the corridor. It's clearly marked. Once you get there, you'll find that there's a waiting room to sit in."

Thanking her, Ed rushed along the corridor following the signs to the delivery suite. Arriving, he felt abandoned. There were no midwives or anyone else to speak to, just a pair of solid double doors with the words 'Delivery Suite' above them. He hesitated. He wasn't sure what he should do. Then, reproaching himself for his delay in getting to his wife, he pushed opened the doors and with purpose, strode inside. Yet there was still no one in sight and it seemed eerily quiet. All he could see was another corridor, which contained a series of closed doors. Ed felt uneasy. It was almost as if he were an intruder. He assumed that Kate had to be in one of the rooms that lay behind the doors on either side of the corridor. However, he knew that he couldn't simply open any of them in an effort to find her. There were bound to be other patients in some of the rooms too. He couldn't just barge in on them.

Hesitating, Ed's thoughts were interrupted by a man's voice to the side of him.

"Have you been called in too pal?"

Ed looked round and saw a small, bearded man, cigarette in hand, looking nervously towards him. He was stood at the open entrance of a small room with chairs around its edge and a small table holding the copies of various magazines in the centre.

"Yes," answered Ed.

"Me too. I'm not half going through some cigs waiting. It's not much fun stuck in this waiting room either. I'll be glad when it's all over," he continued.

Oh," said Ed. "How long have you been here?"

"Three hours now."

"Aren't you going to be with your wife when she has the baby?" asked Ed.

"No. She doesn't want me there. It's my fifth. I haven't seen any of them born. How about you?" asked the man, looking at Ed.

"Oh, this is our first baby together. I want to be with my wife. But there's no one around. I don't know where she is. Do you know where I can go to find out?"

The man raised his eyes to the ceiling and shrugged his shoulders.

"I'm sorry pal, I haven't got a clue. Trouble is," he continued, "they're not friendly at all. I don't think any of 'em like having men around, not even in the waiting room. I'm sure they think that we get in the way. That we get under their feet."

Ed was frustrated. He was finding it incredibly difficult to cope with the fact that he had no information about Kate's condition and didn't have a clue where she was. His concern was starting to turn to anger. How on earth could there be no one around to help him get to his wife?

Noticing Ed's obvious agitation, the man tried to reassure him.

"Come in here and sit down," said the man. "Take the weight off your feet."

"No thanks," said Ed, politely. "If I stand here, someone's bound to come out of one of the rooms and then I can find out where my wife is."

"Okay," said the man.

Walking back into the waiting room, he picked up a magazine and sat back down. Ed thought that he'd sounded disappointed. Perhaps he'd wanted to chat with him to make the time go quicker. But conversation was no good to Ed, he was desperate to see Kate.

Ed stared down the corridor, willing one of the doors to open and a nurse or doctor to emerge who could take him directly to Kate. But everything remained quiet and Ed began to think that he would have no option other than to take the initiative and enter one of the rooms, regardless of the consequences. Just as he was about to do so, one of the doors finally opened and out stepped a midwife. The pair of them saw each other simultaneously, but the response of the latter was not at all what Ed expected. Striding down the corridor, she barked out her instructions to him.

"Now then. What are you doing? You can't be hanging around in the corridor young man. You need to get yourself back into the waiting room."

As she approached him, Ed noticed her fierce looking expression, highlighted by her square, solid jaw and downturned mouth. The midwife had a pasty face, framed by greying hair that was held in place by her hat. She was solidly built and her purposeful stride and haughty demeanour, gave the strong impression that this was her unit and she was used to having her instructions obeyed. Ed stood his ground. Not flinching. He glanced to the side and noticed that the man he'd been talking to, was making himself small in his chair in the waiting room. He was crouching behind a magazine he'd picked up from the table, clearly hoping not to draw the midwife's attention towards him.

"Well?" said the midwife sternly, stopping in front of Ed.

"I'm here to see my wife nurse. Kate Deane. She was brought in by ambulance and the receptionist sent me up here so that I could be with her."

"Well, take a seat in the waiting room," said the midwife, dismissively "and by the way, I'm a midwife, not a nurse."

The woman motioned Ed towards the waiting room and started to turn on her heels, ready to walk away.

"But I need to see my wife," insisted Ed.

"She'll be fine," replied the midwife, without any hint of an acknowledgement for Ed's concerns. "We can't be having you wandering around. There are other women in here. We don't want them being disturbed now, do we?"

The midwife's tone was utterly condescending, hostile even. Her words were like those of an elderly schoolmarm to a wayward child. Ed felt the anger rising inside him. He couldn't understand how this woman could show absolutely no appreciation of the concern he had for his wife. Yet he knew that he had to keep as calm as possible. He desperately needed this woman's help and by losing his temper, he would simply play into her hands and he would be asked to leave.

"I'm sorry," said Ed, sounding as sincere as he could. "I can appreciate that you have lots of mothers to look after, but my wife was rushed in as an emergency. I'm really worried. Her friend is with her. I need to know how she is and I'd like to see her please."

The midwife looked him up and down. She had noted that he was well spoken, which provided her with a slight cause for concern. Perhaps he was connected and could make trouble for her. Therefore, she decided that for now, she would play along with him. Nevertheless, she knew that with other deliveries to contend with, if she ultimately decided to ignore this 'pushy' young man, she would always have an excuse for why she hadn't let him join his wife.

"All right," she said, finally. "You wait there and I'll go and find her and see if she's ready to see you."

She gave Ed a faint and reluctant smile. She turned and walked back down the corridor. Ed had no choice. He had to hope that she would be as good as her word. Yet as the minutes ticked by, he felt that she had made a fool of him. He stood still, his hand nervously rubbing his forehead as he wondered what he should do. Suddenly, from around the end of the corridor, Sarah come into view. Ed's sense of relief was almost palpable. Seeing Ed, Sarah hurried towards him.

"Ed. Where have you been?" she asked. "Kate has been waiting ages for you. She's desperate to see you."

"I've been here all along Sarah. This midwife I saw was supposed to come and tell you and then fetch me, but she's disappeared."

"Well, you're coming now Ed. Kate sent me to look for you. I'll take you to her."

Sarah proceeded back down the corridor with Ed hurrying on behind her. Turning to the right, they walked a little further and then Sarah stopped at a door, opened it and the two of them went in. There, lay in bed in front of them, was Kate. Besides her was a young doctor, together with the very midwife who'd been so unhelpful to Ed. As she turned to him, there was no disguising the look of thunder on her face.

"What are you doing here? I didn't send for you," said the midwife.

"I did," said Kate weakly, struggling to raise herself up off the pillow.

"Well, Mrs Deane. I'm afraid that it's not usual for us to allow husbands into the delivery room."

The midwife looked towards the doctor, looking for his agreement. Much younger and newly qualified, it seemed that he was liable to be intimidated by her. Kate however, didn't give him the chance. She was determined that Ed would stay with her and she beckoned him over.

"Ed, come here."

Ed walked over to the bed.

Holding out her hand towards him, Ed took it in his.

"My husband's staying. It's our baby and I want him here."

Seeing Kate in some distress, the doctor finally spoke up, prepared to stand his ground.

"It's all right, Mr Deane can stay. It's hospital policy now to let husbands be present at the birth. Only, of course, if their wives want them to be."

"But…," began the midwife.

"We don't want Mrs Deane to get upset now do we?" interrupted the doctor. "She's gone through quite a lot already."

Growing in confidence, the doctor was now warming to the task of putting his colleague in her place. Taken aback by his unexpectedly firm approach, the midwife decided to say no more.

"Doctor," said Kate, quietly, "do you mind if I have a word alone with my husband?"

Kate looked knowingly at the young man, who immediately understood that she wished to tell her husband about her condition herself.

"Yes, fine Mrs Deane. We'll leave you for five minutes. Come on."

He beckoned to the midwife and the two of them left the room. Sarah turned to Kate.

"Kate, I'll leave you two together now. You'll be fine with Ed. He can let me know when you've had the baby. I'll go straight round to May's and let her know. She'll be able to look after Rosie tonight."

Sarah bent down and kissed Kate on the cheek and patted her arm. She already knew what Kate was about to tell Ed and that it was something that they needed to share in private.

Left on their own, Kate squeezed Ed's hand.

"Look at me Ed."

Her voice was soft, but urgent. She stared intently at her young husband, fixing her eyes on his. She was in pain, but all her thoughts were for Ed, concerned at how he would react to the news that she had for him.

"The doctors are a little concerned Ed. They think that there could be difficulties for the baby."

"I don't understand," said Ed. "Difficulties?"

"Yes, Ed. There may be something wrong."

Ed closed his eyes. For a moment he couldn't think, unable to take in the meaning of what she had said. Kate could see that he was shaken.

"Ed. Are you okay?" she asked.

Ed looked at her and nodded. Deep down he had always feared the dangers that Kate could face carrying their child, but most of the time he had relegated such thoughts to the back of his mind. He had been so pleased when Kate had told him that she was pregnant, but the most important thing to him now, was that she would emerge safely through the delivery.

"What about you Kitty?" he asked. "You've got to be all right. Rosie needs you. I need you. We can't do without you."

Ed paused, realising that his words may sound selfish, although that was far from his intention. He stroked her hair softly, letting his fingers linger on the top of her forehead, something he would do when she was lay across him on the settee. He knew that she enjoyed him doing it and importantly, it helped her to relax.

"I'm sorry Kitty," he said, quietly.

"Why?" asked Kate, confused.

"For sounding selfish. Rosie and I want you, but because we love you, not because we need you to run around after us."

Ed paused, convinced that he'd now confused Kate more than ever.

"Oh Kitty. I hope you know what I'm trying to say."

Kate smiled weakly and shook her head slowly.

"Edward Deane. You really are puddled. I'm going to be fine and now you've got to be brave. You've got to be strong and help me whilst I have the baby. I need you Ed."

"I know and I would have been here sooner if that midwife hadn't left me out there."

"Well, you're here now Ed. We're together and you're not going anywhere until I've had our baby."

Ed pressed Kate's hand softly. Lay on the bed in her gown, her head and shoulders propped up against the pillows, her hair had been brushed back revealing her pretty face, its beauty not disguised by the occasional look of anguish that signified her discomfort. She was so brave thought Ed. He was so proud of her.

"Ed?"

"Yes?"

"Give me a kiss."

Ed bent forward and kissed Kate softly on her cheek. She patted his shoulder as he slowly raised himself away from her.

"It won't be long," said Kate. "I've been having contractions for a good while now. The baby is on the way."

With those words, the door opened and the doctor and midwife returned. Examining Kate, the midwife seemed pleased. The baby's head was engaged and the delivery, although more painful for Kate than when she'd had Rosie, was progressing normally. For all her awkwardness, Ed could see that the midwife was more than competent at her job and that Kate was in good hands. The doctor too was more than happy to take a subordinate role, aware that his female colleague, although junior in terms of her status, was far more experienced and capable than he. It seemed to Ed that the midwife disliked husbands and fathers, not expectant mothers. Perhaps, thought Ed, it was because she saw the pain that women had to go through in the delivery room, whilst their husbands had only the pleasure of the original conception.

Watching the delivery, Ed was in a state of wonderment. Holding Kate's hand throughout, he looked down at her face, sweat glistening on her forehead and moistening the loose strands of hair that lay on the side of her cheeks. The determined and focused look on Kate's face and a desire not to give into the pain, made her look like an angel sent down from heaven. In Ed's eyes, his wife was nothing short of magnificent. He felt so privileged to be sharing with her, this most wonderful of moments. And then the baby's head had appeared and with Kate's final, monumental efforts, he had joined them in the world, for a baby boy was what they had produced. Quickly cleaned up, the little boy was laid in Kate's arms, the two parents, all too briefly gazing at his little face.

"We're going to have to take him to the intensive care unit Kate," said the doctor. "He's a little blue. He doesn't seem to be breathing very well. You can both come up and see him after you've had a chance to get washed and changed."

With that, their little boy was gone.

Chapter 26

Both Kate and Ed had felt a sense of anxiety at their new son's departure. Although the doctor hadn't given them any indication that the problem with the baby's breathing was serious, the circumstances of Kate's admittance to hospital and the previous warning she had been given by the medical staff, had triggered their concerns. Yet the pair of them were conscious of not upsetting one another and for a time they worked hard to suppress their own fears and keep their thoughts to themselves. Perhaps, after all, everything would be fine.

Kate was washed and changed and the staff were soon ready to take her to the ward. Before they did, Ed prepared to say goodbye. He knew that the rules wouldn't permit him to go with her. It was now late at night and it was well past visiting time. Before he could depart however, another doctor entered the delivery room. He made his way over to the bed and introduced himself to Kate.

"Hello Mrs Deane. I'm Dr Wilson. I saw you on one of your antenatal visits."

"Yes, that's right," replied Kate.

"Is this…?" began the doctor, looking across towards Ed.

"My husband? Yes," said Kate, nodding affirmatively.

"Oh, good."

Wilson extended his hand across the bed. Ed took hold of it and shook it firmly. The doctor seemed tense. It was clear from the concerned look on his face that there was something wrong.

"I'm afraid that I have some bad news for you concerning your son."

Wilson hesitated, aware of how the shock of his words would impact on the young parents. He knew that he would have to give them time to prepare themselves.

Taking stock, Ed sat down on the side of the bed whilst Kate, motionless, stared blankly ahead of her. It was Ed who reacted first. Carefully, he tried to attract his wife's attention.

"Kitty," he whispered.

Very slowly, Kate turned to look at him.

Her face was pale, despair etched into her features.

"Oh no," said Kate, quietly, but with a hint of resignation. "Please God, no."

Slowly, she began to cry, unable to stop her tears. Ed took her hand and then put his arm around her, holding her close, her head pressed against his shoulder. He couldn't bear to witness her pain. He felt so useless, unable to do anything to take away her distress. Gradually though, her sobs subsided. Ed relaxed his arm and as she lifted her head, he   looked closely into her eyes, made red and swollen by a flood of tears.

"Kitty. We need to listen to Dr Wilson," he said, calmly.

For the time being, Ed had forgotten his own thoughts and fears. Kate's tearful reaction had awakened his protective instincts. He had seen her despair and knew that it was his time to be strong. He must protect and support his beautiful wife. And Kate did respond. Her resolve stiffened by Ed's calm assurance, she grabbed his hand tightly and turned to face Wilson.

"I'm so sorry Mrs Deane," said the doctor, "but your baby has cyanotic heart disease."

They were three brutal words that plunged like a dagger into Kate's heart. She instinctively knew that her baby wouldn't be going home.

Ed, just like Kate, hadn't a clue what the condition highlighted by Dr Wilson actually was. Unlike his wife however, he still held on to the belief that perhaps it wasn't so bad, even though the doctor's appearance clearly suggested that it was. Looking at Kate, he noticed that she looked calm, as if she'd simply accepted that they were going to lose their son. Hoping that she was wrong, he looked back at Wilson.

"What exactly is cyanotic heart disease?" he asked.

Wilson, more comfortable now that he could focus his attention on the baby's medical condition, explained the details in the best layman's terms that he could muster.

"It's a problem with the supply of oxygen to the blood. That's why your son looked blue when he was born. It's caused by a heart defect that is present at birth. We suspect that one of baby's heart valves is missing, which means that oxygen isn't being circulated properly around the body."

"Isn't there anything that you can do?" asked Ed.

Wilson looked down at Kate. He could tell that she was numb, devastated by the news. He suspected that she wasn't fully focused on the words he was saying. He sensed that she had known from his arrival that her baby was lost; that she had accepted the inevitable. He now had to make sure that her husband also understood the bleak prognosis.

"I'm afraid that we can't help him Mr Deane. We can keep baby comfortable in the special care unit, but ultimately, we can't act to correct the problem. I'm so sorry."

No matter how many times he had to deliver such terrible news, Wilson found that it never got any easier. Yet in a perverse way, that reassured him. It told him that he still cared. Surrounded by death and tragedy, he'd remained a concerned and considerate human being. He looked at the couple. He could only imagine their grief. His own two children had been born normally, without incident. They had grown up strong and healthy. He could only thank Providence for his own good fortune.

Ed stood silent, digesting the doctor's words. It was a shattering blow. He'd dared to believe that everything could be all right, but now all hope had been taken away from him. He looked at Kate. She was usually so strong, but she was still silent. He knew therefore, that he was going to have to be the one to pose the inevitable, but heart-breaking question.

"How long does our baby have?" asked Ed

"I'm afraid that it's hard to tell exactly," replied Wilson, "but probably, only a few days."

"Oh," said Ed.

"Have you thought of a name for your baby?" asked Wilson.

"Yes, we're going to call him James Andrew."

"That's a good name. It's very Scottish sounding," continued Wilson.

"Yes," replied Ed. "Kate's grandfather was Scottish."

"Oh," replied Wilson.

"Can Kate and I see him please?" asked Ed.

"Of course," said Wilson. "I'll get a nurse to take you both to the unit. I'm afraid that you'll have to look at him through the window tonight, but you'll be able to hold him tomorrow."

With Dr Wilson's departure, the couple were alone once more. Turning his attention back to Kate, Ed put his arms around her and held his wife tightly. There were no words that passed between them. None were necessary. They simply needed each other and embracing in the delivery room, quiet but for the soft hum of the electric lighting, the two felt their union strengthened by their shared, but tragic experience. Hearing the door to the room open once more, the couple parted. They could see that an auxiliary nurse had entered the room and with her, she had a wheelchair. Leaving it by the door, the nurse stepped over to Kate.

"Are you ready to go and see your baby?" she asked.

"Yes, please," replied Kate, nodding.

"Come on then love," said the nurse.

Ed noted that she was friendly and outgoing, so different to the midwife they had dealt with earlier.

Carefully, Kate eased her legs out of the bed and placed her feet on the floor.

"Are you going to be all right to stand?" asked the nurse, slightly concerned. "You've had a tough delivery you know. Do you think you're going to be strong enough?"

"Yes, I think so," replied Kate.

Kate felt tired, both physically and emotionally, but her resolute nature was starting to reassert itself. She was determined to walk over to the wheelchair and sit in it by herself. As Kate tentatively started to straighten up, the nurse sensed her uncertainty and put out an arm to steady her.

"No, I'm fine. Don't worry," said Kate.

The nurse withdrew her arm and watched as Kate slowly made her way over to the wheelchair and settled herself down into it. Bending down to remove the brake, the nurse pushed Kate towards the door which, in anticipation, Ed had opened in order to let Kate out of the room. With Ed following behind, Kate and the nurse advanced along a series of corridors before arriving at the entrance to the baby care unit. Stopping, the nurse applied the brake and asked Kate and Ed to wait. Entering through the double doors, the nurse alerted the staff in the unit to their presence. Returning, she explained the procedures that they had to follow.

"The midwife will bring James Andrew to the viewing window. He'll still be in his cradle. We can't allow you in unless you're wearing protective clothing. We have to keep all the other babies safe from infection. Tomorrow, when we have more staff, we'll be able to sort some out for you. Is that okay love?" asked the nurse, looking at Kate.

Kate nodded.

Shortly after, the nurse asked Kate to stand up. Baby James was at the window. Ed put his arm around Kate's waist and they walked over to get a closer view of their son. He looked lovely. He was in an incubator, covered with a blanket and wearing a little hat and mittens. Kate was desperate to hold him, but knew that she couldn't. She felt Ed's arm around her and looked up at his face. She noticed that there were tears in his eyes. He moved his free hand to wipe them away, not realising that she had already seen them.

Kate looked back at little James. It would have been natural for her to question why such a thing could have happened; why the life of an innocent baby should be so cruelly cut short. But Kate understood that it would do no good to think in such a way. She already knew just how hard life could be and however much she may wish it, nothing was going to change. She felt so tired. She was unable to cry any more. Her mind had gone over all the possibilities whilst she'd sat silently on the bed, as Ed had spoken to Dr Wilson. She knew that there would be no miracle and worst of all, she knew that she wasn't, even for a short time, going to be able to take her baby home with her.

"I'm sorry Kate," said the nurse. "We're going to have to take baby James back now."

The nurse motioned through the window and her colleague slowly took James Andrew away. Ed and Kate's eyes followed her through the window as she approached another pair of double doors and then disappeared through them with their baby son. Sitting back down in the wheelchair, Kate spoke to the nurse.

"Can my husband come back to the ward and sit with me in the day room before he goes home, please?"

The nurse nodded.

"Yes, of course Kate."

It was getting late, but the nurse was no stickler for the rules. She had a family of her own; kids and a husband that she loved. She appreciated that the two of them needed time together, so that they could start coming to terms with what had happened and what still lay ahead.

Arriving at the day room, the nurse applied the brake to Kate's wheelchair and left the young couple alone. Kate, got to her feet.

"I don't like being in this chair Ed. Let's sit on the seats over there."

Kate indicated over to the side of the room where there were some comfortable chairs arranged around a low table. Ed followed her over and the two sat down next to one another. Kate placed her hand on Ed's.

"Hold my hand Ed. Let's just sit quietly for a moment"

Since their arrival at the special care unit, there had been a gradual shift in the relationship between the couple. After a period of despair and anguish, Kate's mind had gradually addressed the realities of their situation. Her maternal instincts, her strength of character, her huge capacity for love, reasserted themselves in the face of this awful tragedy. Ed had been steadfast in supporting her through the initial shock of the revelations about James Andrew. It had seemed to him as if Kate had been on the verge of emotional collapse. Yet he was wrong. Kate was a born fighter and what gave her the strength and resolve to keep going now, was her belief that if she were to wallow in her grief, then she was being selfish. She was a wife and mother and she had to be strong for Ed and Rosie. They were the ones who would find it extremely difficult to cope, if she were to simply abandon them for her own personal grief. As usual, she would have to be a rock for them both.

Kate was now back in control. Ed recognised that her outlook and demeanour had changed. She was coping once more. Ed felt drained. He'd had to be strong for the two of them. He'd assumed the lead in the conversation with Dr Wilson and he'd not really had time to take in the enormity of the news that they had been given about their son. Now, in the quiet of the waiting room, the harsh reality of what had happened was beginning to sink in. Ed began to think that it was all his fault. He couldn't escape the thought, no matter how hard he tried. He shouldn't have allowed Kate to keep working. It had been too much for her and there had certainly been enough warning signs. It had been clear that Kate hadn't experienced an easy pregnancy. He began to think that he should have ignored her and gone to see Arnold anyway. If he'd have been working, Kate wouldn't have had to and then none of this would have happened.

Kate could see the growing look of concern on Ed's face. She knew that it was important for them to confront what had happened together. She felt instinctively that the continued strength of their relationship depended on it.

"Look at me Ed," said Kate, placing her hand on the side of his face and gently turning it towards her.

Ed however, averted his gaze, staring down towards the floor. He seemed unwilling, almost ashamed, to look her in the eyes.

"Ed, look at me," she repeated, insistently. "What is it? What's the matter?"

Slowly, Ed raised his eyes. All too briefly he engaged her attention, before once more looking away.

"Nothing," he replied, uncertainly.

"Yes. There is something Ed. You have to tell me, please."

Ed took a deep breath and held his forehead in the palm of his hand. Kate could tell that he was becoming upset.

"Please Ed," she said softly, pleading for an answer.

"I'm so sorry Kitty," said Ed. "I'm so sorry that I put you through all this. I'm so sorry for baby James."

Ed began to sob, quietly at first, but with increasing intensity. Kate pulled his head towards her and held him close to her breast. She could feel his body heaving, the pain and anguish of the afternoon and night, finally being released in a flood of tears.

"It's okay Ed. It's okay to be upset. It's why I love you."

Gently stroking and then kissing the top of his head, Kate waited for Ed to settle down. Gradually, he became calmer and lifting himself away from Kate, he sat back up in his chair. Kate, once again, was the first one to break the silence.

"You've nothing to be sorry for Ed."

"I have. You couldn't have brought James Andrew into the world without me and I should have looked after you better. If I had, then everything could have been different."

"Don't be silly Ed," said Kate, firmly. "Nothing you or I could have done would have made any difference."

She knew that her husband was intent on blaming himself for what had happened. He was clearly feeling guilty and there was no reason for it. Kate was determined to make him see sense.

"Ed, Rosie and I need you. We both have to be strong. Blaming yourself, when it's not your fault and letting your grief take over, isn't good for you or anyone else. And you're being selfish. We both owe it to baby James to be here for him until it's time for him to go. He's our son and he's beautiful."

Kate smiled reassuringly at Ed. She could see that her words had hit their mark and that he had realised that he too must show resolve.

"You're going to have to go home Ed. They won't let you stay here. Tomorrow, I want you to go and register James Andrew's birth. See May in the morning and take some new clothes and dolls and crayoning books for Rosie. Ask May if Rosie can stay with her whilst I'm still here and explain to Rosie that she'll be coming home soon. You then need to ring your school and the college to tell them what's happened. You've already passed your teaching practice, so I'm sure that they won't mind you missing your last few days. But whilst you're not here visiting me, you'd better get your assignments finished. You have to make sure that there's nothing to stop you from qualifying. You're going to be a teacher, Ed Deane. So, get used to it!"

Ed was shocked. She was so forthright, almost like her usual self. Yet he'd reacted just as Kate had hoped he would, nodding obediently as she gave him her instructions. Kate knew that if their family were to survive the difficult days ahead, then Ed had to keep functioning as normally as possible.

"Come on Ed," said Kate, finally. "It's time for you to go. I don't want to get the nurse into trouble. She's been very kind to us."

Getting up and walking to the door, Kate and Ed shared a farewell kiss. As she watched Ed walking away, Kate was determined that whatever happened, she was going to make sure that she kept her family together.

Chapter 27

Early the next morning, Kate was taken to the special baby care unit. Entering the outer room, she waited whilst a midwife in protective clothing, went in to fetch baby James. Whilst she was gone, Kate was given her own gown and mask to put on. Emerging with her son, the midwife passed him to Kate, who was now sat in a chair. He was beautiful, a product of her and Ed's love. Finally allowed to hold him, she stared into the features of his little face. Around his delicate lips she could see the blueish tinge to his skin, the tell-tale sign of his fatal heart disorder. It was another reminder to her, not that she needed one, that these moments were precious. There was no telling how long she and James would still have together. It was terribly hard for Kate. She felt numb. The joy, expectations and dreams of her child's life in the future; the happy times that they would have together, all these were denied her. She looked at his cute little nose and ears. She was sure that she could see Ed in him. Opening the blanket that was wrapped around him, she placed her forefinger in his tiny hand. Weakly, his fingers wrapped around hers; it was as if he was acknowledging his mother and reassuring her of his love.

"Kate, you need to keep him covered up. You have to keep him warm," whispered the midwife, as gently as she could.

She put her hand reassuringly on Kate's shoulder, but Kate didn't respond. She was in a world of her own, her mind beginning to assess the possibility that perhaps it was all just a bad dream. That the doctors had made a mistake and that they would soon come to tell her that her baby was going to be fine after all.

Softly, the midwife patted Kate's shoulder.

"Come on love, he's getting cold. I'll have to take him back."

Carefully, the midwife put the blanket back around him, taking care to avoid Kate's arms and hands. Finally, deserting her daydreams for the brutality of the real world, Kate looked up and then passed James to the midwife, ready for him to be taken back into the main unit, a room with a controlled, warm temperature.

"He's a handsome little chap, isn't he?" asked the midwife.

"Yes. He's beautiful," replied Kate.

Beginning to find her resolve tested, Kate's eyes began to moisten. Yet she was determined that she would remain strong for her son and at that moment she had a thought. Perhaps she could do more for James than just sit with him. As the midwife reached the double doors, about to depart, Kate called after her.

"How are you feeding him? Can't I?" asked Kate.

"What do you mean? replied the midwife.

"Well, I assume that you're using a bottle. Can't I breast feed him or at least express some of my milk for him?" asked Kate.

The question took the midwife by surprise. She hesitated. It seemed as though she wasn't too eager to respond.

"If baby James doesn't have very long, shouldn't I be allowed to breast feed him?" asked Kate again, unsure whether the midwife had understood her.

"Well… no," began the midwife, uncertainly. "It might spread infections that can be passed on to the other poorly babies in the unit."

"Well, what about if I express my breast milk for you to use when he's being bottle fed?"

Kate was being quietly insistent, but she wasn't about to get a positive response from the midwife.

"I'm sorry Kate. There's still a chance of infections. We'll have to leave things as they are."

"Oh," replied Kate, disappointed.

The midwife proceeded to take James Andrew away through the double doors. At the time, Kate hadn't questioned the look of unease that had been on the midwife's face and the hesitancy that there had been in her voice when she had responded to her request. Much later, when she recalled their conversation, Kate would see the significance of the midwife's reactions. Now however, there was no time to reflect, as the nurse who had accompanied Kate, was eager to get her back to the ward.

"Come on Kate, take off your gown and mask," said the nurse "and we'll get you back. The doctor will be coming to see you soon, so he can decide when it's safe for you to go home."

That was it. Stark and to the point. She would be sent home with her baby slowly passing from this world. Kate wouldn't be allowed to stay with him. She would only be able to see her son at the usual hospital visiting times and there was nothing that she could do about it. Yet Kate hadn't forgotten that she had another child too. Her little Rosie. She wondered how she was feeling now. After all, she hadn't seen her mam since early yesterday morning. She could well be worried and confused, whatever May and Ed had said in order to reassure her. Kate felt guilty, knowing that she couldn't give either of her children the full attention that they deserved.

The doctor, attended by one of the ward's midwives, saw Kate shortly after her return. It wasn't Dr Wilson, but a younger, junior doctor. He was clearly less experienced, yet was confident in his ability to an almost arrogant degree. Carrying out the most rudimentary of examinations, he then directed some questions about Kate to the midwife, picked up her medical chart from the bottom of the bed, looked at it, coughed, cleared his throat and then finally spoke to Kate.

"Well, Mrs Deane. I can see absolutely no reason why you can't go home tomorrow. We'll keep you in for today, just in case, but I think that you're fine."

The doctor smiled at her in a reassuring manner.

Having listened to him, Kate couldn't believe what she had just heard. Neither could the midwife who, embarrassed, looked away. Middle-aged, with over twenty years of experience, it never ceased to amaze her how these young men in their mid-twenties, who'd only just qualified and were still wet behind the ears, treated their patients in such a curt and unsympathetic manner. Invariably unmarried and certainly without children or a family of their own, these young, male doctors, lacked any empathy for the suffering and distress of their patients. Sometimes, it was very difficult for her to hold her tongue; not to put these young upstarts in their place. But she knew that she couldn't. The hospital hierarchy wouldn't like it. He wore a white coat. It wasn't her place to question him. But this time she needn't have worried, the young, working-class woman on the bed was unusual. She had a real presence about her and she was no respecter of a white coat, a stethoscope and a doctor's title.

"I'm fine?" asked Kate, sharply.

"Yes, Mrs Deane. You're fine to go home. There's nothing at all to worry about. You're in good shape."

Again, the doctor smiled, totally unaware of the criticism that was about to come his way.

"I'm fine! In good shape! Are you being serious?"

Kate's voice had hardened. There was an edge that penetrated the doctor's comfortable exterior. It began to dawn on him that things might be some distance away from being fine.

"And your name is?" asked Kate.

"Erm … I'm Dr Stewart."

It was an uncertain reply. His voice no longer sounded assured. His veneer of confidence had been stripped away.

"Well, Dr Stewart. My son is in the special care baby unit, he's without his mother and soon he'll no longer be with us. Tell me. In your honest opinion, do you really think that I'm fine?"

Unable to withstand her biting sarcasm, Stewart looked sheepishly into her face. He wanted to avert his gaze, but he couldn't. Forced to take in Kate's complete and utter look of contempt for him, he was desperate to get off the ward before even more damage was inflicted on his now bruised ego.

"Well? Do you?" continued Kate, fiercely. She was utterly determined that he would give her an answer.

Stewart's eyes dropped to the floor. He was almost paralysed, unable to reply.

"Are you a complete idiot?" asked Kate, harshly.

Stewart once again tried to reply, but he simply couldn't get the words out. His brain couldn't produce them and even if it could, his tongue was stuck in his mouth, unable to articulate the necessary sounds.

Feeling a sense of satisfaction at Stewart's obvious and deserved discomfort, the midwife was nevertheless concerned that Kate may become overwrought. She could only guess at the inner turmoil that the young mother was going through. Kate had made her point. She had put Stewart in his place and made him an object of ridicule in front of the other patients who had witnessed the exchange. It was now best for Kate that she was able to calm down.

"I think Dr Stewart would like to apologise, wouldn't you, doctor?" said the midwife. "I'm sure that the words didn't come out quite how you would have liked them, did they?"

The midwife smiled. It wasn't just a smile of reassurance to Stewart, but also a recognition that she too was being condescending to him. Stewart had been badly mauled. He knew that in Kate he had met his match. It was a shock to the system. This was supposed to be his domain. Around the women patients he was assured and confident. In the male dominated environment of the hospital ward, women were of little consequence, yet here he was made to look foolish and incompetent by this young and combative mother.

Disorientated, Stewart remained silent. Both Kate and the midwife were looking at him expectantly. They had given him a chance to extricate himself from his uncomfortable, embarrassing and ultimately, humiliating situation. Slowly, he nodded and finally found his voice.

"Yes, you're quite right of course. I'm sorry Mrs Deane," he said, looking at Kate. "I didn't mean to cause you any upset. I just wanted you to know that in terms of your own body, it seems that you've had no ill effects as a result of the delivery. So, you are in relatively good health. Of course, your son's condition must be extremely upsetting for you and your family. Please accept my apologies if I've added to that upset in any way. I can assure you that I had no intention of doing so."

Kate looked at him. He was a fool, not worthy of any more of her attention. He could go now for all she cared, rebuild his shattered confidence and, no doubt, be equally conceited and obnoxious with the next young mother he dealt with on the ward.

"I'll leave the midwife here to make the necessary arrangements. Goodbye Mrs Deane."

Turning away, Stewart quickly made his way out of the ward, hoping that he would never have to deal with such an awkward young woman again.

"Kate," said the midwife. "Your husband telephoned this morning to see how you and baby James were. He's coming in to see you at two o'clock, visiting time. When he gets here, you can let him know that he'll need to collect you tomorrow. We can have your post-natal check-up appointment sorted out by then and you'll be able go home with him."

"What about baby James?" asked Kate. "When will I be able to see him?"

"I'm sorry Kate, but you'll only be able to see him at visiting times."

"But I want to be with him, together when it's time for him to go."

"Have you a telephone Kate?

"No."

"Do any of your neighbours have one?

Kate shook her head. Hardly anyone in Ardwick had a phone.

"Well if you ring us on the ward regularly, we can let you know if we think that you should be here."

The midwife felt awful. She knew and so did Kate, how imperfect this arrangement would be. Yet there was nothing else to be done. Kate had to prepare herself, the best she could, to deal with the inevitable passing of her baby son.

Chapter 28

Waiting for Ed to return, seemed like an eternity to Kate. The time moved so slowly. Eventually though, visiting time had arrived and Ed was there. Once the ward doors had been opened, Ed had moved quickly towards her. Kate got up out of her chair and the two of them embraced, clinging to each other tightly, as if they never wanted to let go of one another again. Yet both of them knew that their son was waiting and they were desperate to spend every precious moment that they possibly could with him.

But all too soon, it was time to leave and Ed had to say goodbye. He couldn't understand why the hospital were so inflexible; that despite the tragic situation of their son, they refused to change their rules on visiting. Yet there was no one to whom they could appeal and they had to accept the decision. He knew that it would be terribly hard for Kate when she came home, but he was convinced that she would prove to be as resilient as ever and manage to find a way to cope.

Twenty-four hours later, the inevitable moment came when Kate had to go home with her husband, leaving their son behind. Saying a tearful farewell to James Andrew, the ward staff had reassured her that he was in good hands and that he was in the best place possible. Certainly, Kate knew that there was no way that she could bring him home with her, no matter how much she wanted to. It was therefore with a heavy heart that she left him and returned to Bright Avenue. She knew however, that she had another child to think about. Rosie needed her too and more importantly, she needed her mam back working to pay the rent and put food on the table. Life really was, for someone of Kate's background, made that simple. Somehow, she would have to deal with her broken heart, support her baby son the best that she could and be strong for Rosie and Ed. Kate realised that Ed, no matter how much he tried to persuade her otherwise, was finding it hard to cope. She knew that she had to help him through this. Their prospects of a better life depended on him successfully finishing his course and finding a job. Only then, could the two of them build a secure future together.

The very next day, Kate phoned Arnold at nine o'clock in the morning to tell him that she was out of hospital and that she intended to come straight back to work. Kevin and the punters were aware of the tragedy of baby James and were devastated for her. Yet as far as she could, Kate tried to be her old self, a smiling and friendly face behind the counter.

Soon she had settled into a routine that would continue for the next two weeks. She would spend time with Rosie and May in the morning, then she would go to work, rushing back to see Rosie for tea at May's and then she and Ed would go to the hospital to visit James Andrew. Nevertheless, Kate couldn't help but feel a failure as a mother, unable to meet the needs of either of her children. Concern for James Andrew's terminal condition clashed with brutal financial reality, giving her the sense that she was nothing more than a pawn in some kind of grand plan over which she had no control. She worried about Rosie who was now staying with her nanny full time. It was the only way to give her some stability in her life as Kate and Ed, after visiting the hospital, did not arrive home until late at night. Although Kate spent time with her daughter every day, she could see that Rosie was confused, not sure at all about what was happening and why she wasn't living at home with her mam and dad. In particular, Rosie found it difficult to understand why she couldn't go to see her baby brother at the hospital. Rules and regulations were a mystery to her. Kate was worried that Rosie may feel rejected; but then how could she not visit her terminally ill son, or expect Ed not to do so either? The couple needed to go together. It was an experience neither of them felt able to face alone and the reality was that their shared grief strengthened their love for one another.

On the ninth day, it had been Kate's day off, Wednesday. It had given her the chance to spend some time alone with Rosie, so they took a walk in Ardwick Green Park and then went down to the museum at the University on Oxford Road. It was a long walk for her daughter, but the little chatterbox hardly seemed to notice, so happy was she to be spending time with her mam. Wide-eyed and amazed at the exhibits in the museum, Rosie had enjoyed herself enormously. As they stepped out of the museum entrance and back on to Oxford Road, Kate looked across at the Holy Name.

"Shall we go into the church Rosie? You can light a candle for baby James."

Rosie looked confused. Her daughter was so bright for her age that Kate often forgot just how young she was and how much she still didn't know or understand.

"If we go into the church," explained Kate, "we can light a candle which will mean that Jesus will take care to look after baby James."

"Oh," said Rosie, sounding surprised.

"Do you want to then?" asked Kate.

"Yes Mammy," said Rosie, nodding her head affirmatively.

The two of them crossed the road and walked up the steps leading to the entrance to the church. As they entered, Rosie gazed in wonder at the beauty and splendour all around them. She marvelled at the huge towering arches stretching high up into the roof and the central stained-glass windows behind the altar, that lay at the head of the rows of pews stretching out before them. Moving to the side of the church, Kate found a devotional statue, with a large number of candles that had been lit and placed before it. The candles were all of different sizes, some having burned down more than others. Rosie looked at the rivulets of once molten wax that had run down their sides, giving them a gnarled and beautiful appearance. Taking a fresh candle from a box at the side, Kate showed it to Rosie.

"I'm going to put this with the others. I want you to help me light it, but we'll have to be very careful."

Kate placed the unlit candle on the shelf before the statue. She then took a taper and lit the end from the flame of one of the burning candles.

"Here, put your hand on mine and we'll light our candle," said Kate.

Rosie laid her hand softly on Kate's and then saw it guided away as the taper moved over to the top of their candle, which was soon alight. Seeing the flame splutter into life was fascinating for the little girl, her eyes widening in amazement.

"Ooohh," whispered Rosie, softly.

Her mam smiled, reminded again of how such seemingly simple, but novel experiences, could so completely captivate children who were seeing them for the first time.

"You can let go now Rosie."

Rosie withdrew her hand from Kate's and watched as her mam drew the taper up towards her mouth and blew it out, laying the smoking remnant in a metal container on the side.

"Doesn't it look nice Rosie, together with all the other candles?"

"Yes Mammy."

Kate took hold of Rosie's hand and squeezed it very gently. As the two of them stood together looking at the flickering candle, Kate prayed silently, asking God to care for her son once he came to join him. She prayed for Rosie too, asking God to protect her. Having finished, Kate looked down at her daughter.

"Come on Rosie. It's time we were getting back to Nanny May's. She'll be wondering where we are."

As they turned to leave, Kate saw a priest stood before them. Looking at him closely, Kate thought that he must be about forty. He was going bald and the hair around his temples was flecked with spots of grey. Bespectacled, he had a rather prominent nose and thin lips that soon parted into a smile as he spoke.

"Hello, young lady," he said, addressing Rosie.

The priest had a pleasant voice, a soft Irish accent, so common among many of the Catholic clergy of the city.

Rosie didn't answer. Although the man seemed friendly enough, she was still in awe of her surroundings. The church was huge and unusually quiet and she felt so small and uncertain. Instinctively, she grabbed her mam's hand and gripped it tightly.

"It's all right Rosie. You can answer him," said Kate, reassuringly.

The priest nodded and gave a smile of encouragement to the young girl.

"I'm sorry, she's not been in here before and it's a little new and strange for her," continued Kate, now addressing the priest.

The priest turned his attention to Kate. She was a very pretty young woman. He'd not seen her at the Holy Name before and observing her lighting a candle with her daughter, he was a little intrigued as to why she was there. He wondered whether she may be in need of any guidance or support. Her confident manner suggested to him that she wasn't, yet he knew that when people came in to the church, when they normally didn't, they usually had a desire to experience a spiritual awakening, or gain the sustenance of hope and faith that they felt they might find in Christ.

Hello. I'm Father Michael," said the priest, introducing himself.

"I'm Kate."

"And your name is, young lady?" asked Father Michael, turning to look down at Rosie.

"My name's Rosie."

Rosie smiled back at the priest, reassured by her mam's words and Michael's pleasant countenance.

"Are you feeling well?" asked Father Michael.

"Yes. I lit a candle for baby James," said Rosie. She was more confident now, the conversation taking her mind away from her daunting surroundings.

"Oh," said Father Michael.

He paused. He had no intention of seeking any explanation, unless Kate wished to give it.

"James is Rosie's baby brother. He's very ill in hospital," said Kate, after a moment's silence.

Father Michael waited for her to continue.

"Rosie," said Kate. "Do you want to see if you can draw me a nice picture of the candles and the statue. You can sit and do it on the seat over there."

Yes Mammy," replied Rosie.

Kate took Rosie's drawing pad and pencil case out of the bag she was carrying and handed them to her. Rosie eagerly took them and proceeded to sit on a pew, just a few yards away, before opening them up and starting to draw.

"What a well-behaved and polite little girl you have," commented Father Michael, as he watched her appreciatively.

"Yes, she is," replied Kate. "I'd rather she didn't hear what I'm going to say though. She's a little too young for such things."

Father Michael nodded, he knew that he was about to hear bad news and he prepared himself to react appropriately. It was the hardest part of his vocation. He was worldly wise. He'd not been sheltered, as many priests had been, from the hardships and inequalities of life. He'd entered the priesthood working in a challenging, working-class environment in Liverpool and here at the Holy Name, he ministered to a congregation drawn from some of the toughest and most deprived neighbourhoods in Manchester. Religious platitudes had no place here. People needed hope, but they needed truth and they needed to be treated as individuals. Only in that way could Father Michael provide hope and God's grace to his fellow man. Listening to Kate, Michael learned of the tragedy of baby James Andrew. He was amazed that this young woman could fight on so strongly, caring for both of her children the best that she could. As he listened, he nodded periodically, acknowledging her words and when she had finished, he began to speak.

"Kate, I'm amazed at your strength. I can only imagine what you and your family are going through. I think you're doing everything that you possibly can for both Rosie and baby James. It must be hard for you to accept what has happened to James Andrew; there must be a temptation to feel that God has let you down."

"No," replied Kate. "I don't think that at all. I learned a long time ago that it isn't God who's uncaring and vindictive, it's people who are. People let you down. God doesn't intervene. What's happened to baby James can't be helped, but I know that he'll be going to heaven. God wouldn't punish an innocent baby."

Father Michael was surprised by her response. It was very unusual. Mothers in her situation would either reject God out of hand, or seek reassurance that the loss of their child was somehow part of God's greater purpose. He found that the latter often provided reassurance and comfort, yet he had never been convinced by such a view, for he could see no purpose at all in the taking of a young infant's life. Such things had, in the past, tested his faith and he too, like Kate, had come to the conclusion that bar for the short period of time Jesus was present on Earth, there would be no divine interference in the actions of men or the vagaries of nature.

"I agree with you Kate, but I can also see how your love for your family is a source of hope for them and I believe that through people like you, this world can become a better place. The kind of world that God wants to see."

The two of them stood quietly for a few moments, considering all that they had said.

"I need to be getting back home with Rosie" said Kate, finally. "Thank you for listening to me. It's such a quiet, beautiful place to talk and to think. I know I have to be strong and we will, as a family, get through this and I will be reunited with baby James after he's gone. I have no doubts about that."

Father Michael nodded.

"Rosie," called Kate.

Rosie looked up from her drawing pad.

"It's time we were going now."

Rosie got up off the pew and walked over to her. She held her drawing pad out proudly in front of her.

"Look at my drawing Mammy," said Rosie. as she reached Kate.

Holding it up, both Kate and Father Michael looked at it. They were impressed with the results.

"My, that's a pretty picture," said Father Michael. "You're quite a talented little artist, aren't you?"

Rosie looked shyly at the floor. Father Michael laughed gently.

"Come on Rosie," said Kate, putting the pad and pencil case back into her bag. "Say goodbye to Father Michael."

"Goodbye," said Rosie, weakly raising her hand in farewell.

"Bye Rosie," replied Michael "and goodbye Kate."

"Father Michael. Would you be able to say a prayer for baby James please?" asked Kate.

"Yes, of course I will Kate and for all of you. God bless."

Kate took Rosie's hand and the two of them walked steadily out of the church and back to Nanny May's house.

Chapter 29

The daily visits to see James Andrew had put tremendous strain on both Kate and Ed. They knew that there could only be one outcome and the inevitability of their son's death gnawed away at them and strained their emotions to breaking point. They had no wish for James Andrew to suffer, but still a sense of guilt struck them at every turn. Guilt that they wanted him to remain with them, knowing that he was suffering such discomfort, yet guilt that they desired him to have a peaceful, final sleep, which would mean him taking his departure from this world. Kate increasingly realised just how important it was that she and Ed visited James together. In that way they could support each other through their pain. Only their complete love and affection for one another, could unite them in their devotion to their dying, baby son.

On the fifteenth day, Wednesday June 20th, Kate and Ed once again arrived at the special baby care unit to visit their son. As usual, the two of them put on their masks and gowns and watched as James Andrew was brought into them through the now familiar double doors. Kate took him first. She held him in her arms and gazed at his little face. He seemed calm and content, though moved very little under the blanket he was wrapped in. Every time she'd seen James, he appeared weaker and once again she thought about his feeds and recalled her earlier conversation with the unit midwife. Since then they had told her so little and she never felt sure that her questions were being met with straight answers.

Having held James Andrew for several minutes, Kate looked up to see Ed staring down at their son with tears in his eyes.

"Come on Ed," she whispered. "Come and hold your son."

Ed sat down on the chair next to Kate, who carefully placed James Andrew in his arms. Ed looked down at him with affection.

"He's so beautiful isn't he, Kitty?"

"Yes, of course he is," replied Kate, quietly fighting back the tears. She had no intention of breaking down in front of him. She was determined that they would both be resolute and so their little boy could sense that his parents were there to protect him.

"Come on Ed," said Kate, reassuringly. "James needs you to be strong for him."

Ed, understanding, nodded his head and took in an audibly deep breath, gulping in the air to stiffen his resolve. As the two proud parents looked down together, they saw a sudden movement of James' head. It startled them both, so used had they become to their son's unchanging expression and situation. Bending down towards him, Kate heard a little gasp emanate from his mouth and then nothing.

Kate knew at once. It was a mother's instinct.

"No!"

The midwife, who had been stood at a respectful distance, was startled by Kate's cry and quickly came over to her.

"What is it Kate?"

"It's James."

Ed, startled by Kate's reaction, looked down at his son. He looked so peaceful in his arms. Ed was confused, unable to understand what was happening.

"Ed," said the midwife, urgently. "I need to take James."

Reaching down, the midwife picked him up and quickly made her way back through the double doors. Kate watched her disappear and then turned to Ed. She felt strangely calm.

"Ed. It's over. Our little boy has gone."

The words out, her self-control suddenly collapsed, as she burst into uncontrollable sobbing. Reacting quickly, Ed stood up and threw his arms around her to love and protect her. He knew it was his time now, his turn to be strong. He had to be there for her. When they had received James' diagnosis, he sensed that however much the news had hurt him, his wife's anguish had to be greater than his. After all, she had carried their son for nine months. She had gone through the pain of giving birth to him, only for her joy on his arrival to have been cruelly shattered by the news of his terminal condition. Where new life had brought with it the promise of so much hope, the legacy for Kate had been one of disenchantment. She had fought on, carrying their family through these dark days and now finally, she was reaching out for his help.

Drawing back slightly, Ed took his arms from around Kate's waist. With his right hand he gently brushed a loose lock of hair away from her eyes and kissed her on the forehead. Quietly, he tried to reassure her.

"We don't know for sure Kitty."

"I do Ed," said Kate, slowly beginning to regain some semblance of control. "He's gone."

Ed pulled her close to him again and softly stroked her hair. They stood quietly, each of them with their own thoughts, each of them taking comfort from their embrace, their feelings for one another flowing between them and creating a unity of purpose. It was so still, so silent. They were on their own in the room, the only noise the sound of their own irregular breathing. For a brief period of time, it seemed as if real life had been suspended and that they would be spared the harsh realities of dealing with their son's passing. But it was not to be. Inevitably, the double doors swung open. Hearing them, Ed and Kate separated and turned around. It was Dr Wilson.

"Kate, Ed," said Wilson.

"He's gone, hasn't he?" said Kate, not allowing the doctor any opportunity to prepare the ground; to soften the blow.

"Yes," said Wilson, affirmatively.

"I knew," said Kate.

Wilson looked at her. She was so incredibly brave. Pretty and intelligent too. He'd been told about her reproach of Dr Stewart and he approved of her actions. He sought to offer her some crumbs of comfort, knowing however, that words could appear to be incredibly cheap in such circumstances.

"Kate, there's little that I can say to you both that can alter the distress that you feel right now. Yet you were with baby James when he left us. He wasn't alone and, young as he was, he knew that you both loved him. From the moment they're born, babies can sense love and James could sense it in abundance from you and Ed."

He paused. The couple seemed calm.

"We'll take baby James down to the mortuary and you can see him anytime you want until you finalise the funeral arrangements. We'll get a nurse to take you back to the ward Kate and we'll talk you through what both we and you will need to do now.

"Thank you," said Kate, quietly.

Dr Wilson departed and within a couple of minutes a nurse had appeared. They went back to the ward and with the issuance of the notification of death and letters from the hospital, the young couple set off home. Riding in the taxi to Bright Avenue, Ed clung on tightly to Kate's hand. So much tragedy for someone so young. His wife had buried her first husband and now she would have to attend the funeral of her second child. It was so cruel. The world was so unforgiving. Yet Ed was determined, that together, they would overcome their heartache and their relationship would become even stronger.

Chapter 30

Early on Thursday morning, Ed assumed the difficult task of going to see May before Rosie was awake, in order to tell her about James Andrew. He and Kate knew that May would want to prepare herself before Rosie was given the news.

Opening the back door to Ed, May saw the grave look on his face. His arrival at such an early hour convinced her that he was the bearer of bad news. Inviting him into the kitchen, May stood by the table as Ed told her of James' passing. Ed's disclosure wasn't unexpected. May was well aware of the fatal prognosis for James Andrew's condition. Nevertheless, she still found the news upsetting. Bowing her head, May put her handkerchief to her face in order to dab away the tears that were beginning to well up in her eyes. Ed could see her shoulders rising and falling and heard her gasping for breath as she tried to stifle her sobs. He had never seen May upset before. She was always so assured; someone upon whom he and Kate could depend. Her tears had therefore shocked him, making him aware that his son's death wasn't only a tragedy personal to his parents. In order to console her, Ed put his arm around May's shoulder and patted her reassuringly. It was the first time that he had expressed any physical affection towards her. As May slowly recovered, Ed couldn't help but think how strange it was that it had taken such a tragedy, for the two of them to show their deep concern for one another.

"I wanted to prepare you before Kate and I came to see Rosie," said Ed, in order to break the silence.

"How are you both feeling?" asked May. "Do you need more time to yourselves? I can look after Rosie for longer if you want me to."

It was May's way of coping with the family's loss. She wanted to provide them with practical support and to feel useful. In that way she could overcome her own sense of grief. What's more, she understood how much of a strain the young couple were under. If it would help them to spend more time alone, in order to come to terms with their loss, she was happy for her great granddaughter to stay with her.

"I think Kate's eager for Rosie to come home," replied Ed. "I'm sure she feels guilty that we haven't been able to have Rosie at home. I think that spending the nights with Rosie again, will help her to get back into some kind of normal routine."

"Well, I don't think she had much of a choice," replied May. "Baby James needed her until now; Rosie needs her in the future. Kate's a silly girl, she's never let Rosie down. Neither have you Ed. Rosie's lucky that she's got the pair of you to care for her."

"And we're thankful for you too May. I know we keep saying it, but it's true. I don't know how we could have coped without you," said Ed, appreciatively.

"Don't be daft Ed. Rosie's my great granddaughter. I'll do anything I can for her and for you two for that matter. Now get back round to Kate and I'll see you both later."

Ed returned to Bright Avenue, but before they went back to see Rosie, Ed had the task of having to go to the phone box to let Arnold know that Kate wouldn't be at work for a couple of days. It was a difficult call to make. Talking about his son's death, Ed felt as if he were reliving it. More than that, to refer to James Andrew in the past tense, forced him to confront the finality of his son's departure. To his relief, Arnold understood the grief that the young couple were going through. He had no wish to prolong the conversation more than necessary and told Ed that Kate should take as many days off work as she needed.

Having returned home, Ed found Kate ready and waiting. Quickly, the couple made their way into the alley at the back of Parker Street and then through the gate to May's backyard. Mounting the steps to the kitchen door, Kate pushed it open.

"Hi, it's only me," said Kate, entering the kitchen as positively as she could.

Rosie, sat with a plate of toast at the kitchen table, stopped eating and looked up at the sound of Kate's voice. It seemed an age since she had last seen her and she was overjoyed. Jumping from her chair, she rushed the few steps to her mam and threw out her arms in front of her. Taking hold of her daughter, Kate lifted her off her feet and pulled her face towards her, planting an enormous kiss on her cheek. Holding Rosie in her arms, her daughter's head nestled against her breast, Kate realised just how precious her little girl was. She could watch Rosie grow and develop over the coming years and the two of them would be able to share their joys and disappointments together, as mother and daughter.

"Mammy, why are you crying?" asked Rosie, concerned.

"I'm not," said Kate.

But she was, her eyes were filling up with tears.

"Your mam's been poorly love. It's hurting her to hold you," said May.

It was quick thinking and reassuring for the little girl. Putting Rosie down, Kate stepped over to May and embraced her. Pressing her head tightly against May's shoulder, Kate tried to regain her self-control. She knew that her daughter was about to ask the inevitable question, especially as Kate had insisted from the start, that neither May nor Ed were to give her any indication about how serious her little brother's condition was. As calm as it was possible for her to be, Kate straightened up, stepped away from May and turned to look at Rosie who was now sat on the edge of the settee. The exchange of glances between them now prompted Rosie, in her naturally inquisitive way, to question her mam about her visit to the hospital. Most importantly, there was one thing, above all else, that mystified the little girl.

"Mammy. Where's the baby? When is my new brother going to come home? When can I see him?"

Words from a child. They cut straight to the point and demanded an immediate answer. Kate sat down on the settee and pulled her daughter close in order to give her a short, reassuring cuddle. She had already decided that she would be as honest and clear as she could. Nonetheless, Kate knew that death was an awful and difficult concept for a young child to understand and she was determined that Rosie wouldn't see what had happened in a negative light. Releasing Rosie from her embrace, Kate sat back and slowly began to talk.

"James Andrew, your brother, is beautiful, just like you Rosie."

Kate paused. She took Rosie's hand in her own and held it gently, yet before she could continue Rosie, becoming impatient, spoke up.

"Where is he Mam? Where is baby James?"

May and Ed, impotent spectators in the developing drama, felt their hearts sink. They felt certain that Kate would break down. Rosie's insistent questioning would surely be too much for her. But Kate was resolute. She had lost her son. He had suffered. She wasn't about to let her daughter suffer too. Having to watch her mam disintegrate before her eyes, would be heart breaking for Rosie and Kate implicitly understood that she just couldn't allow that to happen.

"James Andrew is with Jesus Rosie. He's not coming to stay with us."

"But why?" asked Rosie, surprised.

"Because sometimes Rosie, it's what happens."

"But why can't I see him?" asked Rosie.

"You will. Eventually. James will be watching you. He's an angel now."

"Ooooh," said Rosie, with a sense of wonder. "A real angel?" she asked, in a hushed and reverent tone.

"Yes, love. A real angel."

"When will I see him then?"

"Not for a long time Rosie, but all of us will be with him eventually. You, Nanny May, Daddy, me. All of us."

"Oh. I wanted to see him now though," said Rosie, disappointed.

"I know love. But don't worry. He's happy, just like you. He wants you to be a good girl."

"I will," said Rosie.

For a moment Rosie was quiet. She looked down at the floor. Kate could tell that she was thinking. Eventually the little girl lifted her head and turned back towards her mam.

"Can I draw a picture for him Mammy?" she asked.

"Of course, you can. As many pictures as you want and when Nanny May puts them on the cupboard doors, he'll be able to see them, won't he?"

"Yes Mam," said Rosie, feeling pleased with herself.

Getting up, Rosie walked over to the table and began to pick up her pencils and crayons.

"Shouldn't you finish your toast first?" asked Kate. "Nanny doesn't want you wasting it now, does she? Not after she's gone to the trouble of making it."

"Yes Mammy," said Rosie, putting her pencil down and pulling her plate back towards her.

Kate smiled and glancing at May and Ed, noticed their expressions lighten too. It was clear that they had been concerned that her talk with Rosie would prove too upsetting. Now, they were relieved to see that she seemed all right. Kate was well aware of how much her family cared for her and in that sense it did, to some extent, compensate for the suffering that she was going through.

Having spent the morning with May, Kate, Ed and Rosie went back to Bright Avenue. When she'd returned home last night, Kate had found it difficult to settle. As she went through the rooms, she looked around her and could see that her furniture and possessions were in the familiar places that they had always been. It was her home. Yet before she'd been rushed into hospital, she had lived with the expectation that the rooms would be lit up by the presence of a little baby, who would symbolically link Kate and Ed together and make their relationship complete. Despite James Andrew's condition, this feeling hadn't left her until she had finally, with his passing, to accept that he would never be coming home with her. This had given Kate a sense that the house was empty. She felt as if the rooms needed new life breathing back into them and she hoped that Rosie's return would do just that. Arriving back at the house, Kate was eager to spend time with her daughter. She took her into the front room so that they could draw together and play with Rosie's dolls, whilst Ed settled down at the kitchen table to work on the assignments that he had necessarily abandoned over the last few days.

After a short period of play, Rosie started to get tired and snuggled up to her mam on the settee. Kate put her arm around her and started to read her a story. It wasn't long before Rosie's eyes were starting to droop and soon, she was asleep. Laying her head gently on a couple of large cushions, Kate made Rosie comfortable on the settee and covered her with a coat. Kate felt a little better, her daughter peaceful and content; the house once more a home. Leaving the door ajar, Kate walked out into the stairwell and through to the kitchen to check on Ed.

Whilst Kate had been with Rosie, Ed had been struggling. Sat reading a book at the kitchen table, part of his research for his final assignment, he had made little progress. Effectively, he'd read the same paragraph over and over again. He was finding it hard to concentrate and couldn't find the motivation necessary to complete his work. Somehow, his essay just didn't seem to matter anymore.

"What's that you're reading?" asked Kate.

"Oh, nothing really. Just something for the course."

"You're getting on with your final assignment, aren't you?"

"To be honest, my heart's not been in it," replied Ed, rather weakly.

"Ed. This is no time to lose your way. You've got to get it done for all our sakes. Rosie and I need you to."

"I know Kitty. But it isn't easy to simply move on."

Ed's response threw out a challenge and it was one that Kate was determined would not go unanswered.

"No one's asking you to. Neither of us can. But we've both worked hard. For ourselves, for Rosie and baby James too. You can't give up now. In fact, if either of us do, we'd be letting down the memory of our son. Can't you see that, Ed?" asked Kate.

Ed looked at her. She was fixing him with that piercing stare. Her gleaming green eyes reaching into the innermost depths of his soul. He knew that she was right and more importantly, he knew that he couldn't withstand the energy she had summoned to help him concentrate on his responsibilities. Nodding his head rather sheepishly, Ed sighed.

"I love you Kate. I really don't know what I would do without you. You know, I get so worried sometimes," he continued.

"Worried?" asked Kate, surprised.

"Yes. Scared that I'll lose you."

Kate could see that Ed was struggling. His voice was raw with emotion. Losing James Andrew had triggered his subconscious fears. She had always known how sensitive and vulnerable he was and just as she now needed Ed's love and support, she knew that he desperately required hers.

"Oh Ed, you are puddled. Why would I ever leave you? Anyway, how would you ever manage to get on if I wasn't around to sort you out! Chance would be a fine thing! Come on, put your book down and we'll have a cuddle."

Kate turned on the radio. With the music playing quietly in the background, the two of them settled down together on the settee. Kate lay her head on Ed's chest, her shoulder cradled by his arm. They were close. Conscious of one another's warmth and touch. It was comforting and it was love. It was what both of them knew would get them through the difficult days ahead.

Chapter 31

In June 1963, life in Ardwick, as Kate well knew, was anything but easy. The Prime Minister's bold assertion that the British people had "never had it so good," had little relevance to her own life. Waking up on Friday morning, Kate knew that she would soon have to go back to work. There was a funeral to arrange and it had to be paid for. There could be no time to grieve; not yet. Waking Ed, who was lay beside her, the two quickly got dressed and made their way downstairs.

Sat drinking their early morning mugs of tea, the couple contemplated the day ahead.

"Ed, I want you to ring Arnold again and let him know that we'll both be back in work tomorrow."

Ed was surprised and also concerned.

"Don't you need some more time before you go back Kitty?" he asked. "At least until after the funeral. Don't you think it's a bit too soon?"

"Ed. I don't have any choice in the matter," said Kate. "We need the money."

Ed winced, he felt wounded. When Kate had carried on working after leaving hospital, he could believe that it had helped her to gain some respite from constantly worrying about James' condition. But this was different. Now he felt just as he'd done before their son had been born, when he'd had no option but to stand by as Kate continued working until the final moments of her pregnancy. He had felt guilty then, regardless of any reassurances that Kate had given him. Now, deep down, regardless of what Kate had said, he still believed that had he been able to support his wife properly and let her give up work, baby James would still be with them now, alive and healthy. It was of course nonsense. The doctors had said that the defect in James' heart existed early in the pregnancy, but this had made no difference to him. The fact was that there was a part of Ed that wanted to feel responsible; to accept the guilt for what his son and his wife had been forced to go through.

"If only I was working," said Ed.

"You will be soon enough," Kate replied.

"But I'm not now," continued Ed.

"Never mind. We're not going through all that again Ed. I don't want to hear you blaming yourself. Do you hear me?"

Kate rested her eyes on his. She had that determined look, one that made it clear that she wouldn't brook any opposition. It was a clear message to Ed that the matter was closed. Ed sighed and nodding his head, acknowledged his agreement.

"We'll have to get the funeral arranged for James," continued Kate. "We can go to the undertakers today, the ones I used before. They were very nice and helpful and they'll allow us to pay in instalments."

"Yes," replied Ed quietly, "we need to get it organised."

Kate reached across the table and took Ed's hand. Her fingers were soft and gentle. Ed looked into her eyes.

"Ed," said Kate.

"Yes."

Ed waited expectantly for her to continue, but she didn't. It seemed to him that she was weighing up the consequences of what she was about to say. Finally, she resumed the conversation.

"There's something I need to ask you Ed."

"Yes?"

"I want James to be buried, but a plot for a grave is too expensive for us. When Joe died, May had him buried in her family's plot in Southern Cemetery. Would you object to me asking May if we can bury James there too?"

Ed looked surprised. He didn't understand why she felt the need for his agreement.

"Of course, I wouldn't mind. Why would I?" he asked.

"I wasn't sure if you'd be happy for James to be buried together with Joe."

"I don't mind at all Kitty. It's better that James isn't all alone. Joe's part of you, part of Rosie, so in that sense, he's part of my life and James's too."

Kate leaned over and gave Ed a kiss.

"Thank you, Ed."

"What for?" said Ed, puzzled by her reaction.

"Because you're you."

Ed could see Kate's lip beginning to quiver. She was fighting back the tears. He had no desire to see her upset and so continued the conversation and pretended not to notice.

"So, it's settled then. We can ask May if it will be all right when we take Rosie this morning. Come on, we best get washed and changed and get Rosie up and ready."

Kate looked at him. She was surprised by his sudden sense of purpose.

"Come on Kitty. Let's get weaving," continued Ed, mimicking one of Kate's favourite sayings.

Ed smiled at her. Kate shook her head, pretending to be annoyed.

"Just watch it, Deane. You're not too big for me to sort you out you know!"

Arriving at May's just before nine, Ed left Kate to go to the phone box to ring Arnold. Whilst he was gone, Kate broached the subject of James' burial with May.

"Of course, he can, the poor little mite. You're more than welcome. You know that Kitty."

"Thank you," said Kate.

"Ed knows about this though, doesn't he?" asked May.

She was concerned, like Kate had been, that Ed may not feel too comfortable about his son sharing a burial plot with his wife's first husband.

"Yes," said Kate, nodding affirmatively.

"You're sure that he knows that James will be together with Joe?" asked May, in search of further reassurance.

"Yes, May. I've asked him already. I've given him the choice. He seemed pleased that James wouldn't be buried alone."

May looked at her, clearly impressed by what she'd heard.

"I've told you before," said May, "you've got a good 'un there Kitty. It's funny, Joe and Ed. They're just like chalk and cheese. I don't think that you could have been married to two men so completely different. I'm sure that Joe wouldn't have been as understanding as Ed."

Kate said nothing. She wouldn't criticise Joe openly to his grandmother. Even in the darkest days of their marriage, she had intimated nothing of her frustrations and unhappiness to May.

"We'll go to the undertakers as soon as Ed gets back," said Kate, changing the subject.

"What's the undertakers Mammy?"

Kate hesitated and then turned round to see Rosie, sat up on the settee and looking expectantly at her for an answer. Once again, Kate had underestimated just how bright and alert her daughter was. Whilst the two women had assumed that she was busy playing with her dolls, Rosie had also been listening to every word that they'd been saying.

"Oh, nothing important," said Kate. "Just somewhere that Daddy and I have to go whilst you're here with Nanny."

"Oh," said Rosie, slightly disappointed that it wasn't anything more interesting. Turning her attention back to her dolls, it appeared that she had now lost interest in Kate and May's conversation. Rosie's question had however, reminded May that it was essential that the arrangements for James' funeral were made with due consideration for Rosie. Young and vulnerable, she could well become distressed by the occasion. May was sure that her parents would consider this, but to put her own mind at rest, she quietly broached the subject with Kate.

"Have you thought about Rosie and the funeral Kate?"

"I've tried not to," replied Kate.

"Are you thinking of letting her go?"

"I'm not sure. On the one hand, I don't want to see her get upset and she may well do if she sees either Ed or I struggling to cope, but then I don't want her to feel left out. It's so difficult to decide."

"You can leave her here with me if you think it's best," said May, "or Rosie and I could make our own way to the cemetery and meet you there. In that way you don't have to worry about Rosie seeing you both upset in the car."

"Yes," replied Kate. "That seems a better idea. She can still come and be with us, but the journey with you will be better for her. She's still too young to understand that adults can get upset. It could well frighten her if Ed or I were to break down."

"She can seem like quite a tough little girl Kate, but a funeral's a difficult occasion for anyone. Perhaps with her being so young, she won't fully understand what's going on. Then again, she's forever asking questions and it's going to be very difficult to give her answers. I agree with you Kitty. You're going to have to think very carefully about it."

Shortly after, Ed returned. He and Kate kissed Rosie goodbye and set off for the undertakers in Levenshulme. Sat together on the bus, the two of them were quiet, lost in their own thoughts. Ed looked down at the vanilla envelope he held in his hands. It contained the notice of James' death that had been issued to them by the hospital. It seemed to Ed that his son's brief life had been reduced to a mere piece of paper, with little trace of the time that James had been on the Earth. Ed thought about what type of son James would have been. What it would have been like to see him grow up and to be there to help him through the trials and tribulations of life. Yet he knew that he could only speculate. The reality was that James' life had ended here and now and although Ed outwardly supported Kate in her Christian beliefs, unlike her, he seriously doubted the existence of God in a world that could so ruthlessly tear their little son from them. It seemed so unjust. Why should James have suffered? Why hadn't he been given a chance? Surely, if God really cared, he would have made it right for James.

Getting off the bus, the bereaved parents had soon walked the short distance to the undertakers. Kate was aware that she would have to assume the responsibility for finalising the details of James' burial with the funeral director. More resolute than Ed, she knew that she was far better equipped to discuss the arrangements and negotiate payments; after all, she'd had to do it following the death of Joe. To Ed, the need to reach a financial agreement, seemed incongruous in such a setting. To discuss money when a life had been taken. But Kate understood that it was necessary. The funeral director had to make a living and Kate and Ed hadn't the money to pay their bill all in one go. In fact, it would be hard for them to pay in instalments and Ed had already been forced to acknowledge, albeit reluctantly, that the only way they would be able to do so, was by Kate going straight back to work.

The funeral director, Charles Brown, was elderly but impressive looking. He was wearing a traditional black, undertaker's long coat, a grey waistcoat, white shirt and black tie. Tall and thin, he had grey hair and a moustache. Ed couldn't help but think that he looked a little bit like Harold Macmillan. Brown had now been in business for over fifty years. He'd started working for his father when he was just fourteen. His ambition now, was to pass on the family firm to his two middle-aged sons. Yet although his 'boys' had worked with him for many years, Brown still insisted on dealing with all his clients personally. He had been brought up through hard times and he had seen how difficult it was for ordinary working people to meet the costs of bereavement, particularly through the terrible depression of the Thirties. Wise, shrewd and with far more than a modicum of compassion, Brown knew that life had remained equally tough for so many of the families who still lived in Manchester's terraced streets.

Brown doubted however, that his sons viewed matters in the same way. Part of the aspirational post-war generation, they saw themselves as businessmen rather than public servants. He sensed that they had little sympathy for the unskilled and the poor, who were increasingly getting left behind in the new prosperity of the Sixties. Without his business acumen, his sons hadn't the capacity to understand that a generosity of spirit had allowed the family business to thrive. His treatment of his poor clients as individuals; his capacity to be flexible and ease the burden of payment for them, had kept the business going. He knew that these were people who were hard-working and committed to their family responsibilities. It was a badge of honour for them that somehow, they would give their loved ones the best send-off that they possibly could. It wasn't often that he would find himself out of pocket with final instalments unpaid, especially as he took pride in the fact that in his unobtrusive and uncondescending way, he would create a funeral for his clients that would impact as little as possible on their capacity to pay. His experience of people; how they looked, how they spoke, were clues that indicated to him just how much they would be able to afford. He doubted whether his sons, seeing good business as a matter of getting clients to take the more expensive funeral packages, would ever understand the continuing success of his business model.

Observing the young couple sat in front of him, Brown knew that they would need all the help he could give them. He had remembered Kate from handling Joe's funeral and initially assumed that she had come to see him over the loss of an elderly relative. Finding out that the couple had lost their newly born son, he was all too aware of the heartbreak that they were going through. As he and Kate discussed the details, Brown guided her as delicately as he could, subtly encouraging her towards acceptably cheaper options. Having persuaded her that the quality of the least expensive coffin, was almost as good as the higher priced ones, he then addressed a more delicate issue.

"Mrs Deane, with James being a baby and the coffin being small, it's possible for James to travel with you in the car. Other parents, in similar circumstances, prefer their child not to be carried in a huge hearse, where they can seem to be lost and alone. I'd be happy for you to do the same. You've had so little time with James, you might both like to be with him on the final journey."

Brown paused and looked across the table at Ed and Kate. He watched as they exchanged glances. Then Ed nodded and Kate spoke.

"Yes. We'd like that."

It was something that most other funeral directors wouldn't have done. Brown wasn't only showing a real empathy for the parents, but he was also writing off the money he would make from hiring out a hearse. To Brown, that didn't matter and he knew that not only would it provide comfort for Kate and Ed, but that it would also significantly reduce their costs. His heart had gone out to the young couple and especially Kate. She had lost her first husband and now her baby, yet here she was, stalwart in the face of her misfortunes, determined to say goodbye to her son with dignity and love.

Having gone through all the arrangements, Brown informed them of the total cost.

"I can arrange the same instalment periods as before, if you like?" he offered.

Kate nodded her agreement.

"Yes. Thank you," she said. "I'd like to pay a deposit of £20 if that's all right?"

"Yes, that's plenty," said Brown. "It's more than enough."

Kate opened her bag, took out her purse and handed the money to Brown. Taking it, he wrote out a receipt from a pad in front of him and gave it to Kate.

"I think we'll be able to book the chapel for next Wednesday at Southern Cemetery and I can contact them to prepare the grave ready for us. Have you a preference for the morning or afternoon?"

"In the morning please," replied Kate.

Brown left the room to make a telephone call to finalise the arrangements. Returning, he confirmed that the funeral service would take place on Wednesday and that he had booked it for ten o'clock.

Leaving the undertakers, Ed expressed his surprise that Kate had handed over the £20. Ed wasn't aware that they had any extra money. Kate told him that it had come from the savings she still had through not buying James a pram and from her maternity grant, most of which she hadn't spent. Kate had only bought a few clothes to bring their baby home in, waiting to see if she had a boy or a girl before she spent the rest. It was an old wives' tale that it was bad luck to buy the pram before a baby was born and it was why Kate hadn't. Not getting it however, had made no difference to James Andrew. It hadn't seen him born in good health. Kate knew that she was unlikely to be superstitious again, but she was now thankful for the money that had been saved, given that she could now afford a fitting funeral for her son.

Catching the bus home, the young couple had completed their first task in laying baby James to rest. It had been a tough day but together, they had got through it. The funeral had been set for the following Wednesday, June 27th, a day that both of them knew would be even harder than today.

Chapter 32

It was a quarter past nine when the knock came to the front door. It had been a difficult night. Sleep hadn't come easily for either Ed or Kate. Thoughts of the funeral and a recognition that they would be saying a final farewell to their son, played on both their minds. Up at six, they had been dressed and ready for some considerable period of time. They felt numb; emotionally drained. Ed wondered how it would be possible for them to cry any more tears, yet he was sure that they would.

Opening the door, Ed was greeted by Charles Brown, their funeral director.

"Good morning, Mr Deane. Are you ready to go?"

"Yes, I'll just go and get Kate," replied Ed.

"It looks like it's going to be a fine day for baby James," said Brown, respectfully.

Ed glanced up at the sky. He could see a few small, wispy clouds and the sun was shining bright and strong.

"Yes," he replied, nodding in agreement.

Ed had no need to go through to the kitchen though as Kate, hearing Brown's voice, had collected her handbag and was soon stood there by his side. She could see that the car had arrived for them and it was now time to go. Stepping out of the front door of 17 Bright Avenue, Kate could see the closed curtains of the house opposite. Moving her eyes to the left and right along the line of terraces, she saw the picture repeated. It was a mark of neighbourly respect for Ed and Kate's loss. Parked alongside the pavement was a shiny black limousine, with its polished chrome door handles. A tall man in a long undertaker's coat stood by the back door of the car. With a slight bow, he took hold of the handle and opened the door for Kate to get in. Brown, having made his way to the opposite door, opened it and motioned to Ed to get in at the other side. On the long back seat, Kate and Ed could see the small coffin containing baby James. Sitting on either side of it, the couple took hold of one another's hands and rested them along its top, reassuringly holding on to one another whilst symbolically cradling their son. Having closed the doors, the two men got into the front of the vehicle. The key was turned in the ignition and quietly, the engine started. It made a reassuring, quiet purr, like a contented cat, the soft sound soothing the nerves of the car's occupants. The young couple were quiet, lost in their thoughts, but taking reassurance from their physical contact. Ed unconsciously stroked his wife's fingers, which she had placed in the palm of his hand. Kate hardly noticed the changing scenery of people, vehicles and buildings, as the car pulled out into Syndall Street, turned on to Stockport Road and eventually made its way down and across to Southern Cemetery. The funeral service having been arranged for ten o'clock, the roads were now clear of any rush-hour traffic and the journey was a smooth one.

Arriving at the chapel, Ed and Kate got out of the car. Waiting for them were May, dressed all in black and Rosie, who had stayed the night with her. May had explained to Rosie how important it was for her to be quiet at the chapel, so she was unusually subdued as Kate walked towards her. The long bus ride to the cemetery had been exciting for Rosie, but on the other hand it was unusual and together with her nanny's curious attire, had created something of a sombre mood for the little girl. Rosie understood that today the adults around her were sad and in her turn, she felt the same way. Seeing the look of concern on her daughter's face, Kate recognised just how much she needed her and it was this realisation which would help Kate get through the events of the day. It was time to say goodbye to James Andrew but also to thank God for her daughter, who she must continue to do everything that she possibly could for. Her little Rosie. Her little angel.

Kate crouched down and pulled Rosie towards her, giving her a kiss. Getting up, she was joined by Ed. At his side was Sarah. Kate and Ed hadn't expected anyone else to attend the funeral, but as Kate's close friend, Sarah was determined to be there to offer her support. As Sarah stepped forward, the two young women threw their arms around one another and embraced. Ed could see the emotion between them clearly betrayed by the tears that were soon running down Sarah's cheeks. Taking Rosie by the hand, Ed led her over to May, who was standing a few yards away from them.

"Come on Rosie, let's leave mammy and Sarah to talk on their own."

"Yes Daddy," replied Rosie, eager to please him.

"You look very smart Rosie," said Ed, looking at her admiringly.

Rosie looked pleased and then broke into a smile, her first since she had arrived. May had dressed her in a light blue, chequered dress with a white collar and buttons. She had a thin blue cardigan on top, white socks and a pair of new sandals. May had obviously taken Rosie to the shops and bought her the clothes over the last couple of days. With her blonde curly hair adorned with a couple of blue ribbons, Rosie looked lovely. Her nanny had felt that she was too young to be dressed in black and Ed approved. His new daughter was a symbol of life and hope, of radiance for the future and a reminder that in order to honour James' memory, those left behind had a responsibility to make the most of the life that they had been given.

"Did you enjoy the bus ride?" asked Ed, consciously trying to keep the conversation as simple as possible. It was his way of trying to negotiate Rosie's passage through the day, as painlessly as he could.

"Uh huh," said Rosie, nodding her head.

"There were a lot of people on the bus, weren't there Rosie?" asked May.

"Yes. Lots. And there was this man with a white stick who had his doggy with him," said Rosie, responding to her nanny's prompt.

"Was it a nice dog?" asked Ed.

"Yes," said Rosie. "Daddy, can we have a doggy?"

"Well, possibly. If we get a house with a garden. We'll have to wait and see what Mammy says," said Ed.

Before their conversation could go any further, Ed noticed Charles Brown walking over towards them.

"Excuse me Mr Deane. We're ready to take James into the chapel and the minister's waiting for us. If you'd like to let the young ladies know please."

May took hold of Rosie's hand whilst Ed walked over to Kate and Sarah and brought them back to the chapel steps.

Brown motioned with his arm and followed by a couple of pall bearers, carrying the small coffin, led the way into the chapel. The small funeral party followed behind, Kate and Ed holding hands, followed by May, Rosie and Sarah. Entering the chapel, they made their way to the front, sitting down before the minister. James' coffin had been placed to the side and on top of it were two wreaths, one from Kate and Ed and the other from May and flowers from Sarah and Kevin. Beyond the formal part of the funeral service, there was a short eulogy and one that was difficult for the minister to deliver. After all, James had experienced little in his short life. As such, there were no landmarks or achievements for him to talk about. Tragic for the parents, he had no wish to state what was so obvious, the pain that they had gone through. He therefore expressed the hope that the two of them would, through God's grace, find solace and strength through the life they were sharing together.

Ed held Kate's hand firmly. He looked at her, the woman he loved who was such a tower of strength to him. She was so incredibly brave. Her eyes were moist, but she was holding back the tears, determined that she would remain strong for James Andrew. Letting him know that she was there to love and support him.

With the completion of the service inside the chapel, James was taken back outside and on to the burial plot. The Minister led the small party behind the coffin, continuing to pray as they slowly made their way past a succession of monuments on their way to the grave. Seeing the deep hole in the ground, ready to receive James Andrew, Kate's eyes were drawn towards the soil that had been placed to one side. There seemed to be so much of it. It was a stark reminder that her son would soon disappear beneath the ground, reinforcing the finality of his departure from this world. It was the only point at which Kate doubted her ability to stop herself from breaking down. Yet somehow, she was able to fight back the tears.

As the party gathered at the side of the grave, the Minister continued with the service. Kate and Ed stood on either side of Rosie, each of them holding her hand. The little girl was being so good. Sensing her parents' sadness, she had become a little concerned, but now that she was holding on to them, she felt better. In many ways it was a bewildering experience for Rosie. She didn't really understand what was going on and never having seen James Andrew herself, her emotional awareness was only for her parents. It seemed a strange sight to her as carefully, the pall bearers lowered the coffin into the grave. As they did so, she felt both of her parents' hands tighten on hers, making it clear to her that the action had impacted upon them. However, when she looked up at their faces, their resolve to remain strong for both of their children, meant that she couldn't detect any signs of distress. All she could see was a concentrated, steely and determined look on both of their faces.

Reaching the culmination of the service, the Minister took a small handful of soil and slowly sprinkled it into the grave, it landing softly on the top of the little coffin. Rosie felt her parents let go of her hands, as Kate and then Ed picked up some soil for themselves and followed the Minister's example. Recognising that somehow this was an act of great significance, Rosie pulled on her mam's hand. Kate looked down at her.

"Mammy," said Rosie, quietly. "Can I put some in there?"

"Yes love," said Kate. "You'll need to be careful though. I think it's best that I hold your hand. We don't want you falling, do we?"

"No, Mammy."

Rosie crouched down and took some soil in her right hand. It felt dry and crumbly, a result of being warmed through by the sun. Standing up, she held out her left hand to her mam, who took hold of it and the two of them took a couple of steps towards the edge of the grave. Looking down, Rosie could see the polished wooden top with its small brass nameplate. Slowly and deliberately, she released the soil a little at a time from her outstretched hand. She was fascinated as she saw it bounce off the coffin lid, before settling back down again on the surface. Just as she finished, she saw a single red rose drop on to the coffin. She looked to the side and saw her nanny with her arm outstretched, her other hand clutching a handkerchief to her face. Rosie watched as May dabbed both her eyes, before stepping away from the graveside.

"Come on Rosie," said Kate.

Slowly she led her daughter back to look at the wreaths and flowers which had been laid a few yards to the side.

After a brief word with the Minister, it was time to return home. May, Rosie and Sarah walked the short distance to the car, whilst Ed and Kate stood arm in arm at the grave of their little boy, to say their final goodbyes. Out of sight and alone, it was inevitable that the tears would finally come, Kate no longer able to hold them back. Yet they didn't come in torrents but in a few, single tears, which trickled their way down her cheeks. Kate gulped in the air, fighting to keep control. Taking a hanky, she dabbed at her cheeks, slowly regaining her composure.

"Come on Kitty, it's time for us to go," said Ed, softly.

"I know," replied Kate.

Breathing out, she turned, ready to walk back to the car.

"We can come back to visit James with Rosie at the weekends," said Ed.

"I'd like that," replied Kate. "He's not with us now though, he's in heaven," she continued.

"Yes, but when we come here, he'll still know how much we love him," said Ed.

Holding hands, the couple returned to the car to make their journey back to Bright Avenue and continue the difficult task of rebuilding their life together.

Chapter 33

A week had passed. It was the first Thursday in July and Ed had gone to his training college to finalise the official completion of his teaching course. He had been informed that he had passed and that his status as a qualified teacher was now assured. The loss of James Andrew had threatened to undermine his chances of completing the requisite course essays, but the understanding of the course tutors and the insistent support of Kate, had ensured that they were handed in after a discretionary extension had been granted. However, by itself his qualification had yet to secure his family's future and Ed had good reason to feel apprehensive. The fact was that he'd been unable to apply for any of the teaching vacancies that had been advertised on the college notice boards, from the time that Kate had been rushed into hospital at the beginning of June. Ed was now extremely concerned that he'd missed out. Furthermore, Ed felt unable to tell Kate of his fears. He couldn't face the prospect of providing her with such a disappointment after all she had gone through. Ed knew that the vast majority of permanent teaching posts ran from the first of September, the beginning of the new school year. If he hadn't secured a job by then and the end of the summer term was just three weeks away, he would be faced with an uncertain year trying to secure local 'supply' work, with all the difficulties that job entailed. Ed's only other alternative would be to seek employment away from teaching. He knew however, that this was an option that would be unacceptable to Kate.

Entering the college office, Ed walked over to the main desk where he was met by the smiling face of Hetty, the principal secretary. With short grey hair, a pleasant round face and her glasses perched on the end of her nose, the arms of which were connected to a thin chain draped around her neck, Hetty projected a warm welcome to all who entered. A grandmother, who was close to retirement, Hetty's heart had gone out to Ed when she had learned of the loss of his baby son. He was a young man with whom she was impressed. He was always polite and prepared to stop and talk to her when he came into the office. Ed seemed so unlike the other student teachers, products of the new 'teen culture' she reasoned, with their lack of consideration for members of the older generation. It seemed so unfair that such misfortune should have befallen Ed and his wife but today, she hoped that she had some good news for him.

"Ah, Ed!" said Hetty, warmly. "I'm pleased that you didn't leave it any longer to come in. We've had an urgent request for a reference for you and with there being so little time left in the term now, the school wants you to go for an interview as soon as possible."

Ed looked confused. He hadn't made any job applications. How could any school have contacted the college if that was the case?

"I don't understand. Have I been mixed up with someone else?" he asked. "I've not been able to make any applications. There haven't been any jobs advertised."

Hetty looked at him. Ed seemed perplexed rather than delighted. Given the setbacks he had faced over the last few weeks, she wasn't surprised that he couldn't just simply accept the positive news that she was giving him.

"Well, we certainly haven't made a mistake" replied Hetty, "it's definitely you that they want the reference on. I've got some information here to give you about the school."

Hetty, seeing that Ed remained unconvinced, sought to reassure him further.

"Hang on a minute Ed, let me go and get your file and I should be able to explain a little more about why they've contacted us about you."

Hetty knew that she wasn't supposed to divulge any of the contents of the file to Ed. Information on his references, specifically what the requesting school had asked about him, was supposed to stay confidential in order to protect the veracity of the opinions given on the student by the college. But Hetty wasn't, as far as this case was concerned, bothered about the rules. This young man and his family needed all the help that they could get. And she was determined to give it to them.

"It's a good school Ed, a grammar school, out towards Cheshire."

"But why are they interested in me?" asked Ed.

"Why indeed?" replied Hetty. "I'll have to look and see."

Getting out of her seat, Hetty walked over to the filing cabinets at the side of the room. Opening one of the drawers, she ran her fingers over the tops of several folders before stopping and drawing out a file. It was Ed's. Closing the drawer, she walked back to the desk and sat down. Opening the folder, she leafed through the documents inside. Reaching a letter, she stopped and began to move her finger carefully across the lines of words written on the paper. Ed watched closely, fascinated as she unconsciously mouthed the shape of the words as she read them silently to herself. Having read the letter, Hetty then scanned through some additional paperwork. Satisfied, she put the papers back in their place and closed the top of the file.

"Well, it all seems a lot clearer now Ed. Apparently the deputy head at your teaching practice school knows the headmaster at the Grammar. The Head is after a young teacher, a graduate, for the history department and it seems that they've already held interviews but haven't been happy with any of the applicants. You were highly recommended. The deputy at your last school was very impressed with you and told the Head. With time being short, they thought it would be quicker to ask us if we can contact you, as they didn't have your home address."

"Oh," said Ed.

It was clear to Hetty that Ed had still to recognise what an excellent opportunity had so fortuitously come his way. Looking at him, she could see the signs of hesitancy that Kate had so often noticed. Fortunately for Ed, Hetty realised that the young man needed a push.

"Ed. You're going to be available tomorrow, or on Monday, aren't you?

"Available?" asked Ed.

"Yes, for the interview. You can't hang about if you want the job," said Hetty, sternly. She was determined to get the young man's brain functioning once more.

"Well, yes," replied Ed, hesitantly.

"Right. I'm going to ring them for you."

"But I don't know what to say."

"Not you," said Hetty, letting out a sigh. "I'm going to speak to them, get you an interview time and then you can go home and prepare for it."

"Oh," replied Ed. "All right."

Ed felt a sense of relief. Events had been moving a little too quickly and unexpectedly for him. He had been taken completely by surprise by the news that Hetty had given him. He was grateful that she was arranging the interview and most importantly, that he would at least have some time to get himself prepared.

Ed sat and listened as Hetty dealt quickly and efficiently with the school's secretary over the telephone. There was a slight delay as the secretary checked the headmaster's diary to finalise the details. An appointment for the interview having been made, Hetty put down the phone and smiled.

"Ed. They want you there, at the school office, for nine thirty tomorrow morning. They've asked me to give you the copies of the details they sent to us about the school. You need to read through them. Think of some questions that you can ask them. They like it when candidates show some kind of awareness of what their school's about. Why don't you go to the library? You can do it before you go home."

Ed nodded his approval. He was calmer now.

"Yes, I think that's a good idea," said Ed. "Thanks for your help Hetty. You've been very kind. I hope that I can impress them tomorrow. I'd love to get the job for Kate and Rosie's sake."

"Well, you've been recommended to them by your practice school. That will go a long way to convincing them that you're up to the mark. Schools often give more weight to that then they do the College's own references. Nevertheless, your tutors have also been equally as positive about your classroom performance. Just be yourself at the interview and I'm sure that they'll recognise just how promising a teacher you are."

"I hope so," said Ed.

Having completed his preparations in the college library, Ed returned home and then went to May's in order to collect Rosie. It wouldn't be long now before she would be starting school herself, a place all ready and waiting for her at Ross Place Infants in September. Whilst Rosie was busy drawing and colouring in her books, Ed spoke quietly to May as they enjoyed a cup of tea together.

"I've had some promising news at the College today," said Ed, "I've got an interview at a school tomorrow for a full-time job in September. But I don't want Kate to know yet, just in case it doesn't go well. I don't like not telling her, but I just don't want to give her any more worries and I know that she'll be really disappointed if I let her down and don't manage to get it."

"You won't let her down Ed," replied May. "She loves you. She doesn't expect you to be perfect. She knows that you can't always get everything right."

"I know May, but she's done so much to help me get through the course, especially over the last few weeks. I think I would have just given up after James passed away and have failed to qualify, if it wasn't for her pushing me. I'd rather she didn't know about the interview. In that way, if I don't get the job, I won't have raised her hopes, only to disappoint her.

May looked at Ed concerned. She didn't approve of his thinking and was determined to change his mind. She fixed her eyes on his, determined to secure his undivided attention.

"Ed," said May, in a soft, but urgent tone.

"Yes?"

Ed knew that she was about to impart some advice to him and although he felt slightly uncomfortable and was beginning to regret confiding in her, he respected May far too much to try and avoid listening to it.

"What do you feel when you think about not telling her?" asked May.

Ed, surprised by the question, hesitated, thought carefully and then replied.

"I'm not comfortable."

"Why?"

"Because I've always told her about absolutely everything," replied Ed.

And?"

May waited expectantly. Ed remained quiet, taking time to mull over his reply. It was clear to him that she wasn't going to give him the answer, but he knew exactly what she expected him to say. Finally, he responded.

"That's why I have to tell her. No matter what."

"Yes," said May. "The reason that your marriage is so strong, is that you're honest with one another and what you said you were going to do, is a kind of deceit. If either of you withhold anything from the other, you risk destroying the magical relationship that you have. It's precious Ed. Joe and Kate never had that and that was all my Joe's fault. You must promise me that you'll always be open with Kate, no matter what."

Like many women her age, May had a wealth of experience. She had gone through so many challenging periods in her life and as a result of that she had developed real wisdom; a true intelligence when it came to understanding people. It hadn't surprised Ed that she had been able to analyse his character and his relationship with Kate, so effectively. Yet he had never been privy to her criticisms of Joe. In fact, he found it hard to remember a time that she had actually talked about her grandson in front of him. Now, here she was, determined to stop him from damaging his relationship with her grandson's widow. It was a timely reminder of just how much he, Kate and Rosie meant to her and how determined she was that nothing would undermine them as a family.

"You're right May," said Ed. "I do need to tell her and I promise you that I will as soon as she gets home."

"Ed, you don't need to worry so much about Kate. She's a lot tougher than you are. When you tell her about the interview, her main concern will be about how it will affect you if you don't get the job. Kate's a survivor. It's her vocation to look after you, Rosie and the other little ones when they come along, because they will you know."

"I hope so May," replied Ed. "But I'm just thankful that we have Rosie. That's one thing that losing James Andrew has taught me."

"You're a good lad Ed. You've got a kind heart. I'm sure that they'll see it tomorrow. We all can."

May patted him gently on the shoulder and then turned and called over to Rosie.

"Come on now Rosie, it's time to pack away your things and get ready
to go home with your daddy."

Rosie put away the dolls, books and crayons that she kept at her
nanny's and then, giving May a kiss, she walked over to the back door.

"Come on Daddy. We don't want to be late for Mammy coming
home."

"Go on Ed, you've got your orders," said May, laughing.

Saying goodbye, Ed and Rosie went out into the backyard and off
home to wait for Kate's arrival from work.

Chapter 34

Returning with Rosie to Bright Avenue, Ed didn't have too long to wait before Kate arrived home from work. After both he and Rosie had greeted her, Ed set about making her a cup of tea whilst she sat talking to Rosie. Having finished, Ed placed Kate's drink in front of her and then sat down to join her at the table. Kate, who'd been watching Rosie as she coloured in her book, looked up at him and smiled. She loved coming home. She always received a warm welcome from her husband and daughter and it left her in no doubt that she was loved and treasured. Most of all, she never failed to appreciate how Ed would insist that she sit down, take the weight off her feet, whilst he made her a drink. Often, he would have already started cooking the tea for the three of them.

It was so different to her marriage to Joe. His views, a product of his upbringing, had been decidedly traditional and unaffected by any liberal notions of shared responsibilities between man and wife. To Joe, anything concerning cooking and cleaning was the domain of the female and he would have considered it effeminate for a man to participate in such things. Bringing in a wage to help pay the bills and chastising the children, was the extent of a man's familial responsibilities. Ed however, was different and although Kate welcomed his attitude, she knew very well that many women questioned the masculinity of any man who was happy to take on 'women's work' in the home. Kate considered her contemporaries in Ardwick and often felt a sense of despair, even anger, that society had engineered a situation in which women had such low expectations of themselves and their husbands. Yet she knew it was something that wasn't easy to remedy. It was obvious to her that education had to change. She remembered how in school she and the other girls had been instructed in domestic science, whilst the boys weren't. She was certain that this was designed to convince young women that they shouldn't aspire to very much more than becoming 'skivvies' for their husbands and kids.

Looking intently at Kate, Ed reached out and took her hand. Just as he'd promised May, he proceeded to tell her about the interview. May had been right. He had no reason to be worried. Kate took the news in her stride and was realistic about his prospects of success. Looking through the information that Ed had been given about the school, Kate was impressed and clearly pleased that her husband was being considered for such a prestigious job.

"You've already done so well to get offered an interview Ed," said Kate. "The fact that your practice school thought so much of you, means that even if you aren't successful tomorrow, it shouldn't be too long before you're able to land a job. You've got to treat this as a great opportunity. After all, they can only say no and if they do, you'll still be getting interview experience to help you for the next time."

"I don't know Kitty. It's a good, academic school and there's a lot of exam work. Normally they wouldn't give the job to someone as inexperienced as me."

Kate could sense Ed's negativity. She suspected that he was probably trying to calm her expectations and inject some realism into the situation, but she still didn't like it. She was proud of her husband and it annoyed her when he, all too frequently in her opinion, was so self-effacing, often to the point at which he failed to acknowledge his own positive qualities. It made her determined that he wouldn't appear to be lacking in confidence when he arrived for the interview.

"Well, Ed. I'm sorry to disappoint you, but they are considering giving you the job," she said sternly. "You need to go to the interview confident in yourself and your ability. And, anyway, what does it matter if they don't give it you? It's their loss. Rosie and I still love you. Don't we Rosie?"

Kate looked round at Rosie who, hearing her name, looked up from her sketch pad. She had a confused look on her face. She'd been concentrating hard on drawing a picture of a dog, a not so very subtle hint to her mam and dad that she'd love one of her own. As a result, she'd not been listening to their conversation.

"You do love Daddy, don't you Rosie?" asked Kate, once again.

"Yes Mammy," said Rosie, smiling. "Daddy said that we might get a doggy. Didn't you Daddy?"

Both Kate and Ed burst out laughing. The innocence of a young child was the perfect antidote to the concerns and pressures of adult life. Rosie, confused by their reaction, turned back to her drawing.

"There, you see," said Kate, the two of them having recovered from their merriment. "Your daughter loves you. What more do you want? Get there tomorrow and just do your best."

Ed realised that his wife was right. He had been too negative and if he wanted to be successful, he had to show far more self-belief. Once more, Kate had helped him to get matters into perspective.

"Yes, Kitty. I'll make sure that I do my best and if that isn't good enough, then I've just got to accept it and move on."

"Ed," continued Kate, sympathetically. "I know that you weren't able to apply for any jobs and of course, I know that you're worried that another one won't come along before September. But it really doesn't matter. We'll get by. There's always supply teaching available until something permanent comes along."

Ed looked at her. He was surprised by her knowledge. After all, he'd not discussed anything with her about finding a job. Kate smiled as she noted the puzzled expression on his face.

"Don't you think I've been finding out things for myself Ed?" said Kate. "I think you've forgotten that May knows Leslie Lever and he knows the Manchester Education Committee inside out. He told May that you'll definitely be able to join the pool of supply teachers and once you've worked in a few Manchester schools, they'll get to know you and it won't be long before you end up with a permanent job somewhere. So there."

Playfully, Kate pulled out her tongue at Ed. He sat there, a surprised look on his face. Kate shook her head and laughed.

"Don't you think that I care about my husband's prospects?" she continued. "And I'm not beyond asking Leslie Lever to put in a good word for you too."

"No, no," said Ed, embarrassed. "You mustn't do that!"

"Well then, you'll just have to get that job tomorrow, won't you?"

It was now Ed's turn to laugh. She was far too clever for him. In the nicest way, she had proven herself to be an expert in psychological manipulation. She had managed to reduce tomorrow's interview to a matter of relatively little importance, yet at the same time she had made him even more determined to be successful. Significantly though, she'd eliminated the pressure. Kate had told him that she would be steadfast in supporting him. She would always be with him through thick and thin and that, he realised, was the essential nature of his fear. He was apprehensive that somehow his failure to deliver a job in September and with it the prospects of giving Kate and Rosie a better, more secure life, would damage his relationship with his wife and could lead to him losing her. Secure in the knowledge that it wouldn't happen, Ed felt a huge weight taken from his shoulders.

"Ed, we've been through so much already," continued Kate. "We've managed it together. Whatever befalls us, we'll overcome it by always sticking together. I would never have married you if I wasn't certain that I could put my trust in you and know that you would do your very best for me and Rosie. In return, I'll always love and support you, no matter what happens."

Ed leaned over towards his wife and kissed her tenderly on the cheek. He wanted to throw his arms around her, pull her to him and kiss her passionately. But with Rosie around, that wasn't going to be possible. He knew that such things would have to wait until later on.

The next morning, Ed had been forced to leave the house early. He would have to take two buses to get to the school and feeling that it was better to err on the side of caution, he decided to start out very early in order to compensate for any potential delays that may occur on the way. Certainly, he looked immaculate. At Easter, Kate had insisted that he buy a new suit, to be put away in the wardrobe to save for just such an occasion as this. After hearing Ed's news, she had pressed it together with a new, white shirt and a dark blue tie. His shoes were neatly polished and before he'd gone to bed, she'd given his hair a quick trim, using the skills she had picked up as a teenager, working on Saturday mornings for a local hairdresser. Kate had sent him off with a kiss. It was one of the nicest kisses that he could remember. Her lips so soft, so inviting, a promise of what could lay in store for him if he returned successful. The thought made his body tingle. It was the effect that she always had on him. His desire for her hadn't abated. In reality, it had increased with every passing day and he was sure that she knew it. Knew that in every way he was irrevocably bound to her.

Momentarily disorientated by his amorous thoughts, Ed hesitated at the doorstep. He seemed to have forgotten where he was going.

"Go on then. Do you want the job or not?" asked Kate.

"Yes. Yes" said Ed, still in a state of confusion.

Kate laughed and shook her head at him.

"Men!" she said, with an additional tut for emphasis.

She knew however, that her kiss had distracted him. And she'd done it on purpose. Kate was being playful, but had to admit that she quite liked the look of him in his smart, new suit. Most importantly, her parting kiss had given him something else to occupy his mind, besides worrying about the interview. Yes, she was being a tease, but he wasn't just her husband, he was also her lover.

"I'll see you after work Ed. Remember, just do your best."

With her words ringing in his ears, Ed was gone.

Chapter 35

It was one o'clock and the dogs at White City had almost finished. It hadn't been a particularly busy morning at work and as such, Kate had been given a fair deal of time to sit on her stool and read the newspaper. Yet it was hard for her to concentrate. Regardless of anything she'd said to Ed, in order to encourage him to relax, she herself had become increasingly nervous as the morning had progressed. She suspected that his interview would now be over and she naturally began to wonder whether he had been successful. Although it wouldn't be easy for Ed to get the job, she knew that if he did, it would certainly transform their lives. Nervous, Kate couldn't share her anxiety. She hadn't told Kevin anything about today, believing that it was up to Ed. After all, he might feel that it was advertising his failure if he were to return without getting the job. Perhaps, she thought, she should have asked Ed to telephone her. Then again, he might need time to compose himself and would prefer to give her the news personally. It all seemed so very confusing.

"Kate," said Kevin, sat at his desk. "Do you want to go over to the shops and get yourself a sandwich. It's dinner time."

Looking round, Kate realised that normally she would have gone by now. It was clear that the interview was playing on her mind more than she realised. Poor Kevin, she thought. He wanted a sandwich but knew better than to ask her to go and fetch one for him. Their unwritten rule was that he had to wait for her to offer.

"Yes Kevin. I'll go now. Did you want anything?"

"Yes, thanks Kitty. Can I have a ham and tomato and cheese and onion roll please. Here you are."

Kevin handed her some money as she walked over to him.

Picking up her purse from her handbag, Kate looked through the glass windows at the front of the counter and spotted Ed coming through the door and into the bookies. Surprised to see him, momentarily she stopped, staring at him as he walked towards the window. As he approached the counter, Kate could see a broad smile break out on his face and she immediately knew that it could mean only one thing. Ed had got the job. Working hard to contain her excitement, Kate moved towards the door to exit the counter and turned back towards Kevin.

"Right Kevin. I'm ready to go."

Kevin rose from his desk. He hadn't seen Ed and still didn't notice him as he closed the door behind Kate. Walking back to the window however, to cover the till in Kate's absence, he saw Ed and Kate embracing in the middle of the floor. Initially, Kevin had been surprised. All he'd seen was the suit, apparel he wouldn't normally associate with Ed. He was shocked, unable to believe that Kate was kissing another man. Once the couple had parted however, Kevin could clearly see that she had been embracing her husband.

"Hey! We'll have less of that you two. They'll be closing down the bookies for improper behaviour."

It was Sam, who had stood watching as the young couple embraced.

"Get off home if you want to start kissing and canoodling. And who's going to take my bet then?"

"I'll take it," said Kevin.

"I know," said Sam. " He thinks I'm being serious," said Sam, glancing up at the ceiling and smiling at Kate and Ed.

"You're looking smart Ed," continued Sam. "What have you been up to then? Have you just been taken on at Head Office?" he asked. "Watch it Kevin, he's come to give you your marching orders."

Kevin and Kate laughed whilst Ed, as usual, looked a little embarrassed.

"Well, Ed. Are you going to tell them then?" asked Kate.

Ed hesitated as Kate, Sam and Kevin turned towards him. Seeing their eyes fixed firmly upon him, he felt like he was in the spotlight. He hadn't anticipated this at all. He had just come straight from the interview and assumed that he would be telling Kate quietly on her own. Slowly, he took a deep breath.

"I got the job. It's permanent and I start in September."

Kevin and Sam, not privy to where Ed had been, unsurprisingly looked a little confused. As Ed hesitated, Kate stepped in to fill in the details for them.

"He's been for a job interview out in Cheshire this morning, teaching history at a boys grammar school. He's done really well to get it."

"Well done, Ed. Congratulations," said Kevin, shaking Ed's hand and genuinely pleased for him.

"That's why you're looking so smart," said Sam. "That explains it. You've done well kid. Make sure you give 'em a good hiding if any of 'em start."

Ed couldn't help but smile. Sam's reaction was so typical of men who had gone through the Depression and the War. And Ed could understand them. They had seen the emergence of a new teen culture. National Service had gone and too many youngsters, in their opinion, had it easy. It was no wonder that manners and respect had slipped; there wasn't enough discipline they argued. Yet their sentiments weren't ones that Ed shared. Nevertheless, he made no comment and simply nodded his head. Ed knew from experience that if he were to express any hint of disagreement, he would simply be dismissed as one of the new breed of liberal 'do-gooders', who would rue the day when by 'sparing the rod,' they would end up 'spoiling the child'.

Kate was now eager to get Ed on her own. She turned towards Kevin.

"I best get over for our sandwiches. You must be starving Kevin."

Kate took Ed's arm and led him outside. Once on the pavement she stopped and turned to him. Gently, she pulled his face down towards her and gave him a long and lingering kiss. Finally, parting from him, her face broke out into a beaming smile. Ed, captivated by the warmth of her affection, stood calmly, admiring his beautiful wife and feeling a glow of contentment and satisfaction. He was so pleased at Kate's reaction. He hadn't expected it, especially there on the pavement alongside Stockport Road, one of the busiest thoroughfares in Manchester, with so many people passing by.

"I knew you'd do it Ed," said Kate, excitedly. "I'm so proud of you. It means so much. So much to me and Rosie."

Overjoyed, Kate grabbed hold of Ed once more. This time, he eagerly pressed his lips to hers, the two of them holding each other tightly. They could feel the intensity of their love for one another. Parting once more, Ed stepped back and looked around him. At the nearby bus stop he could see the waiting queue of people smiling at the two of them. It was clear that they had been cheered by the young couple's public show of affection. It had brightened their day, bringing them a vision of positivity in an all too challenging world. Conscious of their audience, Ed started to feel a little embarrassed and as Kate continued to look at him, she saw him start to blush. She couldn't help but smile, it was the Ed she loved so much; loyal, unassuming and reserved.

"Come on Ed, we'd best get over to the bakers for Kevin's rolls. You must be hungry too. You can come and have something to eat with me, before you go back home."

Together, the couple walked to the crossing in order to get over the busy road. After all their recent heartache, today they had, for once, been delivered a perfect result. They now shared a belief that they could finally build their new life together. But exactly where that would be, they still had to decide.

Chapter 36

Several days later, as Kate travelled home on the bus after work, there were many questions running through her mind. Ed's new job had provided them, as a family, with new opportunities. However, after the first flush of excitement was over, Kate realised that their imminent change in circumstances, however welcome, was going to provide them with some tough decisions.

Her immediate thought had been that they could move into a new modern home, with an inside toilet and bathroom and perhaps even, central heating. That, just a short time ago, had seemed unthinkable. They could also move Rosie out of the crowded streets of Ardwick and into the airy and healthy suburbs. Kate knew that they would have to rent a house at first but then, with both of them working, they would soon be able to save a deposit and get a mortgage to buy their own property. But Kate was an Ardwick lass and she had never lived anywhere else. The town planners may decry the urban degeneration of the area, but it was still the place that she was proud to call home. Furthermore, the reality provided by Ed's success, had provided her with something of a shock. Although she'd often thought about what it would be like to have a modern house with a garden, deep down she was far from convinced that the situation would ever arise. Consequently, she had never fully contemplated just what it would mean for her to leave behind all that was familiar in Ardwick.

Another concern that Kate had, one that she had previously discussed with Ed, was that the prospect of moving, provided her with feelings of guilt. The shared experience that created such strong communities in districts like Ardwick, forged a sense of camaraderie. It was a tough world and although she would be able to leave it behind, others could not. Her conscience suggested to her that she should stay. Now that they would have the security of a larger income, she could relax her relentless focus on making ends meet for her family and concentrate on fighting for improvements for others too. Nevertheless, she knew that she couldn't neglect her responsibilities to her daughter and the loss of James Andrew had brought that into even greater focus. Rosie deserved the best that her parents could provide and for all her confused emotions, Kate recognised that ultimately, she would never forgive herself if she denied her lively and intelligent daughter, the best possible chance to fulfil her undoubted potential. Therefore, despite her misgivings, Kate accepted that, sooner or later, moving was inevitable.

In the final analysis however, beyond any altruistic motives that Kate may have, her biggest consideration had to be for May. How could they possibly move and take Rosie away from her nanny? Kate loved May. She had always been just like a mother to her. Her unwavering support had been so important in helping Kate to overcome Joe's death. Furthermore, May had accepted Ed unreservedly and Kate knew that they couldn't have possibly coped with the loss of baby James without May stepping in and caring for Rosie. To move, to take her great granddaughter away, the little girl that she idolised, would break May's heart. They might only move a bus ride away but to May, rooted in Ardwick, they might as well have moved to another part of the country. After all, her little Rosie wouldn't just be able to 'pop round' with her mam anymore. The more that Kate thought about it, the more she worried. She was concerned for May. She knew that she just couldn't put her in such a situation.

Collecting her thoughts, Kate rose from her seat as the bus approached Devonshire Street. Stepping down on to the pavement, she quickly made her way home. She was determined that today, Ed would have no inkling of her concerns. After all, they had enough time to decide and regardless of what they did, Ed's job had now brought a sense of security into their lives. There would be no more scrimping and saving, making constant sacrifices to pay the bills. They could now face the world with confidence and certainty. She would wait until Sunday and then, when they took Rosie to the Park, she would make Ed aware of her fears about the consequences of leaving May.

The weather was fine on Sunday and after they had washed and put away the dinner pots, Kate and Ed, together with Rosie, made their way over to Ardwick Green. As usual, Rosie took her pencils, crayons and drawing pad to sit and sketch the flowers and trees. Sitting together on a park bench, with Rosie quietly absorbed in her work, Kate took the opportunity to broach her concerns about May. Ed's response surprised her. It was clear that he'd already given the matter a great deal of thought, as his words sounded as if they were part of a well-prepared speech. One that he'd rehearsed. It was quite obvious that he too was concerned about the impact it would have on May, if they moved away.

"I've been thinking much the same myself Kitty. It's not just Rosie who needs May, we do too. We can't just move. It wouldn't only devastate May, but it would upset Rosie as well. I've been considering the problem though and I believe that there is a solution."

Ed paused. Kate looked at him expectantly.

"It's going to depend though on how you and May feel about it."

Once again, Ed hesitated. It seemed as if he was unsure whether he should put forward his suggestion.

"Go on," said Kate.

"Well Kitty, what I thought was, why couldn't she just move with us?"

"Move with us?" asked Kate, not exactly sure what he meant.

"Yes. We'll have enough money to get a bigger house with plenty of room. So why can't she live with us?"

Kate sat quietly. Ed could see that she was taking time to digest what he'd said. Patiently, he waited for her response.

"It's an idea Ed. Would she want to live with us though? I'm not so sure. Would she think that she was beholden to us? She may do if she doesn't feel like it's her own house. I'm not sure that she'd actually want to leave Ardwick anyway. It'll be a big enough wrench for me if we decide to move and I'm only young. May's spent all her life here and she's never known anywhere else as home."

"But the Corporation have committed themselves to clearing away all the unfit housing," said Ed. "They've already started and most of Ardwick will, sooner or later, be flattened. All of us will have to move in any case, eventually. They're already building new estates at Heywood, Langley and Hattersley. They're all miles away from here and they might not even give her a choice of where she can go. They're going to break up all the old communities. Everyone will be dispersed to who knows where. We can talk to May, tell her that we want her to be with us and not out on her own. How long, if we left and she stayed here, would her friends still remain around her. They're all going to be moved somewhere else too."

Ed had spoken with real passion. Like Kate, he too had a developed social conscience. He had experienced the poverty of Ardwick first hand, yet he had also seen the closeness of the community. He admired their sense of defiance, a determination to make the best of their situation and at all costs, to retain their sense of humour and hope. Ed welcomed the new housing programmes, but he wasn't convinced that the planners were going about it in the right way. It would have been much better, he thought, to refurbish the housing stock and provide families with inside bathrooms and toilets and thereby keep the old, familiar communities together.

"Well, I still think it's going to prove difficult to persuade her," said Kate, "but I can talk to her about it. I can tell her that we've not decided on anything yet, but that we'd like to know what her feelings are about moving away from Ardwick."

"I think it's best if I'm there too," said Ed. "May needs to know that I'm happy about her coming to live with us."

"All right," replied Kate, "but I don't think that you need to worry. May doesn't doubt your good intentions. She's always accepted you as part of the family. She believes in you Ed."

It was decided. They would both talk about their potential plans to May and then see how she reacted. The opportunity to do so wasn't long in coming, as that afternoon they went, as usual, to May's to have their Sunday tea. Sat around the table, it was Ed who told her, eager to let May know that he wanted her to move in with them and that they would find a new home big enough for all of them to live in. As he spoke May sat quietly, carefully considering his persuasive words. Kate could see her purse her lips, her mouth showing signs of a slight frown. There was a pause after Ed had finished speaking. It seemed to last forever, as the young couple waited nervously for a response. Although she would never have told May, Kate knew that there was little chance that they would move with Rosie, if she decided that she wanted to stay in Parker Street.

"I'm really grateful to you both," said May, eventually breaking the silence. "It's so kind of you to offer to take me into your home. You're right to be thinking of moving. There's far more for Rosie away from here. She can have a garden to play in, fresh air and a better chance in life. I'm not sure though that I want to leave here. I've been in this house for thirty years and I've always lived in Ardwick. I'm too old now. I'm not sure that I'd be able to move somewhere else. I don't know that I'd be settled there."

"You're not old May," said Kate. "You've got more life in you than I have."

"I wish I had," replied May, with a smile.

"Mammy. Nanny May is old," said Rosie, suddenly. "Aren't you Nanny?"

Kate, startled by her daughter's intervention, felt deflated. Quite innocently, Rosie had undermined her own attempts to encourage May. Yet almost immediately, May burst out laughing, tickled by her great granddaughter's words.

"There you go, as I always say," said May, struggling to get her words out. "Out of the mouths of babes. Hey Kitty?"

May's laughter was infectious and soon Ed and Kate were joining in. Tears were rolling down May's cheeks. Kate turned to her daughter who, sat with her doll on the settee, had a look of astonishment on her face, unable to understand the reaction to what she had said. Then, in a clear sign of disapproval at their jovial behaviour, she dismissively turned her attention back to her doll.

Gradually settling down, the three adults were now in a more relaxed mood to discuss what, for all of them, would be a huge decision. Kate now realised that Rosie's comment had in fact been a huge help. It was Ed who continued the conversation.

"I understand how you feel May. I wish everyone was going to be given the chance to stay here, but the Corporation's already decided that they're going to level Ardwick. All the terraced houses are going in the next three or four years. They'll force you to move whether you want to or not and when that does happen, we'd want you to come and live with us anyway. So why not now?"

"Yes, I know what you're saying Ed," said May. "I do know what's going to happen."

Ed felt a fool. Of course, she was aware of the plans in store for Parker Street and the rest of Ardwick too. He was now worried that May would think that he was being condescending and that certainly hadn't been his intention. He had just wanted her to see the benefits of moving now, rather than in the future.

"I'm sorry May," said Ed, trying to apologise, "I didn't mean …"

May quickly interrupted him before he had a chance to finish.

"Don't worry Ed. I know that you and Kate are concerned about me. But it's okay. I'll be fine here. It's you two and Rosie that I worry about and the important thing is for you all to go and give yourselves a fresh start."

Kate watched May closely as she spoke. Everything she had said since they had been there had been skirting around what really concerned her. It was something that Kate herself had identified when she had spoken to Ed earlier. As soon as May had finished, Kate addressed her fears head on.

"I know why you're so unsure about moving out of your house May. You think that if you live with us, it will seem as if it's our house and not like it's your own home."

May looked at her without responding. The silence told Kate that it was true. And she was right. May wanted to pick her words carefully. She had no wish to upset Kate and Ed. After all, how many other young couples would be prepared to take one of their elderly 'in-laws' into their own home. Yes, she was Rosie's nanny and she had looked after her, spending more time with her great granddaughter than her own mam had over the last few weeks. But still, she wasn't Kate's real grandmother and to Ed, she was a constant reminder of Joe. Yet such things were of no concern to the young couple. Details that would have undermined the chance of a close relationship with others in similar circumstances, were simply brushed aside by Kate and Ed. May was quite humbled by the respect and affection that they were showing towards her. As such, she knew that she had to relay her thoughts with the utmost precision.

"They say Kitty, that you can't have two women living under the same roof. I wouldn't like to be in your way. It's your home. You need to run it and organise it however you want it to be."

"May," replied Kate. "You're part of our family. You might not live with us, but we're in each other's houses every single day. Rosie stays with you all the time. We rely on you to help bring her up. When we move, Rosie will be in school. You're finally going to have the day to yourself and you'll be able do anything that you want. If you're living with us, you'll be there for Rosie just like now. You can pick her up from school and care for her until we come home from work."

"We're going to get a bigger house May," said Ed, eager to support Kate. "We'll be able to afford it now. We'll make sure that there's a separate downstairs room just for you, so you can get a rest from us and have some privacy whenever you feel like it."

May laughed, pleased to have the opportunity to take some of the seriousness out of the situation.

"Why? Are you that bad to live with Ed?"

Kate laughed too as she saw Ed's face redden, a sign of his embarrassment.

"Seriously May," said Ed, trying to stay focused. "You'll be able to have as much or as little privacy as you want."

For all her light-hearted ribbing of Ed, May could see that both he and Kate were willing her to say yes and so agree to their offer.

"Look," said May, "let me think on it overnight. We don't need to be so hasty, do we?"

"No. Of course we don't," replied Kate.

She nodded at May, realising that their enthusiasm had probably put undue pressure on her, even though they hadn't intended it to do so.

Returning home with Rosie, Kate and Ed hoped that May would, after due consideration, agree to move in with them. Following their conversation with her, both Kate and Ed were more convinced than ever that they couldn't leave Ardwick without her. If necessary, they would stay as long as Bright Avenue and Parker Street remained standing. They reasoned that at such a point in the future, May would be far more prepared to move in with them, rather than be forced to take a small flat on a new estate, in a part of Manchester not of her choosing. Nevertheless, Kate couldn't help but experience a sense of nervousness when she went to drop-off Rosie at May's, before she went to work on Monday morning. She couldn't kid herself. Ideally, she wanted them all to move to a new home together, but it had to be under the right circumstances. May had to be committed to the idea too.

Knocking on and then entering through, the back door to May's kitchen, Kate greeted May who was busy filling the kettle at the sink.

"Sit down Kitty. I'm just putting the kettle on. You've got time for a brew, haven't you?"

"Yes, of course," replied Kate.

Kate sat at the kitchen table, whilst Rosie settled down on the settee to play with her dolls. May began to chat as she stood waiting for the kettle. Small talk about Rosie, the weather and Kate's job. Finally, once the kettle had boiled and the tea was made, she brought two mugs over to the table, putting one down in front of Kate and the other on a mat opposite, where she proceeded to sit down.

"I can see that you're waiting for my answer," said May.

"No," said Kate, trying to appear as nonchalant as she could, but knowing full well that May wouldn't believe her.

"Yes, you are," said May, smiling. "Have you and Ed thought about it more?" she asked.

"No. We'd already thought it through before we spoke to you. We already suspected that you'd have the concerns that you did."

"Just tell me one thing Kitty and answer me honestly," continued May, looking intently at Kate. "If I say that I want to stay here, will it make any difference to you moving?"

Kate paused. It was the impossible question. How could she answer it? If she told the truth, it would be putting more pressure on May, even providing her with a sense of guilt. However, if she lied and said they were moving anyway, which might make May's refusal easier, it would also upset her. Confused about what to say, Kate managed to devise a weak and non-committal response that somehow, she hoped, would suffice.

"There's no hurry at all about us moving May. It's something we can take our time over. Actually, we've already worked out that we can save more money for a deposit to put down on our own house, if we stay here longer. After all, the rents around here are a lot cheaper. That would mean that we wouldn't have to rent a house ever again."

"Yes, I suppose so," replied May, "then again, Rosie will be starting school soon and surely it's better to move before that happens."

Kate looked at May, who raised her eyes and gave her that knowing look. It told Kate in no uncertain terms that she was far too quick for her. May was no fool. She knew that Kate had framed her answer so as not to upset her. Yet, it was the type of response that May had been looking for. She knew now, beyond any doubt, that Kate and Ed were serious about her moving in with them and more importantly, just how much they thought about her. With her recognition of those facts, May's face broke out into a smile.

"You can't fool me Kitty. We have to get Rosie settled and you're going to need me too. You, Rosie and Ed are my family. You mean the world to me and I've waited for this time through all the dark days with Joe. I hoped that he would be able to give you and Rosie a real future and finally now, with Ed, you've got that chance. I want to help you to take it. Ed's right," she continued, "the old neighbourhoods are going. Then, will there still be anyone around me that I've grown up with? I have to move and it seems just as sensible to go now. Yes, Kitty. I've thought about it and I'd like to come with you."

Kate looked at her. As she had spoken, her voice had become increasingly charged with emotion. She noticed that May's eyes were starting to fill with tears. She feared that making her decision had upset May, but she was wrong.

"Are you all right May?" she asked, concerned.

"Yes love. I just feel so lucky to be appreciated."

With that May began to cry, but quietly. Kate walked around the table, bent down and put her arm around May's shoulder. She kissed her on the cheek.

"We're the ones who are lucky May. I don't know what I would have done without you. You've given me and Rosie a chance. I could never have met Ed if I hadn't been able to go to work and I think of all those mornings when you kept telling me that I'd meet someone nice and I took no notice of you. You were right. I owe you so much."

By now Rosie, watching from the settee, was becoming concerned. Her mam and nanny were both becoming emotional. She had noticed May's tears and her first thoughts were that both of them were upset and unhappy. Getting to her feet, she walked over to them and shook her nanny's arm.

"Nanny! Nanny!"

Sensing Rosie's distress, Kate and May broke off from their embrace. May, reacting quickly, sought to reassure her great granddaughter that she was fine. Taking a little handkerchief from the pocket in her cardigan she dabbed her eyes.

"It's okay love. Nanny's just happy, that's all."

Rosie looked puzzled. She still couldn't understand how anyone who was crying, could possibly be happy.

"Sometimes people cry when they're happy Rosie," explained May. "It's called tears of happiness."

"Oh," said Rosie, still looking unconvinced.

"Yes, that's right," added Kate.

Looking at her mam and then back at May, Rosie could see that the two of them now appeared much calmer. Whatever it was that had caused the tears, had gone. Her mind at rest, Rosie returned to play with her dolls back on the settee.

"I'm going to have to get the bus to work May. I'll tell Ed that we can go ahead with the house and try to find somewhere suitable. He's starting on relief at the bookies today, so I'll be picking up Rosie tonight. He's going to work for the next month to earn some extra money. After that, he's going to need some time to prepare for his new school. He's not letting on to me, but I know he's excited about it."

"Well, he should be," said May. "The lad's done well."

Giving Rosie a kiss, Kate said farewell and set off to work. She knew now, beyond any doubt, that her time living in Ardwick was coming to an end.

Chapter 37

A month had passed and the young couple's situation had quickly changed. They had anticipated moving out to the south of Manchester, into Stockport. From there, they could access good bus and train services to both of their jobs. They had searched for a house as far as Bramhall and Hazel Grove, eventually finding a large semi in the former, with enough room for all of them. It was such a surprise for Kate to see how easy it was for them to rent it. How different it had been to when she and Joe had struggled to find a house when they were newlyweds. Their relative youth and Joe's job as an apprentice painter and decorator, meant that landlords, even in the run-down areas of Ardwick, were loath to take a chance on the young couple not paying the rent and then having to evict them. Eventually though, they had found Bright Avenue. It was owned by May's landlord who, recognising her as such a reliable tenant, was prepared to take a chance on her grandson. No doubt, he also believed that should Joe be unable to pay the rent, May would step in and do it for him. Number seventeen though, was still in a mess from the previous occupants who hadn't maintained the property in a good state of repair. May had helped Kate and Joe to convince the landlord that they were prepared to put it back in good order, for which they also negotiated two weeks grace on the rent. Kate had, together with Joe, put a great deal of effort into cleaning and painting their new home. Over a period of time, Joe had been content to use some of his wages, along with Kate's, to buy furniture and furnishings that would turn their house into a real home. Even after Rosie was born and Joe became distant and disinterested, Kate had worked hard to maintain the property. She was incredibly house proud and wouldn't give anyone the opportunity to criticise her in terms of the tidy and spotless state of her home.

The house that Kate was now about to rent was in no such state as Bright Avenue had been. They had applied to rent homes in a far more affluent area and her husband was a grammar school teacher. Kate was, joked Sarah, a member of the middle classes now. A reference from Ed's new school was sufficient for any landlord to happily rent a property to them. Kate accepted the fact that it was the way things were. She could also take satisfaction from the knowledge that their move would give Rosie opportunities that she, as a girl growing up in Ardwick, could only have dreamed of.

Once the house had been found, May and Rosie had been taken to look at it and both of them had given their seal of approval. Rosie was amazed at the size of the garden, so different to the backyard that she was used to at home. It was therefore settled that they would move before the end of August. Rosie was quickly registered at the local Infants School, the deposit and first month's rent were paid in advance and all that was left to do, was for Kate to book the removal van.

The day came and the van arrived on time at seven-thirty. The contents of May's house were loaded first and then it was around the corner to Bright Avenue. With two lots of furniture between them, Kate and May realised that they didn't have room for everything. The two women had to decide what they would leave behind, with their landlord happy to keep the items for the next tenants. The removal men worked quickly and efficiently and by midday, they were loaded up and ready to go. May and Rosie went with them; May aware of where all the items would be put in their new house.

Kate and Ed had remained behind, waiting for the landlord so that they could hand in the keys for the two properties. Stood waiting in the kitchen, Kate had a request for her husband.

"Can you wait here for the landlord Ed, whilst I just have a last look around."

"Yes. Okay."

Ed realised that this was an emotional moment for his wife. He could understand that now the time had finally come for them to depart, she needed the opportunity for some time alone with her thoughts.

Leaving the kitchen, Kate went into the front room, looked around and made her way up the steep stairs and towards the upstairs rooms. Going into Rosie's bedroom, she paused. She closed her eyes and remembered the day when she had first brought Rosie home from the hospital. She'd had the room ready but Rosie hadn't gone into it for several months, her cot placed next to the bed in Kate's room, until she was sure that Rosie could sleep through the night. After that, it had been her room. Here was where she had slept, except on those occasions when she hadn't been well, or had woken up crying after a bad dream and would go into her mam's bedroom to be comforted. Walking into her own bedroom, Kate tried to focus on the happy times. There had been real love in that room when she had first married Joe, but the passion and feeling had died, only to be resurrected with Ed's arrival. He was her life now. Together they were happy and strong. They would be, wherever they chose to live. A new house or location, couldn't alter that fact. Descending the stairs, she heard a knock on the kitchen door. The sound of Ed's voice followed almost immediately, as he welcomed the landlord into the house.

"Well, to be honest," said the landlord, as Kate walked through to the kitchen, "I'm sad to see you go. You've looked after the place well and the rent's always been there on the nail. I have to say Kate, that I thought you might struggle after you lost Joe, but you're a strong 'un lass. And now you're going to Bramhall. I bet you aren't sorry to be swopping here for there!"

The landlord chuckled and Kate and Ed smiled.

"Well, I will miss Ardwick. I've always lived around here," said Kate.

"Yes, I suppose you will. It won't be too long though before it's all gone. The Corporation will be getting around to it soon enough," continued the landlord.

"Have you heard anything definite?" asked Ed.

"Not yet, but I don't think I'll be waiting much longer."

The landlord paused and then walked back to the kitchen door and opened it.

"Well then, shall we get locked up and get off?"

"Do you mind if we go out by the front door?" asked Kate.

"No. Whichever way you like," replied the landlord.

"Did Ed give you the keys?"

"Yes."

"Could I have the front door key to lock it behind us?" she asked.

"Yes, of course," said the landlord, though clearly mystified by her request.

"I was first into the house, through the front door, when Joe and I moved in and I'd now like to be the last one out," explained Kate.

"Oh," said the landlord, "I understand now."

Ed smiled. He knew full well that the landlord didn't. To him houses weren't homes, even the one he lived in himself. They were simply investments; valuable to rent or to be sold on at a profit. He would never think like Kate, that a house was a living, breathing entity. A stage that had witnessed a lifetime of dramatic events and understand that they had a heart, a soul, that they kept secrets and looked after the people who lived in them.

Together, the two men made their way into the front room. Ed opened the door and they both stepped out and through the tiny front garden and on to the pavement. It was a fine, August day and they could feel the heat reflecting off the hot walls of the houses and the street and pavement. Inside, Kate took a last look around the front room and then walked through the door. Stepping down on to the front path, Kate pulled the door to, put the key in the lock and turned it. Removing the key, she handed it over to the landlord.

"Thanks. I'll be getting off now. Good luck to the pair of you."

Quickly, he got into his black Ford Zephyr, which he'd parked opposite the front door. It was the only car on the street and seemed strangely out of place. Only a couple of residents on Bright Avenue owned a car and they had taken them to work with them. The Zephyr's engine soon roared into life and with a honk on his horn to say goodbye, the landlord pulled away from the pavement. As he drove down to the end of the street, his tyres made a rumbling noise as they travelled across the cobbles, the kids playing in the street grabbing their balls and skipping ropes and scattering for the safety of the pavement. Turning left down Syndall Street, he was gone. Quickly, the children returned to the middle of the road, ebbing and flowing like waves lapping back and forth on the beach.

"Well, Ed. It's time we got going," said Kate.

"Are you okay Kitty?" asked Ed, fully expecting her to be upset.

"Yes," said Kate, quietly nodding to him.

"We'll be coming back to see Sarah and we aren't actually that far away," said Ed, attempting to make her feel better.

"Yes," said Kate, "I know we're not. But Ardwick will never seem the same to me again. Not now."

Kate paused. She could see an anxious look on Ed's face. Concerned that perhaps they hadn't done the right thing.

"No Ed," she said, taking his hand. "I'm not sad. I'm quiet, yes. I'm thinking about the past. But, more importantly, I have a future. We all have a future. When I closed that door, it didn't close the door on the past. What I am, what we've shared together here, will always be a part of us. One that we can never forget. But we need to go forward now to new hopes, new dreams. I love you Ed and we're going to build a wonderful life together. I know that we are."

Ed put his arms around her, bent down and kissed her.

"I love you, Kate. You're the whole world to me. I promise I'll never, ever let you down."

"You better not!" said Kate, playfully.

Ed smiled and the two of them, holding hands, walked towards Syndall Street. As she turned the corner, Kate had no need to look back. Now there was only the future; a future that she and Ed would build together.